THE MARRIAGE EFFECT

A WASHINGTON WOLVES NOVEL

KARLA SORENSEN

Cover Designer-Najla Qamber Design www.najlaqamberdesigns.com

Proofreading- Jenny Sims, Editing4Indies

Interior Formatting - Devin McCain, Studio 5 Twenty-Five, www.studio5twentyfive.com

DEDICATION

This one is for the man I married, for the endless support he's given me in this crazy endeavor, even if he has terrible title suggestions for every book I work on.
I love you.

CHAPTER 1
PAIGE

I never thought I'd hit a point in my life where I could be standing in the middle of a gorgeous mansion, surrounded by gorgeous football players, and be bored out of my friggin' mind.

Yet here I was.

"You look bored," my best friend Allie said from where she stood next to me.

I took a sip of my drink, some delicious lemon-whiskey concoction, and sighed. "What makes you say that?"

"Your fingers are doing that annoying tapping thing they do when you're planning an escape."

Sure enough. My fingers were suspended midair, a split second before resuming the rhythmic drumming along the surface of the crystal low ball glass.

"What, pray tell, do you think I'm trying to escape?" I asked her. Some young buck rookie with a puffed-out chest and no neck to speak of strutted across Allie's living room, gave me a full-body once-over, and then jerked his chin up. I narrowed my eyes dangerously and turned away. That kid wouldn't know what to do with me if I gave him a laminated sheet with bullet point instructions and a highlighted map of my body.

"Who knows, Paige?" Allie smiled at someone across the room, probably another young buck rookie who wasn't leering and jerking his chin at her, given that she owned the damn team. "I've never been able to figure out what makes you bolt from point A to point B. Like when did you decide to suddenly quit a successful modeling job? Or move from Milan, or before that, from Paris? Or the handful of other European countries you called home? Or dump the dozens of boyfriends who worshiped the ground you walked on?"

I snorted. "If you think they worshiped anything, you're smokin' something."

If I felt like having this conversation—which, I didn't—I might have been able to tell her that sometimes, I woke up, and everything around me felt stale and musty. That I always hit a point in a job, or an apartment, or a city, or a person, and I desperately needed to fling open the proverbial windows of my life and let in a fresh, bracing breeze.

That desire was what made me up and quit a modeling career that I'd spent the previous ten years building. It's what made me pack my suitcases, grab the first flight from Milan to Seattle, and move into my best friend's house that we now shared with her fiancé and his daughter.

Don't worry, the house was ginormous. I basically had my own wing, if anyone was worried about a lack of privacy.

"You need a job," she said in lieu of an answer from me.

Even though I wasn't facing her, my best friend sensed my eye roll, because she poked me in the general area of my kidneys.

"Yeah, right," I told her. "If I had a job, who would help you set up your fabulous football parties?"

Allie sighed as we watched players and their families fill plates of food from the long table that stretched along the middle of the sprawling deck overlooking Lake Washington.

"I'd hire someone," she said. "You know, the person whose job it is to help with fabulous football parties."

"I'm cheaper."

She glanced sideways at me with a lifted brow.

"You know what I mean," I clarified.

"Aunt Paige can't move out," Faith piped up from behind us. "She's way better at braiding my hair than you are, Allie."

I smiled triumphantly. "Yeah, I'm *way better* at braiding her hair. Did you see the masterpiece I created?"

My little co-conspirator did a twirl in front of us, and Allie laughed. "You're right, I couldn't do that."

When Faith spun a little too fast and bumped into me, I steadied her with a hand on her shoulder. "See, all those years of modeling were worth it just to be able to do the fabulous Miss Pierson's hair."

That was when my BFF, my ride or die, the woman who knew me best in the world, gave me a look that said she saw through my bullshit like it was cellophane.

"I get what you're saying," I told her. "But moving around isn't a crime, you know. Besides, I've been here for almost a year. Shouldn't that earn me some imaginary points?"

Allie didn't make eye contact, a sure sign that she was choosing her words carefully.

But her fiancé beat her to it, sneaking an arm around her to snag a piece of perfectly cut red pepper from the tray in front of us. "Do those imaginary points help you move out?"

"Luke," she chastised.

"It's fine," I told her, narrowing my eyes at Luke even though he couldn't see my face. "He pretends he hates having me here, but he doesn't."

"Don't I?" His voice was dry. "Last week, you walked in when—"

"Okay," I interrupted. "I remember. No need to remind me. I saw everything I needed to see on that couch, and if I must remind you, I turned around immediately and went back to my room." Allie's face was bright red, and I patted her shoulder. "I didn't see much, I swear."

She held up her hands. "I'll drop it. But I think you should find something to do with your time. As much as I love having you here, and Faith does too. You're such a huge help with her during the season."

"But," I drawled.

"But you've got your own life to live too," she said gently.

Allie wasn't saying anything I didn't already know or wasn't already feeling. Normally, I looked without leaping, and given my last leap had landed me in a place surrounded by people I loved desperately, it had taken me longer than normal to feel the itch to move on.

But at the back of my neck, up my spine, and under my skin, that itch was starting to build. My fingers curled up in my palm, ready to grip the window frame and yank it off its hinges. I just didn't know what I was ready for next.

A player called her name, and Allie gave me a tiny smile before she walked away to talk to him. For a year, I'd been an unofficial fixture with the Washington Wolves, the professional football team she inherited when her dad passed away.

I knew most of the players and a lot of the WAGS too. Their kids called me Auntie Paige, just like Faith did. And it was because I came to all these functions, the random get-togethers that Allie liked to host to keep a strong sense of community among her team. Most owners wouldn't throw a house party while the team was in the thick of preseason, but this was her way, and it was working.

I tipped my drink back, then grimaced when it was empty. I started toward the bar with a heavy sigh.

The bartender was filling a glass with ice water, and another with the same cocktail I'd just finished when I approached the bar set up along the edge of the deck. Two broad backs were in front of me, one sitting on a stool and one standing.

The guy standing took his drink and walked away. The one on the stool stayed there when the bartender slid a tall glass of water in his direction.

From the back, I tried to place him.

Dark, dark hair, wide shoulders, and a slim waist. A jawline that could cut glass, from the looks of it.

Young Buck Rookie from a few minutes ago sidled up next to me as I approached the bar, clearing his throat as he did. The guy on the stool turned slightly, and I only caught a glimpse of his profile as he glanced toward us.

"What's up, Red?" YBR asked, puffing out that chest again.

Oh goodie, I so loved the original ones. The ones who decided it didn't matter to ask my name, and instead, commented on the color of my hair in lieu of a polite greeting.

Normally, I'd relish the chance to slice him into ribbons, metaphorically speaking, of course. But today, I was tired.

I set my empty glass onto the bar and sighed.

"Another one?" the bartender asked.

I held up my hand. "Just a second." With a slight turn, I braced my elbow onto the bar and faced YBR. "I'm Paige," I told him in as sweet and docile a tone as I was capable of.

He grinned. "I'm Colt."

"Of course you are," I murmured. His eyebrows bent in confusion. I patted him on the shoulder. "Colt, you seem … nice. You do. But I'm too old for you, trust me. The me from ten years ago would have been thrilled if you approached me by a bar and called me Red, but the almost thirty-year-old me just … really appreciates a man who will ask me what my name is."

His grin stayed frozen on his big dopey face. "You already told me your name, though."

The guy next to me sighed heavily, and the sound was so disgusted, overflowing with the same kind of exhaustion that I was feeling that I almost laughed out loud.

"Yeah," I said. "I know. Nice to meet you, Colt."

I turned back to the bar, risking a glance at the guy next to me. His profile might have been carved from rock for as much as it gave away. He lifted his water and took another long drink. I didn't know what it said about my brain, but I felt a tingle of absurd happiness that he was ignoring me completely.

Hello Challenge, my name is Paige.

As I stood there, I heard the sound of Colt shuffling away.

"I think you broke his heart," the bartender said, flicking her eyes to where Colt had just been standing.

"Highly doubtful," I answered. "He's a twentysomething professional football player. I think his *heart* will mend just fine before the night is over."

"Another lemon rosemary bourbon sour?" she asked, wiping the surface of the bar with deft movements.

The large frame of the man sitting next to me shifted slightly, and I tilted my head in his direction, wishing I could see his face more clearly.

"What's he drinking?" I asked.

"*He* has a name," his grumbly, rumbly voice answered. "And after that little speech, don't you think it's a bit hypocritical that you didn't ask what it is?"

The second I heard him speak, his name clicked into place in my head.

Of course.

That voice was one not heard often because he stayed under the radar, hated doing any press, and was, without a doubt, one of the best safeties in professional football. The casual football fan wouldn't have any clue who he was. He could probably walk through most cities in America and not be recognized.

But I recognized his voice all the same. The first time I heard it, I thought that someone yanked it from the pits of hell, but in a really super-duper sexy way.

Before I turned, I pulled a stool out and perched on it. Then I pivoted to the side so I could see him fully.

"Logan Ward," I said, appreciating the slight start of surprise he gave when that was the next thing out of my mouth. His eyes flicked in my direction, and oh goodness, they were green. That was not something I knew about him, and it pleased me to the depths of my very bored soul to discover it. "See? No hypocrites to be found at this bar."

He didn't say anything, only took another drink of his water.

Everything in me screamed to wait, to allow him to be the next to talk, but honestly, I was never the best at listening to the voices in my head that tried to curb my more irrational impulses.

"Do you think I broke Colt's heart?"

"Nope."

"Do you think he'll remember my lesson when he approaches the next woman he wants to talk to?"

"Nope."

I laughed. "That's a shame."

Finally, Logan turned his chin far enough that he was almost, sort of facing me. Now that was a face that a camera would love. Strong jaw, straight nose, eyes so bright and thickly lashed that I was only a little jealous. It was also a face I hadn't seen very often, save behind his football helmet. He rarely made appearances at the social functions.

"Do you critique every man who approaches you?" he asked.

"No," I said easily. I shrugged one shoulder. "But the thing is, most women feel like they can't be honest when a man comes up to us in a social setting and says something stupid or annoying or cheesy. And my thing is, how will they ever learn? We're taught to smile and be nice and be charming because that's what a good girl does. But if a guy comes up to me and smacks me on the ass and hands me a drink that he so graciously bought, shouldn't I be allowed to tell him that I don't particularly appreciate the gesture?"

Logan answered that with a lifted brow. "Yes, you should."

"Thank you. If I had daughters, I'd want to teach them to be kind but also be honest about how they should be treated. If I had sons, I'd want to teach them how to be respectful of the people they want to speak to. Do you have sons or daughters, Logan?"

As I spoke, he started shaking his head, the tiniest beginnings of a smile on those firmly sculpted lips. "I have sisters. Lots of them."

"And you're not drinking?" I teased.

"I don't drink." His mouth settled into a firm line.

He stood, pulling some cash out of his wallet and tucking it into the tip jar.

"Leaving already?" I asked, feeling an irrational tug of disappointment.

"Yup."

"Aren't you going to ask my name?" I said.

His eyes stayed steadily on mine as he put his wallet into the back pocket of his dark cut jeans. "Who says I don't already know it?"

My mouth popped open as he turned and walked away.

I was about to go after him, about to follow the instinctual tug that wanted to keep that particular interaction going, when my cell phone buzzed from the pocket of my dress.

A number I didn't recognize flashed across the screen, but it was the same East Coast area code where my parents lived.

"This is Paige," I said, turning away from the noise of the party.

"Paige McKinney?"

"Paige McKinney," I confirmed.

The man on the other end of the line exhaled heavily. "You're tough to get a hold of. The last number and address we had on file for you was in Milan."

I grimaced. If it was a possible modeling job, my agent would've been the one to contact me. "Not for the last year or so. Can I ask why you're trying to track me down?"

"Miss McKinney, my name is Robert Ford, and I represent the estate of your late aunt Emma McKinney."

My head tilted to the side, and I walked around the side of the deck to find a pocket of quiet. My aunt Emma, crazy though she was, had been one of my favorite people when I was younger. She'd passed away, childless and as kooky as ever, about six months earlier, but this was the first I'd heard about something in regard to her estate.

"Okay. What can I help you with?"

"Well, it's how I can help you. Your aunt was ... unconventional, as you know, and she had very specific wishes in regard to her estate and holdings."

I found a bench and sank down onto it. Aunt Emma's "estate" was also known as a living museum to the late 1800s. She'd kept the place, small and immaculate, in a constant state of readiness for Jane Austen's ghost to pop up from the grave and visit her.

Like, for real.

Her obsession for that time period was in her dress and the things she ate. She eschewed most forms of technology, which was why we'd barely kept in touch when I moved overseas.

"Okay," I said slowly. "What wishes are those?"

"We were instructed to wait until after the will went through probate and all taxes were paid upon her death to see what was left. The house itself is to be donated to the Delaware Historical Society because of the incredible details she was able to preserve over the years."

Preserve, obsess over, whatever he wanted to call it. I rocked my neck back and forth and sighed. I couldn't imagine what my aunt might have left me. She lived so frugally, never traveling, never doing much of anything, really. Maybe it was an antique tea set. Or her favorite corset.

"That makes sense," I said politely.

"But she named you as the primary beneficiary of her financial holdings with only one caveat to be able to inherit."

I narrowed my eyes. "What's the caveat?"

"You have to be married."

I burst out laughing. "That's funny. I'm the furthest thing from married, and I have no desire to change that right now." I was still shaking my head. "What did she leave me, anyway?"

He cleared his throat. "A little over three million dollars."

I bolted off the bench. "Three million dollars?"

"That's correct."

"How?" I pressed a hand to my suddenly racing heart. "This doesn't make any sense."

Richard sighed. "I was as surprised as you, Miss McKinney. But apparently, she was very smart financially and made good investments at the right time. And she felt very firmly that, as you know, the family inheritance be passed down to someone married."

"Holy shit," I breathed, remembering conversations with her when I was maybe eleven or twelve. About how back in the 1800s, if there was no male heir, and none of the daughters were married, the family estate would almost pass to the nearest male relative. Good Lord, she was crazier than I remembered. "And she can do that? Just leave the money sitting there until I get married? That's nuts."

My brain was spinning like a top.

"It may be, but it's her money, her decision." He cleared his throat again. "And it won't just sit there. If you don't find a husband within the allotted amount of time, the money will pass on to your cousin Collins."

"Oh, fuck that," I breathed. "That little twerp? No way."

If my cursing fazed good ole Robert Ford, he didn't show it. I sighed and took a seat on the bench again.

Collins had always been an annoyance more than anything. I was an only child, he was an only child, and while my parents couldn't really be bothered much by my presence, his doted on him. That doting led to a spoiled, sulking child who turned into a spoiled, sulking adult. And considering he had about as much intelligence as a radish, I was absolutely not going to walk away from that money and let it end up in his pocket.

"Okay, Robert. Let's go over this from the top."

Suddenly, I wasn't so bored anymore.

CHAPTER 2
LOGAN

WASHINGTON WOLVES

Things I didn't have time for: mouthy redheads with million-mile-long legs who made me want to sit and talk to them when I shouldn't have been at the party to begin with.

That was why I walked away from Paige McKinney, best friend to the woman who owned the team I played for, and that was why I didn't look back at her.

Most of the guys on the team thought I lived under a rock because of how little I took part in things like this, but even if I did, I'd know who she was.

It was laughable that she thought I might *not* know who she was.

Not only was she a permanent fixture with the team, but she'd been on the cover of the *Sports Illustrated* swimsuit edition twice in the last ten years and featured in the spread five years in a row. It was impossible to avoid that tidbit about her, considering the guys passed those magazines around like they were the Holy Grail.

The second she turned and faced me, I wanted to pour bleach into my brain so that I could forget the shot of her that I remembered best, arms crossed over her chest, red hair flowing down her back, two sandy handprints on her ass as she smiled at the camera.

So yes, the fact that I wanted to sit and talk to Paige meant that it was absolutely the last thing I should've been doing.

The last time I wanted to talk to a woman who interested me, I ended up agreeing to play her fake boyfriend, only to discover that her real boyfriend was a teammate of mine.

"You heading out, Ward?"

I paused when Luke, the only guy who'd been on the team as long as I had, spoke to me. He was on the couch showing something to his daughter, Faith, who was only a few years younger than the twins.

The twins who had been blowing up my phone for the last hour, and the reason I knew I should be leaving.

"Yeah, I need to get home."

He smiled in understanding. Before Allie, he'd been as antisocial as me. "Need or want to?"

I grimaced.

It was enough of an answer for him because he laughed. "Come on, man, it won't kill you to stay for another ten minutes."

"That's what you think," I mumbled under my breath.

My phone buzzed and then buzzed again, and I pulled the phone out of my pocket with a sigh. The two texts from earlier were still on my lock screen.

Isabel: How much does a new iPad cost?

Isabel: Tell Claire that she's not allowed to touch my stuff. SHE BROKE MY IPAD AGAIN. And if she says it wasn't her, she's lying.

Isabel: Lia totally broke her own crappy tablet. I saw it happen. PS this is Claire.

And those were joined with a new one, from the actual owner of Iz's phone.

Isabel: OMG GET THE TWINS THEIR OWN PHONES PLZ, THEY KEEP STEALING MINE.

Me: Iz, they're not getting their own phone. You know 13 is the earliest they're allowed one. I'll be home in an hour, okay? See if Mrs. Connor can fix the iPad.

Maybe staying at the party for five minutes wouldn't kill me. The thought of four females—ages twelve to sixteen—in possession of their own cell phones absolutely would. I sank onto the couch across from Luke and his daughter, the one who would probably never harass him about broken iPads or stealing phones or wanting McDonald's for dinner. I silenced my phone, determined for once, to spend fifteen minutes socializing with one of the few guys on the team who didn't annoy the hell out of me.

"You look tired, Ward."

I pinched the bridge of my nose and laughed under my breath. He had absolutely no idea. No one on the team did. They had no idea how tired I was. That down to the marrow of my bones, I was exhausted and had been for over two years.

Staying under the radar suited me just fine, for exactly that reason.

Media outlets didn't really care about me. Fans didn't snap my picture when I walked down the street. And none of my teammates knew that I was the legal guardian for my four younger half-sisters.

None of them knew that my dad's second wife, younger than him by about seventeen years, decided to go "find herself" in parts unknown a couple of years after he died. That when she left, she handed off all four girls to my care with a signed note that said: "Logan is their guardian, XOXO, Brooke."

Instead of handing him any of that information, I just nodded. "Yeah, I am."

"Doesn't get any easier as we get older, does it?"

Faith beamed up at her dad. "Daddy is the third oldest quarterback in the league."

I smiled. "That right?"

She nodded. "Only Drew Brees and Tom Brady are older, but Daddy definitely looks the oldest of all of them."

Luke wrapped an arm around her shoulders, playfully clapping a hand over her mouth while she giggled. "No one asked you, Turbo. Why don't you go find Allie or Aunt Paige, okay?"

It was on the tip of my tongue to tell her where Aunt Paige was, but I didn't need Luke questioning how I knew.

"It's too early in the season to look that beat," he said as she scampered away. "We're barely out of the preseason."

"I know. I can usually make it to week eight before I feel like I need a weeklong nap."

"My knees are killing me already."

I rubbed my neck. "It's my shoulder. That pick six last week in Arizona had me sore for days."

"Well, yeah," he said on a laugh. "When their tackle flattens your ass right before you stretched your arm past the line, it'll have a negative effect on multiple body parts."

Even though we both laughed, it wasn't all that funny. Every year, it got harder to recuperate. Every game, every week of practice, pushed our aging bodies to the limit. Muscles and ligaments shoved past the brink of what they were designed to endure.

And if my physical body went through a beating every week, that was absolutely nothing compared to the mental exhaustion I was feeling because of four small, stubborn, dark-haired young women.

Luke and I talked easily for a while longer about the games being played tomorrow, the ones we'd actually be able to watch since it was our bye week. Faith came and went a couple of times, and teammates would come and talk for a couple of minutes before wandering off to other conversations.

"Man," Luke said, rubbing the back of his neck, "I can't believe it's almost six. How old do I sound if I say I'm ready for bed."

"Old," I told him with a grin. I pulled my phone out of my pocket, surprised that much time had passed. My lock screen was flooded with texts, and the second my eyes snagged on the first one, I felt the color drain from my face.

"Shit," I whispered. "Shit, shit, shit."

"What's wrong?" Luke asked.

Isabel: Why didn't you answer your phone?? Molly got in a car accident. Uncle Nick is here. I SWEAR I didn't call him. I think stupid Mrs. Connor did.

Isabel: He's really grumpy.

Isabel: LOGAN, ANSWER YOUR DAMN PHONE. We're at Virg Mason

Isabel: Sorry. I'll put a dollar in the swear jar. Don't blow a gasket, she's going to be fine. BUT OMG WHERE ARE YOU

The last one had the blood freezing solid in my veins.

Nick: Thanks for finally screwing up big enough. I'll take it from here.

"I gotta go," I said unsteadily, shoving my phone in the general vicinity of my pocket and standing so fast that my head spun. "My sister … she's in the hospital."

He stood. "Are you okay? I can drive you, which one is she at?"

I was already heading toward the door, heart racing, mind racing, everything … just everything inside me racing to not feel like such an asshole for silencing my stupid phone. "She's at Virginia Mason, and no, I'm good thanks. Uhh, just tell Allie thank you for the invite."

My keys were out of my pocket before I reached the front door. As I sped down the highway to the ER at Virginia Mason Hospital,

I tried not to let my mind immediately veer to worst-case scenarios.

"Shit," I whispered for the fortieth time in the last thirty minutes. If any of the girls could hear me, I'd owe a fortune to the swear jar by the end of the day. The swear jar that was Molly's idea, I thought, trying to swallow past a giant lump of fear. I'd briefly seen her that morning as she stumbled into the kitchen, bleary-eyed and looking for coffee.

"Have fun at your party," she'd told me, punching me in the shoulder as I walked out of the kitchen. "Don't be mean to anyone."

"I'm never mean," I said back, mussing up her dark hair.

My eyes burned hot, and I blinked rapidly. She was *fine*.

I swear, if she wasn't, if her injuries were more severe than Isabel's texts indicated …

My hands tightened on the steering wheel, and I took a few deep breaths to steady my thoughts.

It was easy enough to logically talk myself out of any panic. The hospital didn't call me. No police officers had called me. Isabel hadn't said anything about a serious injury in her texts, and neither she nor Mrs. Connor had left me a voicemail. That was good. It went a long way in my head.

But there was an entirely separate part of yourself that logic couldn't touch when you were the one responsible for the people you loved most in the world. That part of me, my heart, whatever, couldn't stop imagining Molly with a breathing tube or pale in a hospital bed with bandages covering her face, and I had to grit my teeth to the point of breaking as I finally approached the hospital and jerked my truck to a stop in an empty parking space.

I took a moment to remind myself that she was probably fine, but it wasn't easy.

Once I was inside, I'd let none of them know that those fears were bouncing around in my head. I'd walk into the room, and no one would have a single clue that inside my skin, my bones were rattling with the need to be assured that she was okay. That the people in charge of her health were competent and doing their jobs, and watching her with the same love and care that I would.

I ran into the ER entrance off Spring Street and gave my name and Molly's name to the security guard behind the desk. He gave me a polite smile and curious look at my face. I had to breathe steadily because I'd probably lose my shit if he asked if I played football. Thankfully, he didn't; he just buzzed open the door and told me where to go.

The waiting room was a buzzing hive of activity, but everyone was too focused on their own issues to look at me as I strode quickly through the room.

"Nice of you to show up," a voice very much like my own came from behind me. The teeth-gritting and deep breathing were back in full force, but I kept my face blank as I turned to face my younger brother. He was a mirror image of me, the only differences being a couple of inches in height, about thirty fewer pounds in muscle, and his face was clean shaven.

Defensive answers pricked the tip of my tongue, but I let them roll away unsaid. "Is she okay?"

Nick slowly lifted one dark eyebrow. "Define okay."

I kept my eyes steady on him but didn't take the bait. It never went well if I took whatever bloody chunk he was trying to use for me to emerge teeth-first out of the water. After a second, he rolled his eyes.

"She sprained her wrist from the impact of the airbag, and they need to check for a concussion, but she's alive, and she's coherent. Is that okay enough for you?"

I didn't answer, showing him my back so I could go see my sister, but I felt my shoulders deflate with instant relief.

"Hey," he said as I started walking away. "This is it for you, Logan. I'm filing a petition for guardianship. You can't have shit like this happen on your watch and still think you're the best choice for those girls. They should be home with me and Cora. We can provide them with a stable environment, two parents who are home at five for dinner around the table."

Whatever relief I felt fled, leaving in its wake a slow stretch of cold dread. We'd had this argument so many times over the past two years, but he'd never really had enough ammunition to actually try to bring it before a judge.

Two years ago, the first time he'd tried, he didn't live in Washington. Hadn't moved into their school district. Wasn't married.

I looked at him over my shoulder, not giving him the satisfaction of igniting my temper. "They're not going anywhere."

"Forgive me if I don't take your word for it. I'm going outside to call my lawyer right now, asshole."

"Prick," I mumbled. "I hope she charges a lot."

He scoffed, muttering something under his breath that I ignored as I turned down the hallway that led to Molly's room. Outside of it paced Mrs. Connor, a grim look on her slightly lined face. When she saw me, she stopped short and glowered even further.

"Over an hour, Logan," she said. "We've been trying to reach you for over an hour."

I held up my hands. "I know. I didn't … I didn't hear my phone. I got here as soon as I could."

She sighed heavily and adjusted the strap of her purse over her shoulder.

"What did the doctor say?"

Mrs. Connor glanced into the hospital room, where I could hear the chatter of girls, the soundtrack of my entire damn life, and smiled tightly. "Well, he wouldn't tell me much, considering I'm not their parent or guardian," she said pointedly, then looked down the hall where Nick had passed me. "But I guess I can't blame him, considering I was the person *locked in the bathroom* while she snuck out of the house and met her friend in order to day drink."

"What?" I roared.

A couple of nurses at the nearby desk gave me dirty looks, and then from the now silent hospital room, I heard a stage whisper, "Oh shiiiiit, you're dead meat, Molly."

I blinked a few times, my entire brain a frozen block of confusion. "You … how did you get locked in the bathroom?"

The smile tightened even further. "That would be the twins."

My hands curled into fists, and I felt like I was one new little revelation away from growling like a trapped bear. "Okay. Okay, this is fine. I'll … I'll talk to them. They're now grounded for a month, and … wait, Molly was drinking?"

Mrs. Connor held my eyes, and for the first time, I saw a flash of compassion. But it was fleeting. "Logan, I feel sorry for you, I really do. They're a handful, and I know you're doing your best, but I can't put up with this anymore. The Vaseline in my shampoo bottle was cute and everything, but I'm fifty-two. I don't have it in me to try to rein them in. Today was too much."

"Mrs. Connor, please." I stumbled over my words, the growing realization that I was about to lose my fourth housekeeper in a year had my tongue not working properly. "I'll give you a raise."

She patted my shoulder. "Sometimes, some things aren't worth the money. Consider this my notice. I promise I won't ask for a recommendation."

And then she was gone.

While I stood there gaping after her like a water-starved fish, two small bodies entered my peripheral vision.

I pinched my eyes shut and counted to ten before I felt someone's thin arms wrap around my waist.

Sighing, I used my hand to smooth down Lia's unruly hair before her twin sister joined in.

Little craps knew I couldn't truly get mad while they were hugging me.

"Claire, Lia," I said quietly as I leaned down to kiss each of them on the head, "you're grounded until you're twenty."

Claire lifted her chin and hit me with the full force of her blue eyes. "That's an excessive amount of time, Logan. That means you'd have to deal with us at home for *eight years*."

"I think you'd crack after one," Lia chimed in, voice muffled from where her face was buried in my stomach.

"I think I'd crack after two weeks," I admitted, feeling incredibly exhausted. "Go sit on that bench, okay? Don't move until I come back out here."

"We won't," they said in unison and skipped over to where I'd pointed. I pinched the bridge of my nose and walked into the hospital room.

Isabel, the only sane member of the household besides me, was sitting on the edge of Molly's hospital bed, fingers flying over the screen of her phone. Molly was pretending to sleep and doing a terrible job of it, based on the way she was attempting to gauge the look on my face through slitted eyes.

"Isabel," I started, and she held up a hand to stop me.

"I know. You need privacy. I already called Nan and told her what happened."

"Thanks, kiddo."

She lifted her eyes briefly, then rolled them when she saw Molly pretend to snore. "And I'm texting her now about Mrs. Connor flying the coop. She's getting a ticket ASAP."

Knowing that my mom would be on her way from Florida soon had the iron grip around my stomach loosening a little, so I nodded. "Good. That's good. I can stay home tomorrow. Coach will be fine."

"No, he won't, but he can't fight you on it without the players union breathing down his neck."

I shook my head. "Are you sure you're only fourteen?"

Her smile was small, and it looked so much like my own that my heart turned over in my chest. "Last time I checked."

"Thanks for calling Nan."

Isabel shrugged as she stood from the bed. My eyebrows popped up briefly at her eye-blindingly bright ensemble, but what the hell did I know about teen fashion? "It'll be good to see her. Maybe it'll get Nick off your back too." She whistled. "He was in a *mood*."

The fact that she had to deal with any of this shit felt incredibly unfair. Of my four half-sisters, Isabel was the most like me. She saw what needed to be done and did it, and she kept her emotions leashed in if the rest of the room was erupting, just to make sure everything was taken care of. She'd been that way since birth.

When my dad married someone seventeen years younger than him for his second attempt at marriage, back when I was just starting college, I never imagined that it would result in four unexpected siblings over the next six years. I was nineteen when Molly, that little shit fake sleeping in the hospital bed, was born. I never imagined then that she would turn me prematurely gray.

Isabel exited the room, giving me a condescending pat on the back as she passed.

After she was gone, I waited a couple of seconds to see if Molly would so much as flinch. "I know you're awake," I said quietly.

Molly pinched her eyes shut even harder, and I fought my smile. Her wrist was wrapped tightly, already in a sling that fastened around her neck.

"I'm so fucked, aren't I?" she said in a tremulous voice.

"Language," I admonished.

She sighed and opened her eyes. They were big and pleading and about to overflow with tears.

"Hey," I said gently, grabbing her good hand with mine. "I'm glad you're okay."

One tear spilled over, and she let it slide unchecked down her cheek. "It was scary."

I nodded. "I bet. What happened?"

"I was driving us back to Cici's house in her car, and be-because she was buzzed, she was laughing really loud, and I swear I didn't have a drop to drink, and I was distracted, and I didn't see the car pull in front of us." She sniffed and laid her head back on the hospital bed again. At sixteen, Molly had moments when I could see the woman she'd become. This was one of them.

Even though she looked heartbreakingly young and pale and fragile in that hospital bed, I saw the sketch of what she'd look like in ten years. In twenty.

"Molly," I started, and her tears increased steadily. "Hey, come on, Mol, you're killin' me here, but you cannot expect to sneak out during the day to drive around with a friend who's drinking and have there not be consequences."

"I know." She sniffled. "I was just sick of being stuck at home with them. They're so freaking crazy, and they don't give me my space, and they don't understand what it's like to be my age. They're babies, Logan."

A nurse entered the room and smiled at me before checking Molly's blood pressure and oxygen level. While she was asking her how her pain was, I reached into my back pocket to grab my phone. The pocket was empty. I whispered a word that would probably cost me a week's pay into the swear jar. It either fell out in my truck, or it was still back at Luke and Allie's place.

"I'll be right back, okay, Mol?"

She nodded and smiled a little. The nurse gave me a lingering appreciative glance, which I ignored.

"Iz, I need to borrow your phone real quick."

From where she sat on the padded chair, she gave me a level look.

"Remember who pays for that phone before you give me looks like that," I told her.

She rolled her eyes and gave it to me. I tapped out the number for my lawyer, and considering how much I paid her per hour, I was disgustingly happy that she picked up right away.

"Hey, Logan," she said into the phone. "What's up?"

"What's up is my brother is pissed, and he's got good reason to be," I snapped immediately.

"What happened?"

She was quiet as I gave her the short version, then quiet after I'd finished.

"Shit, Logan," she whispered. "You better start talking. Right now."

CHAPTER 3
PAIGE

Allie pressed her fingers to her temples and stared at me from where I sat numbly on the deck. I hadn't moved since I hung up with freaking Robert Ford the freaking jerk who just sent me into a tailspin.

"Holy shit," she whispered.

"Yeah."

"Like … a *husband*." Allie blinked rapidly as she said it.

"Yeah."

Then she threw up her hands. "What is it with us moving here and inheriting weird ass things with weird ass conditions?"

"Right? I wondered the same thing." I gave Lake Washington a narrow-eyed look. "Maybe it's like a curse or something."

Allie flopped on the bench next to me and slung an arm around my shoulder. "It's probably not. We both know that rich people are crazy, and they do even crazier things with their money." She nudged me. "At least you didn't inherit a sports team. There's no massive, life-changing learning curve to cashing a check."

I sighed and dropped my head into my hands. "Maybe not, but I do have one minor problem. Because of the time I lost with the will going through probate, I have six months to find a husband. Six months! If Aunt Emma weren't dead, I think I'd kill her myself right now. She always hated how independent I was. I just never realized how much."

She set her head against mine as we sat there in silence. The party was still holding strong, but where we were tucked around the corner, it was quieter. Which was good, because I was not in a party mood anymore.

"What are you going to do?" she asked.

"Place a classified ad," I said glumly. "Retired model seeks trophy husband. It should be interesting to see what kind of responses I get."

Allie laughed. "Honestly, when I told you earlier that you needed a job, I never thought you'd be forced to turn to husband hunting."

I fake sobbed, but really, I wanted to actually sob because it felt horribly unfair.

Luke came around the corner, holding up a cell phone. "Hey, Logan dropped this on the couch, and Faith just found it. I hate to ditch you with the hosting duties, but he had to rush to Virginia Mason because one of his sisters was brought into the ER, so I think he'll want this."

Allie smiled. "It's okay, he needs his phone. I'll manage."

I looked back and forth between them, then glanced back at the house full of people. "I'll bring it."

His eyebrows lifted. "You sure?"

"Why not? I don't really feel like being here anyway." I stood and took the bulky black phone from him. "This will be a good distraction."

"Thanks, Paige," he said.

"No prob. I'll just drop it off and then drive aimlessly around Seattle until I'm hit with a bolt of divine inspiration."

Luke gave Allie a confused look, which she waved off. "Ohhhkay then," he said. "Good luck with that."

Luck. I didn't need luck. *I needed a husband*, I thought grimly.

I'd gotten a lot of annoyed looks in my day, but this hospital security guard was about to top the list.

"Ma'am, without the name of the patient, I can't let you through those doors."

My teeth clamped tightly together as I breathed in, and then out through my nose. When Luke took me up on my offer to bring the lost phone, I bet he didn't imagine that I'd end up in a battle of wills with a stern looking man wearing a shiny badge.

"Sir, I understand you're doing your job, but I really just need to bring him his cell phone."

He looked at the cell phone in my hand with an uninterested flick of his eyes. "That piece of metal and plastic doesn't mean you're allowed through those doors. It could be your phone for all I know."

Did I just growl? The pop of his eyebrows made it seem like I did.

This dude had no clue who he was messing with today because the last freaking thing I wanted to deal with was another person trying to push their will onto me.

OKAY FINE, he was abiding by the rules of his job, but he sure made a convenient scapegoat when I imagined Collins skipping happily to the bank to cash *my* inheritance check.

I could feel people watching me, and at least one person was waiting behind me to try to get through the same doors that were currently barring me from Logan Ward.

Holding up a finger to the unimpressed guard, I dug into my purse and pulled out my phone, complete with sparkly rose gold case.

"No, because this is my phone. I would never use this awful, bulky black case because it's impossible to hold." I lit up the lock screen of mine, a shot of me and Allie from when we lived in Milan. "See? That's me. My perfect little fingerprint unlocks the phone. I can't do that with Logan's."

I pressed the home button to no avail. All it managed to do was light up the screen and show a picture that had a lump curling up into my throat. Logan was smiling, his handsome face pressed against four others of the young girl variety, all bearing a striking similarity to his. When I showed the guard, he narrowed his eyes.

"You recognize him, I know you do. That's because he got here like," I huffed, "I don't know, an hour ago? Come on. He needs his cell phone."

He stared impassively through the glass separating us.

"Logan Ward," I said. "His sister is here. How would I *know that* if I didn't know him?"

"You're not going in there without the patient name. Sorry, lady. You'll have to call him and tell him you have his phone."

"Call him on what? The phone is in my hand," I hissed, shoving a hand through my hair. It snagged on my ring, and I cursed, untangling the piece of costume jewelry from the offending strands. When my hand dropped to the counter, I stared at the ring for a beat. It used to fit my middle finger, but because I'd gained a little weight since I stopped modeling, I'd moved it over to my ring finger.

The finger you put a ring on when you're engaged.

Holy spitballs, I was a genius. Actually, Sandra Bullock was a genius, and the forty-seven times that I'd watched *While You Were Sleeping* were about to pay off in spades.

I sent a brief look skyward, hoping that Aunt Emma was sending me good juju from beyond the grave.

I sighed dramatically, giving an apologetic glance over my shoulder at the woman waiting not so patiently, and the guy to the other side of her, who was also giving me a not-so-polite stare. Gawd, I thought the people in the PNW were supposed to be nice. "Listen, Mike," I said, gentling my voice to something sweet and wistful and very Bullock-y, using the name on his badge. "I just need to give my fiancé his phone, okay? He was worried about his sister, and in his haste to get here, I didn't catch which sister it was. And it's not like I can text him to ask."

He glanced immediately down to my ring finger. I held it up so he could stare. The aquamarine surrounded by tiny gemstones looked about as much like an engagement ring as anything else did these days.

"You're Logan Ward's fiancée?" he asked.

"Yes." I sighed. "Please, I just need to give him this, and I'll be on my way, I promise."

"You're *engaged* to Logan Ward?" a voice asked from behind me.

Well, shit. This plan didn't allow for eavesdroppers.

I turned, eyeing the tall, dark-haired guy behind me, waiting just beyond the entrance to the emergency room, his phone in hand as he stared at me. He had Logan's eyes and hair, and I felt a pinprick of panic spread like frost over my stomach. "Uh-huh." I held up the phone so he could see it. "Just need to give him this."

"Let me see the picture," he said.

"Why should I show you?"

His eyes narrowed, and holy hell, when he did that, he looked like Logan. "Because I'm his brother."

The frost turned to giant, dangling, stab-you-in-the-stomach-when-they-fall icicles, but I kept my face even.

I tapped the lock button and turned it to face him. His features gave absolutely zilch away. "What are his daughters' names?" he asked, lifting his chin at the picture.

The security guard shifted, watching us with interest.

"He doesn't have any daughters," I answered, folding my arms over my chest. "Those are his sisters."

My obvious non-answer hung between us, and I mentally whispered another prayer to Saint Aunt Emma, who was hopefully now my corset-clad guardian angel, that I'd be able to pull this off.

Because if pressed on the names, I was screwed. And not in the good way.

He watched me, eyes looping over my face and then down my body in a way that I did not particularly appreciate. I didn't know who this dude was, or why he was baiting me, but really, I just wanted to have my little duty done with so I could go back to the party.

WWSBD?

I'll tell you what Sandra Bullock would do … she'd never let something like hospital security deter her, or random family members who had the audacity to question your tiny little fib.

"You don't know her?" the guard asked, eyeing me suspiciously.

If he looked suspicious, then the less-than version of Logan was appraising me like I was one step above a hooker.

"No," he said. "But my brother and I aren't close. It'd be just like him not to tell me something like this."

About three years earlier, I did a photo shoot in the Bahamas where the photographer told me within five minutes of meeting me that my boobs were too small and he hated my freckles. If I could deal with him half-naked while I frolicked in the icy cold ocean, then these guys were a cakewalk. I lifted my chin and met his gaze square on.

"Can I go through now?" I asked the guard, my eyes not leaving what's-his-name. The longer I looked at him, the worse his features got. If Logan's jaw was knife sharp, then little bro's was made out of playdough.

Unfortunately, he was as undeterred by my attitude as I was his. He smiled in a way that I didn't like very much. It was snaky and slimy, and it reminded me of Collins. "I'll take her back to find her fiancé."

All manner of F words flew through my brain because Logan was about to murder me for this. I didn't even know him that well, and I knew he'd want to kill me.

"No, it's fine. I can find him," I insisted. There was just the slightest edge to my easy-breezy tone because this was not how I imagined this working out. Like at all. "We were at a work party when he got the call, and he left his phone by accident. I was just going to drop it off and head back."

His eyes turned speculative with a hint of hard. "You'd leave him while Molly is in the hospital?"

Warning! Warning! Danger ahead!

Bright red sirens went off in my head, and I desperately, so desperately wished I could back up and choose any word except fiancé.

"You know Logan," I said slowly. "He likes his space." It was the right thing to say. I saw it in the annoyance that flashed across his features. "If he wants me to stay, he'll ask."

Brother Ward swept his hand toward the glass doors. "After you." When he nodded to the security guard, the glass doors unlocked with a click, then swept open.

The main waiting area of the emergency room was packed with people, some slumped over in chairs waiting to be seen and others pacing with their phones glued to their ears. I heard tears and a few moans. And at that moment, surrounded by people in pain, people who were suffering, I wanted to be anywhere else.

I should have let Luke take the damn cell phone.

I should have kept my mouth shut when I was talking to the security guard.

Should have, would have, will never do anything like this again, I thought as I followed Brother Ward—who was jerk enough not to tell me his name—down a hallway. Whatever. He'd help me find Logan, and it would all be done, and I'd never, ever, cross my heart say I was someone's fiancée to gain entrance somewhere.

"So," he said as we walked, "how did you and Logan meet?"

At least this was something I could answer honestly.

"Through the team," I told him, keeping my eyes straight ahead.

"I'll bet you know all the players," he answered dryly, then snorted.

It was that *snort*, the derision was so thick that I felt my hand curl up in a fist.

"I do," I said breezily, purposing lengthening my stride so that he had to speed up in order to keep pace with me. "My best friend is really involved there."

"Is she now?" he muttered.

"Yup." I popped the "p."

"Let me guess, head cheerleader?"

Gawd, I could take him out with one quick elbow strike to his Neanderthal head.

I clucked my tongue. "So close." I glanced sideways at his smug grin. From this angle, he didn't look very much like Logan at all. "Owner."

There was a satisfying hitch in his step when his head snapped in my direction. "Who is?"

"Allie Sutton, my best friend, is the owner of the Washington Wolves." I gave him a tiny smile when his face flushed red. "So I guess, in a way, you're right. She's the biggest cheerleader they have, isn't she?"

Brother Ward clenched his jaw as we turned a corner down another hallway.

I saw Logan before he did, and my skin prickled at the sight of him.

He was so tall, imposing just by existing. One of his biceps popped fantastically as he rubbed a hand over his forehead.

I cleared my throat loudly, which brought Logan's head up. His eyes narrowed in anger at his brother, which was interesting enough that I noticed it, even through my buzzing brain. But when they landed on me, the anger turned to unfiltered, quite obvious confusion.

Yeah, buddy, welcome to the club.

"Logan," his brother said in a snide voice. "I stumbled upon your *fiancée* out there. Sounds like you've been keeping a few things to yourself, eh, brother?"

CHAPTER 4
LOGAN

I learned a trick in college, and I became superstitious about doing it before a big game, before any big tests, and it worked so well that I took it into the pros with me. Every time I stood in the backfield, waiting for the kickoff, waiting to watch what a runner would do when he caught the ball, I still did it.

Breathe in for four beats. Hold it for four. Breathe out for four.

It slowed my racing heartbeat, steadied my nerves, and focused my thoughts.

Watching my asshole brother walk down a hospital hallway with Paige freaking McKinney behind him, looking like she'd just kicked a puppy, I wished I could've taken the time to do my breathing trick. Slow my racing brain so that all the really big things shrunk down to a more manageable size.

But my brain was already in hyper speed, even before I'd seen them, the phone call with my lawyer still circling around my thoughts like a pack of hungry vultures. Breathing tricks would do no good right now.

Paige held her hands up in supplication and clutched in one of them was my cell phone. *"I'm sorry,"* she mouthed.

"Aren't you going to say anything?" Nick asked, looking back and forth between me and Paige. She'd smoothed out her face, giving him a small, painfully polite smile.

"Thanks," I answered, voice tight and terse. "You can go now."

He scoffed. "If this is some stunt you're pulling, I don't buy it. It's awfully convenient that the moment I have the exact ammunition that I need against you, she shows up claiming to be your fiancée."

His first mistake was taking a step closer to me.

His second mistake was pointing a finger and coming within a fraction of an inch of touching my chest.

"Back up, Nick." I narrowed my eyes. "Now."

My brother was a jerk, but he wasn't stupid. All he was willing to concede was about a foot of space, but at least I could breathe easier without him right in front of me.

Paige's eyes were huge in her face.

They were so blue. I hadn't noticed that at the party. I'd been too busy trying not to look at her.

"If you think I'm stupid enough to fall for this, you're wrong. Those girls are better off with me, Logan, and I'll spend as much money as I have to, to prove it."

I crossed my arms in front of my chest because no way was I saying a single word until he was gone. There would be no refusal, no admission until I found out what the hell was going on.

"You done?"

Nick ran his hands through his hair and blew out an exasperated breath. "You're impossible, you know that? I don't want to fight you on this."

"Then don't." I propped my hands on my hips and glared at him. Behind Nick, Paige rubbed a hand over her forehead, but wisely, she stayed quiet.

His mouth opened to argue, then he closed it again after looking over at Paige. "I don't know what your role is in all this, but trust me when I say you don't want to be involved. Not with him." Nick pinned his glare on me again. "The courts will be hearing from my lawyer on Monday, I can promise you that."

Even though there were sounds all around us, coming from various rooms, alarms and beeps and doctors and nurses milling around, as Nick stalked off, silence bloomed awkwardly between me and Paige.

She cleared her throat, and I took a second to pinch my eyes shut, try to figure out exactly what she might have gleaned from that interaction, and what I was willing to tell her.

Also, why the hell did Nick think she was my fiancée?

"So," she drawled, "you forgot your cell phone."

I stared at her.

She popped a hip out and stared back. "Luke found it on the couch after you'd driven off."

My eyes narrowed, and she huffed.

"Listen, if you're going to stand there and stare at me all day, I'll just go." She held it out between us. When I didn't immediately reach for it, she rolled her eyes and stepped forward, pulling my front pocket out with the tips of her fingers so she could shove the phone in. I swatted her hand away and tucked it into my back pocket where it was supposed to go.

I crossed my arms over my chest as I leveled her with a glare. "Why does my brother think you're my fiancée?"

The woman who manhandled my pocket disappeared in a blink, transforming into some meek, politely smiling creature who looked nothing like the Paige I'd spoken to at the bar, what? Only two hours earlier?

"Oh"—she laughed—"that. It was just a misunderstanding. Kind of."

I stared her down, much in the way I'd stared down my brother. She set her jaw and mirrored my position.

"Paige."

"Why didn't *you* correct him?" she asked. "You could've told him it wasn't true."

Breathe in for four. Hold it. Out for four.

I glanced sideways and caught sight of a small sitting area tucked around the corner. Laying a gentle hand on her elbow, I started steering her toward it. Before we sat, I saw one of Molly's nurses carrying a chart.

"If Molly needs anything," I told her, "I'll be over here."

She nodded and gave Paige a frank, assessing stare. Recognition lit her face, and she hustled off.

Shit.

Paige perched on the edge of one of the chairs, carefully crossing her long legs. She smoothed the edge of her bright blue dress, which seemed so much shorter now that she and I were sitting alone in a hospital than it had at the party.

Everything about her seemed amplified, the longer I looked at her. Her hair was a deeper, more vibrant red. Her legs longer. Her lips fuller. Eyes bluer.

I hated it.

"Security wouldn't let me in because I didn't know the patient's name," Paige said. Her fingers played with the edge of her skirt, and she wouldn't meet my eyes. "And I just … you know that movie *While You Were Sleeping*?"

I raised an eyebrow.

"Right," she continued. "I'd explain it, but you won't care anyway."

"Paige."

She took a deep breath. "I told the security guard I was your fiancée so he'd let me through. Since I had your phone, it seemed like a logical thing to do at the time."

I covered my mouth with one hand, my elbow propped on the top of my leg while my brain raced furiously. In my silence, Paige kept babbling. Something about Sandra Bullock and gaining weight and rings, but only about half of it made sense.

All I could hear was my lawyer's voice in my head, the last thing she told me before I hung up.

Unless you've got a spouse hiding in the woodwork somewhere, Nick has everything *he needs to be granted guardianship.*

There were no spouses hiding anywhere, but sitting in front of me was a woman who'd proclaimed herself as just that, or a future one, at least. Paige's face and my sisters' faces all blurred together in my head, and I struggled to separate them. Nick's words, the weight of them that I couldn't ignore, coupled with my lawyer's not so subtle suggestion, had an idea forming that absolutely terrified me.

Paige lifted her eyes, and what surprised me most was the look of apology I saw there. "I didn't know your brother was behind me."

I nodded. It all made sense. Perfect, ridiculous sense.

"Also," she continued, "he's a giant dickwad. I wanted to punch him in the throat after about six seconds."

I huffed a laugh under my breath. She didn't know the half of it. My brother was the exact replica of our father. An entitled, image-driven prick. Nick loved the girls, in his own way, but the thought of them being raised in that world, the world I hated so much as a child, by Nick's equally entitled, equally image-driven wife, had my blood boiling over.

How did I even attempt to explain all this to someone who had no clue what she'd just inserted herself into?

Despite what she'd just laid at my feet, an offering she had no idea she'd made, I struggled to find the words to say to her.

Probably because I was struggling to admit out loud what I needed to do. I could hardly admit it in my own head.

Being quiet wasn't new for me. I'd always been that. Always been the guy who led by example, not by barked orders. The lion who never needed his roar, so to speak.

But sitting across from her, I wanted these words to come easily, but even *thinking* them felt insane. Felt like the universe was sitting back and laughing hysterically on my behalf.

Not all that long ago, I was pretending to be someone's boyfriend. And now … I was contemplating asking Paige to do a whole lot more than that. If I wasn't five seconds away from puking, I might have started rocking in a corner.

"Why was he so mad at you?" she asked.

I breathed out slowly, folding my hands over my stomach as I settled into the too-small chair. Those words were, unfortunately, quite easy to find.

"He wants something that I have." I shook my head. "Four somethings, I guess."

Her eyes tracked over my face. "Your sisters?"

My head dropped back onto the chair as I stared up at the white ceiling tiles. "Yeah."

"So you're like …"

I kept my eyes aimed up when I answered. There was no particular desire to see the look on her face when I told her something I'd managed to keep under the radar for more than two years. "Their legal guardian."

Paige was quiet for a couple of seconds as she processed. "And he wants to be."

"Yeah. He and his wife do."

"And you *don't* want them to be," she clarified.

I dropped my chin so she could see my face again. "Definitely not."

She cupped her cheeks in her hands and stared at me. "And me saying I was your fiancée was …" *Was what?* I wanted to ask. Because I had a few words I could drop into that particular empty space.

Perfectly timed.

Brilliant.

Crazy.

Fate.

Paige didn't say any of those things, though. "It was really stupid, wasn't it?"

I closed my eyes and wiped a hand over my mouth. I didn't know why I thought Paige would make this easy on me. Why I thought her mind would follow the same path that mine was.

Probably because that path was certifiable, padded cell insanity.

Except it wasn't. Not at all.

"I just … didn't think, really. I'm so sorry, Logan. I don't blame you for being furious."

I dropped my hand and stared at her.

"Oh my gosh, would you say something? You're starting to freak me out."

"I'm not furious," I told her.

She blinked a few times. "You're not?"

"Nope."

Paige sat back and exhaled audibly. "Well, that's good. I thought you'd flip the hell out on me, tell me I should think things through better, blah, blah. That's what Allie tells me all the time."

"Oh," I interjected, "you *should* think things through better, but I'm not furious."

"Well, that's good." Her eyes narrowed suspiciously. "Why? You're not exactly Susy Sunshine, if you know what I'm sayin'. I figured you'd be breathing fire right now."

I leaned forward and plucked her hand from her lap, turned it side to side so I could study the ring. When she sucked in an audible breath, I kept my eyes down because I didn't want to know what was on her face. The skin of her long, graceful fingers was smooth and soft. No callouses like the ones covering mine. No scars from broken fingers or skin that had been ripped off by an overzealous lineman.

"Nick is an asshole," I told her as I studied her fingers in mine. "But he's married. He works a job with normal hours. During the season, I probably work a hundred hours a week. My housekeeper just quit, the third in a year. And under my watch, my sixteen-year-old sister just got in a car accident driving around with her drunk friend, so he's going to try to take them from me because of it."

Paige's chest rose and fell with increasing speed. Her pink lips were full and open slightly as she watched me. The bridge of her nose was covered with light freckles, and it worked. All of her separate pieces, they worked really, really well together.

"He's better on paper," she said. "That's what you're trying to say?"

I nodded. "Yeah. He checks a lot of boxes that I don't."

A blanket of quiet fell between us, and I saw the wheels turn behind the bright blue of her eyes.

"What is it that you need, exactly?" she repeated, slowly pulling her hand out of my own.

Her eyes held mine. Turns out, I didn't even need to say the words or try to figure out the best way to say it. She finally tore her gaze away, and it landed on the ring.

"Ohhhh," she drawled. "You need a fiancée."

"Actually," I said slowly, gauging the finely featured face in front of me, "I need a wife."

Paige's face stilled, then the last—absolute fucking last—thing I expected to happen happened.

She smiled.

"Perfect," she breathed.

CHAPTER 5
PAIGE

If someone at the hospital were awarding gold stars for being in the right place at the right time, I just won the biggest, brightest, shiniest one in the world.

Logan Ward needed a wife, and I'd just pronounced my role as exactly that to the one person who would be most pissed off about it.

He went stock-still at my unconscious answer. Absolutely nothing processed through my brain before the word fell off my lips.

"What's perfect?" he asked. Those broad shoulders squared up like I'd just aimed a gun at him, and he was bracing for impact.

"You need a wife," I repeated, watching as his eyes darted past my shoulder.

"I," he started, then took a deep, steadying breath. Those green, green eyes met mine bang on. No avoidance, no guilt, no beating around the bush. "Yeah. I do."

I sat back in my chair and appraised him.

I'd never put much stock in what kind of man I'd want to be my sorta fake, sorta real husband. Mainly because this was a situation I never would've been able to conjure up in my wildest dreams. Certainly not as of twenty-four hours ago.

Did I want to marry Logan Ward?

What I knew of him could be condensed into a few easy bullet points.

-great defensive player

-shoulders that rivaled a redwood tree

-jaw that could cut glass

-face that would photograph like a freaking dream

-had the conversational dexterity of a piece of cardboard

And now, I could add two more.

-needed a wife because he was some sort of guardian angel/white knight/brother of the decade

-exactly what *I* required to cash my inheritance check from Aunt Emma.

Oh shit, if I ever doubted the ability of our loved ones to grant their own wishes after death like some warped fairy godmother, I didn't doubt it anymore.

Aunt Emma wanted me to get married.

Aunt Emma would manipulate me beyond the grave in order to keep me from being alone like she was.

And the same day I found out about her antiquated little scheme? Aunt Emma dropped a freaking husband in my lap.

How hard could it really be to pretend I was attracted to the most attractive man I'd seen in a while. Not even most attractive physically, it was the fact that he was the least annoying man I'd conversed with in the past year. Those things were of equal weight in my eyes, honestly.

Hot? Wonderful.

Not an annoying asshole? Even better.

Logan was giving me the same frank appraisal, like he needed to decide the same thing about me.

"Sounds like fun," I said after a minute. "I'll be able to channel some of those acting classes I took but never did anything with."

He blinked. Then blinked again.

"What?" I said with a casual shrug. "You need a wife, right? If you can believe it, I find myself in need of a husband."

"You …" Logan narrowed his eyes. "What?"

I smiled patiently. Not everyone processed as quickly as I did. "Think of it as a mutually beneficial legal arrangement."

Again, he sat back in his chair like I'd used both hands and shoved with all my might. "You can't be serious right now. You walked in through those doors ten minutes ago, and you're ready to *marry* me?"

"Well, not right *now*." I eyed him. "Why are you being so weird about this? It was your idea."

Logan tipped his chin up and breathed slowly. "I don't know. Maybe because I didn't expect you to be so not weird about it. It's freaking me out."

"You are so fascinating," I said quietly.

He sighed wearily.

"Okay, let's focus. You need a wifey so that Nick the dick can't take the girls, right?"

His level stare was as much answer as I got.

"Great. I need a husband to cash an inheritance check from my crazy Aunt Emma."

Those green eyes narrowed to slits. "Seriously?"

I waved my hand. "It's a whole thing. I can explain later. But the bottom line is that I have no interest in trying to dive into the world of dating and swiping and idiot men in hopes of finding a diamond in the rough. You and I can fulfill what the other needs." I sat back and spread my arms wide. "Easy peasy. Besides, you're not hard to look at. I could do worse."

His jaw worked back and forth. "I don't know. Even thinking it felt crazy, but hearing it out loud …"

"Aha!" I pointed my finger at him. "So you thought about it before I said it."

Logan leaned forward and dropped his head in his hands. "This is insane. We haven't even discussed it, and you've got your mind made up."

"What do you think we're doing right now?"

His head lifted. "What?"

"Discussing it," I explained. "We're discussing it. Pros and cons, blah, blah."

"Yeah, except you're not giving me any cons." His eyes tracked over my face. "We'd be married, Paige. Living together. If my brother doesn't think it's real, then it's pointless. Not to mention my sisters. Anything I do, I'm doing for them. No offense, but your reasons don't factor in when I think about why I'm willing to commit fraud."

"Geez," I muttered. "Don't hold back or anything."

A sound resembling a groan came from deep within that big, broad chest. "I need to call my lawyer. I can't think about this until I hear what she has to say."

I waved my hand at him. "Sure, fine. Let's do it."

Logan looked around. "Actually, I'm going to go check on the girls first."

I started to stand. "Want me to come with?"

"No," he answered firmly. A little too firmly.

My arms crossed over my chest. "I'm going to have to meet them eventually."

He raised an eyebrow. "We haven't even agreed to this yet, so for right now, no, you don't need to meet them. They've had enough people disappear from their life. I'm not going to introduce you until we've got everything hashed out, contracts signed, and a plan set."

The faces on his phone screen flashed through my head, and I had my first moment of pause. These were young, impressionable girls, apparently without parents. I thought about my aunt and how she'd mothered me when I was younger because she had no one else to transfer all that love to. I thought about Faith, braiding her hair just a handful of hours earlier.

Slowly, I breathed out, then nodded. "Makes sense."

Logan tilted his head, clearly surprised at my capitulation.

"You're a good brother, Logan."

At my praise, he sighed again, unfolding that long, strong body from the chair. He looked down at me, then shook his head a little. "I don't feel like one right now, but thanks. I'll be right back."

I settled into my chair and leaned my head against the wall.

Allie would flip her shit when I told her this, and the image was enough to bring a smile to my face.

She was the one who told me my new job could be to find a husband.

The thought of marrying Logan, to help his sisters, to keep Emma's money out of Collins' douchey little hands, felt like standing on the edge of the Grand Canyon. Terrifying and heart-hammering exciting. Doing this, even though we had stuff we had to work through, seemed like a no-brainer.

But it was still a helluva leap into the unknown.

I hadn't had a boyfriend in years, so it's not like my prospects were plentiful. Most men I met, especially in the world I'd left behind—an ocean over—were plenty interested in banging a model. When someone looked at you like you were an empty vessel, it was not a feeling you forgot anytime soon.

Briefly, I allowed a shudder to skate down my skin. That was the part of modeling that I didn't miss in the slightest. People like Allie, who saw straight into my crazy-ass soul the moment we met, were few and far between. And since I'd moved to Seattle over a year ago, I hadn't felt any desire to find a man. Not even for a temporary release because I could handle that on my own, thankyouverymuch.

The sound of heavy steps had my head lifting, the sight of Logan heading toward me had my tummy flipping.

This was no boy. No pretty-faced model with razor-sharp cheekbones and a waist smaller than mine who would constantly be worried about which one of us looked better.

The space of the hallway seemed to shrink simply because of the sheer size of him.

His eyes were pinned on me, resolute and unwavering.

"Everything okay?" I asked, standing as he approached.

Logan nodded, his jaw clenching once. "I had to fork over cash to send the three not currently hospitalized down to the cafeteria to ensure we've got some privacy. They'll bleed me dry before they hit eighteen, I swear."

I smiled at that. "How old are they?"

A doctor and two nurses rushed past us, forcing Logan to take a step in my direction. He smelled like clean soap.

His fingertips scratched along the edge of his jaw when he answered, a rueful smile touching the edges of his usually unsmiling lips. "Molly, the reason we're here and the one currently grounded for life, is sixteen. Isabel is fourteen going on forty, and the twins, Lia and Claire are twelve. If any one of them will turn me prematurely gray, it'll be those two."

Unbearably charmed by the way he spoke about them, I tilted my head, imagining that thick, dark hair cropped short against his head threaded with silver. Without thinking, my fingers reached up to brush against the short, soft strands. He stilled, watching me carefully.

"Silver Fox would be a killer look on you."

Belatedly, I realized I was doing some serious scalp fondling when we definitely had more pressing matters to attend to. I dropped my hand and cleared my throat. "So … shall we call your lawyer?"

Logan stared at me for a beat, and when he opened his mouth to speak, the words had me grinning unexpectedly.

"You're tall," he said.

"You're just realizing this?"

He blinked, coming out of whatever stupor had allowed him to say the words. "I was sitting when we talked at the party. I just … didn't realize it until now."

"Models usually are." I tipped my head down toward the floor. "And I gave myself a bit of a boost today."

His eyes tracked down the length of my legs to the three-inch cork wedges fastened around my ankles.

"Right." His voice was gruff and rough, and if he wanted to blow my house down, I would not have argued with him. "I talked to my lawyer right before you showed up, so she'll probably answer."

While he pulled up the contact information, I noticed an empty conference room just down the hall. I touched his elbow and pointed at it. The phone was pressed to his ear while we walked into it, and I shut the door behind us.

Logan set the phone down and punched the button to put it on speaker. A tinny, indistinct female voice came over the line.

"Hey, Logan. Everything okay?"

I perched my butt against the edge of the table, and Logan took a seat in front of the phone.

"Remember when you asked me about having a spouse hiding in the woodwork?"

Silence pulsed on the other end of the phone. "Yes."

Logan stared at me for a second, closed his eyes, and then turned his face back to the phone. "What if I told you I suddenly found myself engaged?"

Whoooboy, that sounded really, really officially official. My heels tapped furiously on the floor as I waited for the lawyer to say something.

"Well," she started, "I would tell you congratulations. And I would also tell you that if there was a hypothetical relationship for the purpose of maintaining custody of your sisters, then that hypothetical relationship would need to be ironclad. Married in front of witnesses, with all the correct paperwork filed, and I'd strongly suggest against a Vegas wedding because it would be the kind of thing that Nick would point to as hasty and unplanned, especially for you. Hypothetically," she repeated firmly.

Got it. Don't admit you're committing fraud out loud to your attorney.

Logan pinched the bridge of his nose. "I hate Vegas, so that's not a problem."

"Another thing to consider, hypothetically, is that you couldn't get married tomorrow and then break up in six weeks. In the state of Washington, Nick can challenge the custody ruling once every twelve months, if he feels like he's got a case."

Ahh, yes. One minor question that needed to be answered. How long, exactly would we need to stay married?

I rubbed at a spot on my chest, and Logan's eyes honed in on it.

"Well, Molly is sixteen, so once she's an adult, she can make her own decisions, but," his eyes flicked from the nervous tell of my hands up to my eyes, where they stayed, "I don't know if my future spouse is ready to commit to being here until the twins turn eighteen."

The lawyer hummed thoughtfully. "I don't know if that would be necessary. Once Molly is eighteen, that means the younger siblings have a third choice presented to them. Theoretically, if she could provide for her sisters, she's as viable of an option as he is. Not only that, but don't you plan to retire in two years? Once you're home full time, and Molly is a legal adult, he doesn't have much of a leg to stand on."

"Makes sense," he said, eyes still unwavering on my own. My skin prickled when I realized that I refused to look away.

Two years.

Two years.

Living with him.

My heart pounded at the thought, and I promise you, it was not the bad kind of pounding.

In the background, I could hear the shuffle of papers. "Logan, I won't bullshit you, if you turned up married on the first possible business day, it would be really difficult for your brother to prove that removing your status as guardian makes the most sense for the girls."

I tipped my chin up and breathed out slowly.

"You're sure?" he asked, voice low with charged emotion.

"Bottom line, the courts love stability. They've been with you for years, and that's no small thing."

My head snapped toward Logan. *Years?* How the hell had he managed to hide that?

If the media had any idea, he'd be the subject of an E60 documentary in a freaking heartbeat. Women all over the country would suffer mass swoonage at the thought of this beautiful mountain of a man stepping up and taking care of four adorable girls, fighting to keep them, and doing everything he could to protect them.

That was when the shiny little light bulb lit up over my head, complete with a bright *ping!* sound. No wonder Logan avoided the media at all costs, why he fought tooth and nail against putting himself front and center. Why he eschewed all social media, anything that might point the limelight in his direction.

Because he was protecting his sisters.

My whole body went soft and melty, something that did not happen to me outside of holding puppies or kittens or eating a freshly baked donut or something.

The fact I was ready to jump into hypothetical matrimony because of a check with a shit ton of zeros behind it suddenly felt a little cheap and brittle, brassy under the light of what Logan was doing.

I took a deep breath. That didn't matter. I could do a lot of good with that money, and I would.

"So this will work, won't it?" I asked. "We can pull this off?"

The lawyer went quiet at the sound of my voice. "Uh, yes. I think so. You two certainly have things you'll have to discuss privately, but that's nothing I need to be involved in. Your reasons for doing this are your own, and how this hypothetical marriage looks from day to day is your own business as long as you're living under the same roof. You're okay with that, Miss, umm, may I ask who I have the pleasure of speaking to?"

Logan turned in his chair so that he was facing me, his arms crossed over that wide chest. His face was blank, but his eyes burned green into mine.

Maybe I was standing at the edge of the Grand Canyon, but if I was going to leap, it would be the most epically beautiful leap of all time.

I took a deep breath, in and out, and once again. Then I jumped.

"You're speaking with the future Mrs. Logan Ward."

CHAPTER 6
PAIGE

"No."

"Yes."

"Paige," Allie said slowly, "when I told you to husband hunt, I didn't mean to marry the first man who spoke to you."

I flopped back onto her bed and sighed. "You're being dramatic. I talked to at least six humans of the male variety before I saw Logan at the hospital."

My attempt at humor was lost on my best friend, who carefully sat on the edge of the bed and gave me one of those "mom looks" that I hated. I couldn't even blame it on her acquiring a future stepdaughter in the form of Faith because even in the years when we shared a flat in Milan, I'd gotten more than a few of these looks.

"I understand that the thing with your aunt threw you for a loop, but you barely know Logan."

I rolled on my side and punched the pillow under my head so I could see her more clearly. "This is a perfect setup, and you know it."

She huffed. "I know no such thing. It's *marriage,* Paige."

"So what? People get married for all sorts of reasons. And get divorced for even more reasons than that. I have three million reasons to hitch my wagon to Logan's, so to speak."

"What about love? What if you meet someone the day after you marry Logan, and boom, you're the wifey and can't do anything about it." She laid down next to me, positioning Luke's pillow to mirror the one under my head. With her blond hair pulled back from her makeup-free face, she looked exactly like she did when I met her a handful of years earlier. Our knees touched, and I smiled a little, thinking back to when we used to talk like this after I finished a show or a shoot. "You're closing the door to the possibility that someone else could make you happy, and that makes me sad for you."

"I've been here for over a year, right?" I asked. "Not a single man has made me look twice, except Logan."

"Yeah, because he ignores you. He sets off your prey instinct because he's not drooling and fawning and being an idiot."

"Exactly," I said feelingly. "It's not going to be a hardship to marry a hot football player for a couple of years. I get a nice house to live in, he'll be gone all the time during the season, and I'm out from under your roof, so I won't feel like a mooch anymore—"

"Except that isn't a good argument because you're inheriting three million dollars," Allie interrupted. "Pretty sure you could buy your own place."

"Allie," I whined. "Stop interrupting my justifications with logic."

She smiled, but her eyes still held that horrible worried look that made me want to clap my hands over my face so I wouldn't be able to see it.

"Hell, no. And you want to know why? Because this is exactly what you always do. You make these massive life decisions without thinking them through." When I did cover my face with my hands so that I couldn't see her, she reached over and yanked them down. "You can't say that I'm wrong either."

"Trust me, I've thought this through. Even his lawyer thinks it's genius."

"Of course, his lawyer thinks it's genius. It saves her the work of going to court." Allie sighed. "Paige, you found out about the money this morning. The time stipulation your aunt gave you is … unfortunate, I'll give you that. But it's not impossible."

"It's insane," I interjected. "You can't say it's not insane. Trying to find, date, fall in love, and marry someone the old-fashioned way is not happening in the next year. I can barely decide on what kind of food to order in a restaurant, let alone settle on someone forever, you know what I'm sayin'?"

She gave me a look.

"Seriously. So I Tinder or Bumble or whatever else there is out there, and I have six months' worth of duds. Do you know what that does to any guys who come next? Talk about pressure. I wouldn't want to put myself through that, so I definitely can't ask it of them. And I refuse to give that little weasel Collins a penny of Aunt Emma's money."

Allie rolled to her back and folded her hands over her stomach. The way she was staring at the ceiling almost had me fist-pumping. Not that I needed her blessing or whatever, but there was something to be said for your best friend looking you in the eye and saying, *I understand why you're doing it.*

"I just … I think you'll regret not taking a few days to think about this." She turned her head and stared at me. "The whole 'leap before you look' thing is kind of your pattern lately. You know that, right?"

I rolled my lips between my teeth, but of course, she wasn't finished.

"Like when you moved to New York the week after a talent scout told you that you might have a future in modeling."

I pointed a finger at her. "That worked out quite well, don't you think?"

"Or when you moved to Spain, and Amsterdam and Paris and then back to Spain and then Milan because your agent makes a comment about which fashion designers would love your look."

My eyebrow rose imperiously. "Are you complaining about

that flat you shared with me? Because those designers footed the bill with how much they paid me."

"Or when you quit said modeling job without any backup plan, no notice, and hopped on a plane to Seattle to be the hair braider at the Pierson household." Her eyebrow did its own little show, probably more imperious than my own, because dammit, she wasn't wrong. I just … didn't understand the need to hash them out, point by point.

Yes, I moved to NYC on a whim, and my family thought I was batshit crazy, but it gave me a fantastic career.

Yes, I moved to Paris to see what would happen because New York was feeling stale, and it was an amazing experience.

Yes, I'd shuffled country to country for a while because nothing quite felt right.

As for the quitting, eh, she wasn't wrong about that either.

Blech. Anytime someone wanted to sit me down and dissect feelings and the why and why not, I instantly started imagining ways that I could physically maim myself in order to avoid it.

But this was Allie. This was my person. Even though the thought of it made me want to gouge a pencil in my eye, I took a deep breath.

"I was done," I told her. "I was tired of the shitty parts of it and less and less excited about the good parts. Tired of the posing and photographers yelling at me, tired of having clothes yanked on me by asshole assistants. Tired of not being able to live on pasta if I felt so moved. Or work out more because I'd 'look too athletic.' Besides, at twenty-eight and some change, I basically have one foot in the model graveyard. And you can only take so many years of people suggesting the cigarette and cocaine diet before it starts wearing on you."

She grinned. "Oh my gosh, remember that one girl at the Dior show, maybe two years ago?"

My belly shook from laughing. "She almost walked the runway with white powder lining her nostrils. I thought Maria was going to have a heart attack." I wiped under my eyes. "I'll never forget the new creative director swiping under that chick's nose, trying to get it all off before she walked."

Allie sighed. "I get why you were ready for a change. I really do."

"But ..." I drawled.

"But I still don't understand why you have to rush into this. What's a week to think this over going to hurt anything?"

"It won't hurt me, but the sooner we get married, the sooner Logan's brother is off his back."

"I can't believe none of us knew about his sisters." She shook her head. "I mean, I knew he had sisters, so did Luke, but that he has custody of them is a totally different ball game. It's amazing that he's kept this under wraps for so long."

"I know," I said quietly. "Makes sense why he's such a jackass about talking to the media. The more you talk, the more people want to hear."

We both knew that lesson well. Allie more than I did.

"Four girls," she mused. "That's ... I can't even imagine."

"Right? It says a lot about the kind of guy he is." I sighed. "That helps me feel okay about doing this, even if you think I'm crazy."

"I don't think you're crazy, Paige." She gave me a side eye. "It's my duty as your best friend to ask the hard questions, even if I understand why you're saying yes to this."

Ugh. It was her best friend duty. I'd asked her some hard questions myself when she decided to keep the team after her dad died, especially because going into it, she knew roughly zero about football.

"What about the girls?" she asked.

I smiled. "He showed me their pictures, so at least I know who is who now in case some overzealous security guard or nosy asshole brother starts quizzing me."

"I mean, what will they think about all this? Are you ready to basically be a surrogate mother to four girls of that age group?"

Her words were kindly spoken, but I still felt an unwelcome zing of defensiveness.

"I won't be their mother," I said quickly. She gave me a look. "I'll be their friend. Their half-sister-in-law."

"Semantics," Allie countered. "You said it yourself, Logan will be gone a lot during the season. You'll hardly see him. Who do you think will be in charge?"

I shifted on the bed.

"Where will you sleep? Will you be sharing a room with him?"

My eyes narrowed in her direction. I didn't have the answers to those questions, and she damn well knew it.

"Are you signing a prenup? An NDA? Are you allowed to have sex with other people?"

"Oh my gosh, okay," I burst out, my face going hot the exact moment she said "sex" because I didn't think about having sex with other people. I thought about having sex with Logan. "I'm going over there tomorrow so I can meet the girls when they get home from school. I pinky promise to write a list of questions so that your tender little heart can feel better about all the things my intended and I will discuss."

She smiled. "Thank you."

I rolled my eyes but couldn't help but smile back. "It'll be fine. You'll see."

"Well, when you come to me freaking out because you realize what the hell you got yourself into, I'm going to remember this conversation and gleefully rub it in your face."

"Like all good friends do," I said sagely.

We were still giggling about that when Luke walked into the bedroom. He froze at the sight of me in his bed with his fiancée.

"Luke," I cried. "I'm moving out, aren't you excited?"

"Yes," he said instantly, which earned him a glare from Allie. "When is the blessed event occurring?"

At his choice of words, I dissolved into laughter again. Allie covered her face.

"What?" he asked.

I took a deep breath and propped myself up on my elbows so I could see his face. "As soon as I marry Logan Ward. So maybe two days?"

His mouth fell open. His eyes darted from Allie to me, back to Allie and back to me, when she nodded slowly.

Luke lifted his hands. "I just … I don't want to know. I want no part of this."

He backed out of the room, which made us laugh even harder.

"This is such a bad idea," she said between giggles.

I swatted her. "It's a *fantastic* idea, Allie Sutton, you just wait and see."

CHAPTER 7
LOGAN

"Why don't you wait for me in the car, Mol?" my mom said.

"How come I have to do school pickup with you? I'm the patient here. It should have been in the doctor's note to stay away from those two little psychos as long as possible, if you ask me," she said, itching underneath the strap that hooked around the back of her neck, which held the sling still holding her wrist immobile. The doctor suggested wearing it for the first day or two after they'd released her.

I sighed. That had happened only the day before. *All* of this had happened in the last twenty-four hours.

"In the car," my mom repeated, raising one silver eyebrow.

The girls might not have been biologically related to the woman who gave birth to me, but they loved and respected her as if they were. Molly pouted but did as she was told.

When the door closed behind her, my mom gave me a concerned look. "Are you sure about this?"

"What am I supposed to do?" I asked wearily. The night before had proven sleepless, all of my racing thoughts, endless questions and concerns manifesting into hours of tossing and turning, trying to contain those anxieties within the boundaries of my California King. If I could keep them there, it felt more manageable. Because if I let my mom, or the girls, or even Paige see how much this stressed me out, I'd lose my tenuous grip on my sanity.

"I don't know, son," my mom answered. "You know I agree that you're the best place for the girls. I think your brother and that woman would drain all the sweetness right out of them, but you're marrying a stranger. How is that the best option?"

I braced my hands on the butcher block countertop of my kitchen island and hung my head, trying to stretch out the tight muscles in my neck. "Mom, I'd give you the same explanation that I gave you last night when you got here."

She held up her hands. "Okay."

"And she's not a stranger," I said. "Paige has been living with Allie and Luke for over a year. She's at a lot of team events. She helps them with Faith and does some stuff for Allie's foundation, too."

Even though I was often on the outskirts of the social aspect of the team, my mom knew who everyone was. She'd met Allie at a few of the games she came to over the last year. Anytime we played in Florida, or one of the bordering states, she was there. Allie always made sure to tell us that out-of-town family members were welcome in the owner's suite, and my mom had taken her up on that offer once or twice.

"I know you're worried, Mom." I lifted my head. Sure enough, her softly wrinkled face was bent in concern. She hadn't slept well either, by the looks of it. "But Paige has her own reasons for doing this. It'll work."

"And you don't think the twins will scare her off?"

For the first time all day, I smiled. "I think Paige can hold her own. She's feisty."

"Well," she hedged, "that's good, I think."

I nodded. "It is."

My mom looked at her watch. "How long do you need us gone?"

"Uhh, Paige should be here in about ten minutes, and I don't think we need much more than an hour to talk stuff over."

She looked over her shoulder at the front door when Molly honked the horn on her rental car. "You got it. We'll stop for ice cream or something after I pick them up. If traffic's bad, that should give you plenty of time."

"Thanks," I said. She came around the island and gave me a brief hug. Even though she was about eight inches shorter than me, she lifted up on her tiptoes to plant a kiss on my cheek. "I'm sorry your brother is an asshole."

I laughed. "He's your son too."

"That's the thing about being a parent," she said as she hooked her purse over her shoulder. "You can love them forever and still know when they're an asshole."

"Like when the twins locked the housekeeper in her bathroom?"

"Exactly like that," she answered with a smile. "He's like your dad, and that's not his fault. It's my fault for marrying the original asshole."

With that parting shot, she waved and walked out the front door.

While I waited for Paige to arrive, I took a deep breath and pulled out a notebook, jotting down a few things that I wanted to make sure to cover. There was something about her that scrambled my normally orderly thought process.

Probably because she was so … unexpected.

I'd met a lot of football groupies over the years, it was an unavoidable aspect of the job. Some were normal everyday people. Some in high profile jobs like Paige used to have. As much as I hated to think of her that way, Paige looked like a groupie but definitely didn't act like one. When I thought back to the day before, listening to her school Kingsley on how to speak to a woman, I grinned. She wasn't rude, but there was no room for him to misunderstand her meaning.

There was some part of me, buried deep under my misgivings,

that knew Paige would be good for the girls. It was the largest steadying force through all of it. The fame, though mine was less widespread than someone like Luke, or a handful of other guys on the team, wouldn't faze her. The spotlight wouldn't motivate her. Nor would my money, if this inheritance thing was any indication.

Instantly, I felt better. Simply allowing those thoughts precedence over the others, the ones who kept screaming at me that we were insane, soothed some of the raw, sleep-deprived edges inside me.

There was a knock on the front door, and I took a quick glance around the large kitchen that led into the family room, making sure it was still neat and tidy. When I walked to let her in, I caught a glimpse of red hair through the plated glass on the side of the mahogany door.

I inhaled for four. Held for four. And when I opened the door to see Paige waiting for me, I let it out slowly.

"Honey, I'm home," she said with a small quirk of her lips.

My eyes closed briefly at her voice, which pried open the cracks to allow my less pragmatic thoughts to slip through again.

This is insane.

What are you doing?

You can't marry her.

Look at her.

Paige stepped forward and laid a hand on my chest. My eyes snapped open at the gentle contact, and I felt the same tightening of my skin when she touched my hair in the hospital yesterday.

"Hey," she said. "It'll be fine. Trust me."

I swallowed, then stepped back to let her in the house. Instead of a small party dress and a face of artfully applied makeup, this was casual Paige.

Her mile-long legs were covered in light-colored pants. She wore a simple black tank tucked into the waistband, and her fiery hair was contained in a simple ponytail at the top of her head. If she had makeup on, it wasn't much. Nothing to adorn her in the way of jewelry.

And still, she was kick-to-the-balls stunning.

"Your house is beautiful," she told me as she wandered through the entryway into the kitchen.

"Little smaller than what you're used to." Why did my voice sound like that? Had someone sent my vocal cords through a woodchipper before I opened the door?

She smirked over her shoulder. "You should've seen my flat in Milan. The entire thing could fit in my bedroom at Luke and Allie's."

I nodded, not sure what to say to that. She'd traveled all over the world. Been on the cover of dozens of magazines. Her best friend was a billionaire. And I was about to show her around my fairly modest four-bedroom home in the suburbs.

Modest by NFL standards, at least. Certainly compared to Luke and Allie's home on Lake Washington.

But I didn't need a mansion. I'd much prefer to have a fat savings account and robust financial portfolio.

Paige set her small purse on the island before she pulled out a stool. She perched her chin on her hand and appraised me slowly.

"I like that shirt on you."

My brows lowered when I looked down at the basic gray Henley I'd snagged from my closet. "Thanks?"

Her lips curled up in an amused smile. "Compliments make you uncomfortable, don't they?"

I cleared my throat and crossed my arms over my chest. "I don't know. I've never thought about it."

"That's a yes if I've ever heard one."

"Whatever. We need to talk about a few things before my mom gets back from picking up the girls from school."

"Molly went back already?" she asked.

I shook my head. "Doc wanted her to stay home for at least one day. We'll see how her wrist feels tomorrow, but I think she can go back. No concussion, thankfully. They cleared her soon after you left."

"Good," Paige said. Her eyes snagged on the pictures hanging on the fridge. She stood from the stool and went to study them. On Lia's insistence, there was one picture of the girls with their mother, taken about a year before she left. Their dark hair and the shape of their eyes were identical, all five of them. It was a slight blessing for me that they didn't look like our father. If I searched hard enough, I could see a bit of him in their smiles, which resembled the same one that I had.

Paige didn't ask any questions as she studied the snapshots of my life, pinned to the surface by the kitschy magnets that Molly liked to collect. It felt incredibly intimate, allowing her to look freely. It was further than I'd let anyone get in years.

When she was done, she turned and set her back against the fridge. "I'm guessing you have a list of things to cover, don't you?"

I felt my face get warm. "Why do you say that?"

Paige tilted her head. "Do you realize that when I say something about you, instead of saying that I'm right, you deflect. Do you have a problem admitting when someone pegs you correctly?"

When my mouth opened to change the subject, I paused. My eyes tracked over her face, searching for any hint of malice or joking, but she was genuinely curious.

I answered slowly, trying very hard not to filter my thoughts. If this was going to work, even have a chance of working, she and I would have to be honest with each other. "I guess it's been a long time since someone has tried."

Paige nodded. "I can see that."

"Usually …" I cleared my throat when the words wanted to shrink back down into my throat and stay hidden. "Usually, I'm the one on the edges observing and not the one being observed. No one pays much attention to me."

She laughed. "Oh, I very much doubt that."

"Really?" I asked dryly. "I live with four young women. Who do you think is the center of attention?"

"I'd wager they all fight for that spot."

"All but Isabel, yes." I shook my head. "She hates being the center of attention."

"So she's like her brother then."

I sighed at her correct observation. "She is."

Paige licked her lips and glanced over at the family room. "Can we sit somewhere more comfortable?"

I gestured for her to go first, and then followed her into the large room. We'd redone it shortly after the girls and I moved in. They each had input, which was why the framed art on the wall was slightly eclectic, why one end of the couch had throw pillows with pink sparkles on it, and why the large square ottoman in front of the long, gray L couch was covered in fuzzy white fur.

Paige stared at the décor, then back at me. She picked up a light pink pillow with yellow tassels around the edge. "I'm … surprised at this."

Now it was my turn to laugh under my breath. "I allowed each of them to pick something out when we moved in. The couch was my decision, but I wanted this to feel like home to them, not just me."

The way she stared at me made me shift uncomfortably.

"What?" I snapped.

Her smile was pure amusement. "I really want to compliment you right now, but I'll refrain."

"Thank you."

Paige took the edge of the couch with a long chaise. Her legs were almost the same length as the cushion, reminding me again how long they were. "So what do we need to discuss to make you feel less like bolting right now?"

"Don't *you* have anything you feel like we should discuss?" I asked, instead of acknowledging how annoyingly accurate all her little observations were.

She shrugged those slim shoulders. "I feel like a lot of these things will work themselves out. Sure, I think we need an NDA and a prenup, so no one accuses me of being a gold digger, but beyond that, I'm not too worried."

"You never know, they might accuse me of being the gold digger, given your inheritance."

Paige laughed. "Oh, please. One quick Google search would dissuade that. You make far more in a year than I'll get from that one inheritance check." She looked around the house. "Not that you can tell by the way you live."

"Complaining already?" I asked, only the slightest edge to my voice. The edge might have been slight, but she heard it.

"Nope. I don't need a huge house. Just making an observation that you live below your means, which I can appreciate."

I exhaled. "I try. Raising four girls isn't cheap, and I never want to feel strapped. I don't have much in the way of endorsements, but I try to touch as little of my salary as possible with what I do get."

"I'm the same. I lived off the payment I got for a watch company for about two years."

My eyebrows lifted. "Must have been a nice watch."

"Oh, the watch was ugly as hell, but they really wanted me for their spring campaign." She sighed dramatically. "That was my unicorn year. Back when I was still a baby model, and everyone wanted to use me. That was the same year I did *Sports Illustrated*. The older you get, the more infrequent those gigs become."

It was impossible not to do a quick scan of her insane body, the same one we'd all seen in the skimpy bikinis, or even less. "You look exactly the same as you did then," I admitted quietly.

"Thanks, but the modeling industry can be pretty harsh if you're not one of the one name models."

My face must have given away my confusion.

"You know, the girls who only need one name to be identified. Gigi or Bella or Kendall."

"I have absolutely no idea who you're talking about."

Paige bit down on her smile. "I didn't expect you to." She waved her hand. "Anyway, I didn't come over here to discuss my defunct career in front of the camera."

"No," I admitted, smoothing my hands down the tops of my thighs. "I agree with the NDA and the prenup, and my lawyer has already started drafting those. You can send them to your own lawyer once they're done and review any language you don't like."

She nodded. "Sounds good."

The page of my notebook only had a few things scrawled across it. But the top one, the one I'd underlined and circled, stared up at me.

"You'll be the one with the girls once the season starts," I told her. "I'm gone all the time, and as you know, we travel a lot. I don't expect you to be their mom, but you're still in charge for those sixteen weeks."

She inhaled, then exhaled, maybe doing a little breathing trick of her own. "I know what I'm getting into."

Did she, though? Yeah, I had a feeling that Paige would be a good influence, teach them things that I was incapable of, but no matter what she thought, this wasn't just a temporary roommate situation.

"I know I'm already asking a lot, Paige. But when I retire, when this is done … please don't just disappear from their lives." I held her eyes, let her see the weight of what I was asking. "Not completely. It will be hard enough on them. I don't want them to feel abandoned by another person."

Paige nodded slowly. "Of course."

"Thank you." My shoulders sagged in relief.

She smiled. "Unless they hate me. Then they'll probably pack my bags for me."

I rubbed my forehead because yeah, that was a possibility too.

"Speaking of packing and moving," I said, "as far as living arrangements, it's unavoidable that we share a room. The girls need to think this is real too." The thought of it, looking over at Paige as she was comfortably settled on the end of my couch, had that knot of nerves twisting up inside me again. By myself, that California King felt plenty big, but I couldn't imagine sharing the space with her. "I've got a couch that we haven't been using, it's a fold out. I can move that into the master, and the girls wouldn't have any idea that I'm sleeping there."

"*You're* going to sleep on a fold-out couch?" she asked disbelievingly. "That's stupid, Logan. I can sleep there."

"No way. I'd feel like an asshole. I know you've got your reasons for doing this too, but my mom would flay my skin off if she knew I was making you take the couch."

Paige lifted one perfectly manicured eyebrow. "Your mom would rather have you share a bed with your fake wife?"

"You won't be my fake wife," I corrected, standing because I couldn't handle sitting anymore. "You'll be my real wife."

Her mouth snapped shut at my tone.

I kept going because all the thoughts from last night started tumbling around with the thoughts from before she got here. Why this should work. Why it might explode in our faces. How we could pull it off. Sharing a bedroom. Lying to the girls.

"Paige, you'll be my real wife. You'll have a ring on your finger, and not that fake one that got us here. One I'll buy for you. One I'll give you in front of a very real judge, in a real courthouse, in front of real witnesses. In the eyes of God and the law, you and I will be husband and wife. You'll be here, helping me take care of those girls, and none of it will be fake." My heart was thundering in my chest because with every word, I felt my thoughts spinning wildly.

Paige stood slowly. "Hey, it's okay."

How? I wanted to yell, but I swiped a hand over my mouth. She'd have all sorts of reasons at the ready for why this would work, why it would be fine, all the answers to how we'd be able to pull this off without a hitch. My eyes pinched shut because the entire thing felt like I was stepping out into the black without a safety net. No clue what was waiting for me. Every facet of my life since the girls became my responsibility had been planned out, and even when things came up, I never questioned my next step or the decisions I needed to make.

Because I knew what was right. I knew what I needed to do.

When her hand touched my face, I let out a slow breath. Another one landed on my chest, over my heart.

"It's okay," she said again, her voice so close that I finally opened my eyes.

"Is it?" I asked roughly.

Her fingers, still on my cheek, were cool and firm. "You think too much, Logan Ward."

The laugh that escaped me was rough and uneven. She didn't know the half of it. Before I made any decision, I'd already played out a dozen outcomes in my head, including this one. But as each outcome felt equally as likely to materialize, I couldn't find solid enough footing to move forward.

"Look at me."

I did, and those blue eyes were so close to mine that my heart started pounding for a completely different reason. Her fingers on my chest curled into the material of my shirt.

"What are you doing?" I asked quietly, even as my hands settled onto the curves of her hips.

"Answering one of my own questions," Paige said. "And getting you out of your head while I do it."

That was when she pushed up on the balls of her feet and kissed me.

I was so stunned that I froze, for just one protracted pulse, before my hands curled around her hips and pulled her closer. Paige sighed into the kiss, tilting her head to the side and deepening it.

Her mouth tasted like something sweet when I pulled her bottom lip into my mouth, and the hand on my face slid around to the back of my neck, where her fingers dug into my skin.

It had been so long since I'd kissed anyone that this small moment with Paige felt reckless and selfish. She pushed her body closer to mine, and my arm wrapped around the entirety of her waist. Her tongue slicked along the edge of my lips, and it snapped the fog in my brain when my first thought was *taste, more, suck, want.*

I pulled back but kept my arm around her.

Her eyes were foggy, her lips pink from the pressure of mine.

"Did that answer your question?" I asked.

She blinked up at me, then stared down at my mouth. "Uh-huh."

I stepped back and took a deep breath, willing my body's unwilling reaction to her to settle down.

"Why'd you do that?" I asked. We still hadn't touched the topic of sex, with each other, or otherwise. But suddenly, "otherwise" felt like something impossible and infuriating.

Paige slid a hand over the top of her ponytail as she watched me pace like a caged animal. Her lips curved up.

"I refuse to kiss my husband for the first time in front of that real judge and those real witnesses."

I nodded. "Right."

The sound of my mom's car jarred me out of thoughts of beds and lips and tongues.

"Is that them already?" Paige asked, the first flicker of nerves covering her face.

"Shit," I whispered. "They must not have gone for ice cream."

Paige smoothed her ponytail again. "Then let's meet my new sisters."

Even if her bravado was slapped on quickly, I appreciated it as the girls piled into the house with a burst of sound. I watched Paige's face at the high pitch, the giggles, the arguing. She never so much as blinked.

When the twins rushed into the family room, it took a second before they noticed the woman standing next to me. Like mirror images, they froze at the sight of Paige.

"Whoa," Lia said.

"Is she the new housekeeper?" Claire asked, just as wide-eyed as her twin.

Isabel strolled in behind them, her eyes narrowed on our guest. "She doesn't much look like a housekeeper."

"Iz," I admonished gently.

"What does a housekeeper look like?" Lia asked. "I mean, she's got hands and arms and legs and stuff. That's kinda all you need, right?"

"And a brain," Claire interjected. "You can't be an idiot."

I held up my hands when Isabel rolled her eyes. "Okay, that's enough."

Molly and my mom came in last, and Molly froze when she caught sight of Paige.

"Oh. My. Gosh." Her voice was breathy, and her eyes as wide as saucers. "You're … you're Paige McKinney."

"She's a *famous* housekeeper," Lia whispered to Claire.

Paige bit down on a smile as did my mom. Then she nodded at Molly. "And you must be Molly. How's your wrist feeling?"

"Totally fine," she rushed to say.

My mom raised an eyebrow. That was a slight change from the girl who earlier that morning who said she'd probably have to skip school for an entire week because the pain was "unbearable."

"We're a bit early," my mom said, giving me an apologetic look. "I was the only one in the mood for ice cream today, so we came straight home."

Ahh. Well, at least they didn't rush through the door about two minutes earlier, or introducing Paige would've been a whole lot more awkward, especially when I thought about the way she'd been pressed up against me. If I licked my lips, I'd probably still taste her.

Which was why I didn't.

"Girls, I'd like to introduce you to Paige, who is *not* the new housekeeper. Paige, this is Molly, Isabel, Lia, and Claire."

Paige smiled at them, but only three/fourths of them smiled back. Lia and Claire immediately surrounded her, peppering her with questions about why she was over, how tall she was, if she was afraid of spiders, and whether she was allergic to anything.

I stemmed that line of questioning with a stern look.

Molly was so star struck that she simply stared at Paige with a dreamy smile on her face.

That made me clear my throat because I hadn't anticipated any hero worship, but I guess that was to be expected.

And to the surprise of no one, Isabel hung back, observing the unfolding situation with obvious suspicion on her pretty face. I walked over to her and slung my arm around her shoulder. Briefly, she froze but then softened into my side.

"Is she your girlfriend?" she asked. The question was quietly spoken and heavy with wariness, but I wasn't surprised. Out of the four girls, Iz was the one who bore the most scars from when their mom left on her permanent journey of discovery. Lia and Claire, so far, had weathered it well. Molly struggled the first year but bounced back to her old self with the help of friends. But Isabel, more than the rest of them, still struggled with abandonment issues. Worried when I left for away games. Constantly searched for reasons people would leave, so she could be prepared for it when it happened.

"She's important to me. Important enough to me that I wanted you guys to meet her," I answered truthfully. I'd be doing so much lying in order to protect them, more than I liked to dwell on, but I'd be as honest as I could.

"She's pretty."

The words were said with so much acid that I grinned, leaning down to drop a kiss on the top of her head.

"That's not her fault." I squeezed her shoulder. "You're pretty too."

The droll look she gave me had me choking down on a burst of laughter.

From where I stood with Iz, I watched my mom introduce herself to Paige. As they spoke for a couple of minutes, Molly hanging on every word like it was pure gold falling from Paige's mouth, I felt myself relax.

The twins had settled on the floor, already unimpressed with our new visitor. Even Isabel smiled when Paige turned to them and asked if *they* were afraid of spiders because she had a pet tarantula to show them.

As they squealed, Paige winked at me.

This will work.

The thought was so clear and so steady that I took my first full breath since I found out about Molly's accident yesterday. Before I went to stand by Paige, I squeezed Isabel's shoulder again.

"Trust me?" I asked her.

It took her a second, but she looked up at me with solemn eyes and nodded.

My mom and Paige were talking about a place they both liked downtown when I approached.

Paige gave me a curious look, and I nodded meaningfully. Without thought, I grabbed her hand in mine and slid my fingers between hers.

Molly gasped, eyes lighting up.

"There's a reason I invited Paige over," I said. The twins went quiet on the floor, and Isabel watched us carefully. "I know this might seem sudden, but I promise you—all of you—that I would never do something like this unless it was exactly right."

Not a lie. Not romanticizing the situation. From the look on Paige's face, she knew it too and understood. Her fingers squeezed mine.

Molly sucked in a breath and held it. She looked one second away from exploding into a bomb of heart-shaped glitter.

"I wanted you to meet her because Paige has done me the great honor of agreeing to become my wife."

Molly screamed, flinging herself at the two of us.

Paige was laughing as she hugged my exuberant sister. My mom smiled, but her face still held a small edge of worry. The twins grinned at each other. Isabel narrowed her eyes, despite the encouraging nod I gave her.

This will work, I repeated.

This *had* to work.

CHAPTER 8
LOGAN

WASHINGTON WOLVES

"Never thought I'd be your best man," Luke Pierson said. He was straightening his tie, just like I was.

The mirror in the courtroom bathroom was free of smudges, but the bathroom itself was outdated.

"Trust me when I say I never thought that either." I gave him a look in the mirror. "No offense."

"No other choices, huh?"

I shook my head. "Well, my closest friend is probably a fourteen-year-old girl, so no. And don't you dare tell Isabel that. She'll hold it over her sisters forever."

The look in his eye was pure "dad mode" at my answer, and it made me twitchy. Like he was proud of me or some shit.

"You sure about this?" he asked.

The times Luke and I had spent in deep conversation about something unrelated to football in the last eleven years was approximately five minutes. And those five minutes started when he walked into the men's bathroom at the county courthouse after Allie told him he'd need to stand for me at our civil ceremony.

Which meant I had no intention of unpacking the reason I was marrying his fiancée's best friend for legal reasons.

"Yup."

He shook his head but didn't argue with me.

Even though we'd played together in Washington for over a decade, we weren't close friends. We were co-workers who understood that you wouldn't be best friends with everyone you worked with. Most guys on the team understood what their role was—we trained hard, played harder, and did our jobs. That didn't require socialization outside of the locker room, which was something most casual fans didn't understand.

Luke wasn't my boss, despite being the official leader of the team on the field. Everyone knew the team quarterback. But I was a defensive captain, and I'd been in that role as long as he'd been an offensive captain. The guys who played on each line looked up to us, respected us, and valued our opinion about what should happen when that ball snapped, and the clock started running.

His position might be more well known, and he might be the kind of guy who covered magazines, but in the world of the Washington Wolves, we were equals, and none of our teammates would argue with that. That was why he kept his mouth shut. It wasn't his place to talk me out of it because I wouldn't have listened anyway.

Knowing that I was less than an hour from Nick being off my back completely had me feeling so much better. Paige meeting the girls the day before went as well as I could have hoped. My mom watched them so I could go to the courthouse and get our marriage license. With a few minor strings pulled, thanks to my lawyer, we were able to get married only two days after Paige walked into the hospital, before the courthouse even opened, so Luke and I could still make it to practice on time. Outside of that bathroom, Paige was waiting for me with my mom and my sisters. Allie too.

The girls all but refused to go to bed the night before, their excitement over my announcement was so profound. Over our dinner of takeout Chinese, I'd even caught Iz smiling a couple of times when Molly peppered Paige with questions.

Paige had done amazingly, handling their exuberance with

ease and taking Isabel's wariness equally in stride. She asked questions but didn't push. Answered in the same way, not shoving herself or her success in the girls' faces. When Molly asked about some perfume ad that she'd done with some actor, at the lift in my eyebrow, Paige simply smiled and told her that he was a complete professional, and it was as good of a day at work as any had been.

All the paperwork came through quickly, signed that morning by both Paige and I once she was able to review both documents. No changes had been needed, which helped us be able to get married the same day the ink dried on both our signatures.

Luke was still quiet when I finally gave up on straightening the knot in my black tie and dropped my hands to the ceramic sink in front of me.

I glanced sideways. "Any tips you want to pass along on how to live with Paige?"

He laughed under his breath, then sighed. "That was a little different for me, and you know it. She had a room on the opposite side of our house."

I gave him a look. "I know that. Just making small talk."

"Yeah, I guess I don't recognize that coming from you," he said dryly. Luke scratched the side of his face and thought for a second. "She doesn't like to cook, I'll tell you that. And I had to stop screwing my fiancée on the couch because Paige likes watching ESPN until midnight."

"Dude," I groaned. "Please stop."

He laughed. "You're the one who asked."

"Keeping the Allie comments out of it, please."

Luke held up his hands. "Sorry."

"It's fine."

"You know, as much as I liked to hassle Paige about living with us, Faith adores her, and I trust her with my daughter. That's no small thing."

It wasn't. Everyone knew that Faith was the center of Luke's world, always had been. And it was the most perfect thing he could've said to me at that moment. It struck right at the heart of why I was doing this.

Before I could tell him what that meant, the door to the restroom inched open.

"Is everyone decent?" Paige asked.

Luke rolled his eyes but opened the door for her. "It's the men's room, Paige, you shouldn't be in here."

She answered. I think. Her lips were moving. But I couldn't hear a word because of how she looked.

Her hair was falling down her back in some elaborate mess of curls, and I liked that it was a bit messy and completely unbound. The dress skimming her body was simple and beautiful, nothing flashy or overtly sexy, but the swells of her cleavage under the white fabric had my mouth going dry. Her lashes were thicker and darker than they'd been the last time I saw her, and I wondered how long it took her to get ready, or if Paige could spend ten minutes and end up looking like that.

She gave me a wry smile and didn't look away from me when she spoke to Luke.

"May I have a moment with my groom?"

"In the men's room?" he asked.

"Good thing I have a big strong quarterback to play bouncer at the door for me," she said, patting him sharply on the back. "Just a couple of minutes."

Luke sighed but did as she asked.

"What are you doing in here?" I asked. Why was it that every time she did something to surprise me, I sounded like I hadn't tried speaking in five years?

Her eyes tracked down my chest. "You look nice. But your tie is crooked."

I opened my mouth to tell her that she looked more than nice. That she looked stunning. Take-my-breath-away beautiful. But the words jammed in my throat when she stepped up to me to shift my tie into place.

Something glossy and pink was on her lips, and whatever it was smelled like cherries.

"I just … wanted to make sure you weren't getting cold feet." Her fingers stroked down the length of my tie, and my entire body tightened. Paige's eyes lifted to mine when I didn't answer. "I'd hate to be jilted at the courthouse, you know."

The admission, holding the slightest edge of vulnerability, had me lifting my hand to touch the end of her hair. Against my fingers, those red, red strands were soft. She sucked in a breath and held it.

"No cold feet," I told her.

No cold anything. Not for miles and miles. Nowhere in the same galaxy that I was currently residing in, actually.

"Good." She smiled. "Shall we?"

Paige turned to the door, and before I knew what I was doing, I grabbed her elbow and whipped her back around to me. I yanked her body into mine and took her lips in a fast, hard kiss.

This was the one moment I'd allow myself. Just the one.

Instantly, she melted, her hand sliding up the front of my jacket.

After the ceremony, we'd firm up these lines, I promised myself. We'd define what was allowed and what wasn't. But for right now, the slick, sweet slide of those cherry lips on mine was too much to ignore before we embarked on this huge thing together.

Allowing my tongue to slip briefly past her lips, I touched mine against hers. It was cool and wet, and I pulled back to rest my forehead on hers. Paige was breathing hard, and I was too.

I wanted nothing more than to take a selfish, decadent moment with her and let her steady the thoughts in my head, which she seemed to have a knack for. Wanted nothing more than to count the notches on the ladder of her spine, which I could feel through the thin material of her dress.

"Now I've had my first kiss with my future wife before we're in front of a judge," I said.

She laughed, just a puff of air that I felt against my lips. "Touche."

"I got you a ring," I told her.

Her eyes stayed focused on my mouth while I reached into my jacket pocket. "Yeah?"

"Nothing fancy." It was hard to get words around everything I was feeling. The pounding of my blood after the kiss, quick though it was, the smooth, cool edge of the ring that I'd slip on her finger shortly enough. The fact we were in this position in the first place.

Paige took a deep breath, and her chest brushed against the front of my suit. "I don't need fancy. You're sure you don't want a ring?"

I nodded. "It would bug me while I play."

"Right." Her fingers traced the knot of my tie. "I like this."

I wasn't sure if I answered, or hummed, or just kept trying to feed oxygen in and out of my lungs. I never should have kissed her. It muddled my brain at a moment I needed to be sharp and clear-headed.

Maybe that was her effect on me. Something I couldn't afford in what was arguably the most precarious time in my personal life.

I stepped back slowly. "Ready?"

Paige smiled. "Ready."

We left the bathroom together, and at the annoyed expression on Luke's face, I almost laughed out loud. The girls were huddled around my mom, chattering excitedly. They each wore a nice dress, and Molly had done the twins' hair. Isabel looked nervous, but her eyes sparkled just a little when Paige and I approached.

Allie approached us and touched Paige's shoulder. "You might want to touch up your lip gloss."

Paige laughed, swiping a finger under her bottom lip and giving me a look of consternation. Isabel rolled her eyes, and Molly beamed.

"Gross," the twins said in tandem.

My mom hid her laugh with a cough.

A stern looking bailiff opened the courtroom door. "We're ready for you, Mr. Ward."

Paige and I led the way into the empty room, another favor granted to us courtesy of my lawyer. We didn't want gawking fans or anyone snagging a picture for social media.

The girls took a seat in the front row with my mom. Allie stood behind Paige, and Luke did the same for me. When Paige turned to face me, she kept a tight hold on my hands with her own.

The judge stood before us with her hands clasped in front of her stiff black robe. "Shall we get started?"

I nodded at her, squeezing my fingers around Paige's. She smiled.

"Weddings are wonderful, aren't they?" she asked, smiling at Paige and me over the rim of her glasses. "It's my honor to be here today to officiate the marriage of Logan Michael Ward and Paige Katharine McKinney. I'm told that you'd like to get straight to the point, with no pomp and circumstance, which is just fine by me."

I nodded, as did Paige.

The judge smiled at both of us. "Logan, do you take Paige to be your wife?"

I let out a slow breath, holding Paige's eyes as I said the words. "I do."

Paige blinked, her cheeks turning a soft shade of pink.

"Paige, do you take Logan to be your husband?"

"I do," she answered immediately. I heard Molly sigh happily.

The judge smiled at her quick answer, then turned to me. "Do you promise to love, honor, cherish, and protect her, forsaking all others and holding only unto her?"

"I do."

Paige grinned, considering we still hadn't covered that particular part. But she agreed just as readily when the judge asked her the same thing. When the judge signaled, I slipped the simple gold band around Paige's slender finger. She swallowed roughly when I did. Only the slightest flush of pink on her cheeks gave her away as anything other than cool and confident, the woman who put a man three times her size in his place because he didn't ask her name. Who stood up to my brother without knowing a single thing about him. Who jumped headfirst into this plan because she couldn't think of a single good reason she shouldn't.

That woman was standing before me, the literal blushing bride. And she was mine.

The judge glanced back and forth between us and smiled slightly. "Logan and Paige, by the power vested in me by the state of Washington, I now pronounce you husband and wife." Over the whistling and whooping from our small gathering, her smile widened. "Congratulations, you may kiss your bride."

Paige was laughing softly, and before I could move, she slid her hands up my chest and around my neck.

How did we already know how to do this so easily? I wondered, lowering my mouth to hers for a quick, soft kiss. Before I could pull back, she nipped at my bottom lip. My hands tightened around her waist, and I pinched her side, which made her yelp in laughter.

That was when my mom snapped a picture. My hands around my brand new wife with her laughing happily as she looked up at me.

"Look, Logan!" Claire yelled, running up to show me. "Isn't this a good one?"

"It is," I agreed, glancing over her head at Paige.

"Maybe we can put this on the fridge," she suggested, smiling shyly up at Paige.

The enormity of it, of what we'd just done, dropped like a brick of concrete over me, and I saw it do the same thing to Paige. Our eyes locked, and I held my breath while I tried to slog through the wave of icy cold panic.

"I think the fridge is a perfect place," Paige answered when I couldn't. She leaned down to hug Claire. "Maybe we can go to the store after school tomorrow and find a wedding magnet."

Claire ran off to show her sisters, and Paige leaned up like she was going to kiss me on the cheek, but she whispered in my ear instead.

"Breathe, Logan. Just imagine me naked any time you start to freak out. I can almost guarantee I'll be doing the same about you."

I laughed under my breath, enough to cause every set of eyes in the room to stare in my direction, from that one tiny sound. Apparently, no one expected me to laugh at a time like this.

"Is that supposed to help?" I muttered.

Paige gave me a loaded look over her shoulder as she went to accept a hug from her best friend. I blew out a breath slowly, trying to decide if this was the best idea I'd ever had or the absolute fucking worst.

CHAPTER 9
PAIGE

There was a rapidly growing list of strange thoughts that I was having on my wedding day. Added to it was *Logan has a thing against throw rugs.* I hadn't noticed it when I visited the other night, but it was glaringly obvious as I stood in the middle of his massive bedroom.

Our bedroom, I supposed.

The floors were a beautiful, gleaming wood in a warm, welcoming tone, which was a theme throughout his whole house. There was beautiful craftsmanship in the frame of the bed, the crown molding, the staircase leading up to the second floor, which we shared with the girls.

While the décor in the lower level was a mishmash of all five of them, this space was pure Logan. Clean and tidy, not a single thing out of place or cluttering any of the surfaces I could see.

The colors were neutral but warm.

But honestly, with the soaring ceilings and light walls, the long stretch of open space from the door to the edge of the bed, the room could use a nice rug. True to his word, he'd moved a large sofa along the back wall of the room, and I tried not to think too hard about who would be sleeping there when he got home from practice.

I shook my head and went to hang the last of my shirts in the walk-in closet. Logan's clothes were neatly organized by color, not that he had many. Other than the red in the team colors, Logan stuck to whites, grays, and black. Lots of athletic shoes, stacks of crisply folded Wolves T-shirts and sweatshirts. A few college jerseys, Ohio State, which made the monochromatic nature of his clothes even clearer. The red, black and white from both teams matched perfectly, almost like he'd done it on purpose.

Footsteps echoed down the hallway, and I popped my head out of the closet when I heard his mom, Nancy, call my name.

"In here," I told her.

She was a kind woman, clearly still processing this whole turn of events.

"Never thought I'd spend my son's wedding day helping my new daughter-in-law unpack," she said, carefully folding a cashmere sweater.

I smiled, but inside, I was having a *holy shit, I have a mother-in-law* moment.

"I'm sure Nick's wedding was a bit more traditional."

Nancy sighed and took a seat on the bench next to the shelves of Logan's shoes. My heels looked so starkly feminine in comparison, which she must have noticed too because she picked up one of my nude Louboutins and then set it back in place.

"Nick and Cora had a beautiful wedding," she said carefully. "Everything was perfect."

I tapped my finger against my thigh. Was I supposed to pry? Because I kind of wanted to.

"This must not be easy for you," was what I settled on.

She leaned her head back on the wall and gave me a sad smile. "It's not. But I understand. Why Logan is doing this, why he wants to have the girls with him."

"Nick was … not thrilled during our run-in at the hospital."

Her eyebrows lifted briefly. "I imagine not."

"Why do they hate each other so much?"

"Oh, I don't know if they hate each other. Or at least it's not the word I'd use." She shook her head. "They're so different. Always have been. Nick is very much like his father. Everything is about how you look, appearances, and image, and being perfect. Belonging to the right groups and clubs and owning the nicest things. Logan hated that about his dad. Hated that he married a woman just a couple of years older than Logan because it made his father look younger. I think he'd do anything to make sure those girls aren't raised in that world."

It was the world Allie was raised in, which was why she and Luke worked so hard to try to keep Faith's childhood as normal as possible.

"And Nick doesn't hate Logan?"

"Oof, that I don't know about. He hates losing, hates feeling like he's less, somehow. Hates feeling like Logan is better than him because of the success he's achieved. The fact that Brooke chose Logan to watch the girls before she bolted makes him feel like just another competition where he came in second." She smiled sadly. "I think he loves the girls in his own way, but it's the same way he'd love a trophy that he could snatch away from his big brother. Something he could show off and mold into anything he wanted."

As we sat in the big closet, I struggled against the feeling that I'd jumped into the deep end of a pool without checking to see if I could swim first. One deep breath and then another, and the feeling receded. It would be fine. I'd always had a knack with the pre-teen age bracket, and if the first night or the wedding earlier in the day had been any indication, the girls were already on board. That was the hard part. Nick would be dealt with easily enough just by the fact that we were married.

"Did you get along with Brooke?" I asked, unable to stem my curiosity about a woman who'd walk away from her kids like that. And the woman sitting in front of me, who'd stepped in to help even though she didn't share a shred of DNA with any of them.

Nancy chose her words carefully before opening her mouth. "I didn't really know her before my ex passed away. Only what I'd heard from Logan and Nick. His funeral was only the second time

I'd ever met her. It … was a lot for her after that. It was clear she'd never had to be responsible for so much."

"Even though she had four kids?"

Her nod was slow. "I believe she loves them, but not everyone understands or can accept the full, overwhelming kind of sacrifice that it takes to be a good mother. Even before my ex-husband—Logan and Nick's father—passed away, she struggled with it. They had more than one nanny and a housekeeper." She held up a hand. "Not that there's anything wrong with having help, mind you."

"Of course," I said. "They must have been a lot of work when they were little."

She laughed. "Oh, they still are, as you'll find out. I love them, I truly do, more than I ever could have imagined, but they're a handful. Especially the twins."

Right. I'd find out because Nancy was leaving the next day. I blew out air through pursed lips and took a seat on the floor, facing her as I crossed my legs in front of me.

"It's amazing that you're willing to help out," I told her. "Not every woman would step up to do what you've done for them."

I saw Logan in her answering smile. "Family is so much more than blood. But I think you understand that."

I nodded, thinking of Allie, Luke, and Faith. Of Aunt Emma, of my parents. All family to varying degrees, different kinds of love, different definitions of what the word meant. My parents loved me in the way that they'd always allowed me to do whatever I wanted. Their love was in the way they stayed detached, the way they nodded and smiled no matter what I told them was next up on my life's docket. They held down their side of the continental United States, and I held down mine, and the space didn't faze either of us.

Aunt Emma seemed to be the only one who bridged the gap between biological family and my friends.

There were no shared genetics, but Allie was in my blood. I'd stand down a moving truck for her, for Faith, maybe even for Luke, simply because of what he meant to both of them.

"It's amazing you're willing to help out," she told me quietly, using my own words. "Not every woman would step up to do what *you've* done for them."

My face felt warm, and I glanced down at the floor. I wasn't sure why, but her gratitude made me feel uncomfortable. "It's nothing. I'm sure Logan told you I had my own reasons."

She hummed. "He did."

"Plus," I said breezily. "I was ready for a change of scenery. And your son makes for some very pretty scenery."

As intended, it made her laugh. "Okay, okay. I'll let you chase me off with comments about my son's looks."

After she stood from the chair, Nancy paused, then leaned down to drop a kiss on the top of my head. I closed my eyes against the feeling that swept over me.

"I'd never do such a thing," I said under my breath. Apparently, I wasn't very convincing because she smiled.

Her blue eyes sparkled in my direction before she walked out of the closet. "Yeah, you would."

I stood and brushed my hands down the front of the tank. "Want me to pick up the girls with you?"

"It's okay. I like doing it, and I wouldn't mind the time with them before I leave. Not sure how soon I'll get back now that you're here."

I exhaled heavily, trying to think through what else I wanted to accomplish before she got home with them. "Okay."

"Besides, I think Logan will be back soon. Practice usually gets out a little early on Wednesdays, and I think you two could deal with some time alone."

I gave her a loaded look. "Now, don't try to make this into something it's not."

"I'd never do such a thing," she said over her shoulder.

If I sounded unconvincing saying the words, then she was the worst actress in the entire world. I was still shaking my head long after she'd left the room.

Alone in the house, I looked down at myself and wondered if I should change before Logan got home. *It was our wedding day, after all,* I thought ruefully.

Thankfully I'd never imagined my wedding day all that much, so coming home after the perfunctory ceremony with my mother-in-law, then changing into leggings and a tank top so that I could unpack didn't exactly shatter any romantic expectations.

Wandering into the large master bathroom, I gave my appearance a brief once-over and then shrugged. My hair was piled on top of my head, my face wiped clean of the makeup I'd allowed Allie to do earlier that morning. So what if I'd be welcoming my brand spankin' new husband home wearing a tank that said *I have never faked a sarcasm in my life.*

I smiled because I had a feeling Logan wouldn't appreciate the sentiment. If anything, he'd get that mildly annoyed look on his face, exactly as he had when I told him to imagine me naked anytime he started freaking out about what we'd done.

"What are you smiling about?" a deep voice asked.

I jumped, slapping a hand on my chest as I whirled around. "Holy shit, I didn't hear you come in."

His lips were tilted in an amused little half-grin, but my eyes only snagged there for a split second because this was my first time seeing the "just home from practice" Logan.

It was a good, good look on him.

Clearly, he hadn't taken the time to shower afterward because his chest was covered by a Wolves shirt with the sleeves ripped off, showing glimpses of the muscles stacked along his sides. His hair was damp and messy, and the gray shorts hung nicely off his trim hips.

"Umm," I said, then licked my lips. "What was the question?"

He sighed, stepping past me to lean over the sink that he flipped on. Logan splashed some water on his face, then snagged a towel. A lone drop of water slid down the side of his throat, and I watched it. I watched it go *all* the way down.

Did he get hotter in the hours he was gone? Or was this some weird marriage pheromone that my body naturally started pumping out now that I was legally bound to this spectacular specimen?

"You need to stop looking at me like that," he practically growled.

I blinked heavily, trying to snap myself out of it. "Sorry."

He snorted. "No, you're not."

At that, I smiled. "You're right."

Logan rolled his eyes a little and walked out of the bathroom. I followed.

"My mom picking up the girls?"

"Yeah. She helped me unpack my stuff. I kind of just moved your things around, so I hope that's okay."

He shrugged, glancing briefly into the closet before meeting my eyes. "Fine with me."

"Why do you hate throw rugs?" I asked.

If Logan was thrown by my random question, he didn't show it. "When the twins were younger, they tripped over the edges constantly. Spilled things on them all the time because they have a fundamental issue staying seated while they eat. Figured it was easier to just get rid of them."

Well, wasn't that just the most adorable thing I'd ever heard. I tried to stop my smile, but I couldn't.

"Don't look at me like that." He sighed. "It's simple logic."

"Mmkay."

Logan propped his hands on his hips and looked around the bedroom. "If you want to buy a rug, go ahead. Just try to keep anything pink and sparkly out of this one room, please. I've got enough of it everywhere else."

"Mmkay." Marriage pheromones, man. They were racing through my bloodstream at a shocking speed as though someone had unleashed some wild mustangs or something and off they went, manes flying, hooves pounding, kicking up storms of dirt and dust as they ate up the ground in front of them.

And why shouldn't I entertain thoughts about my hot, sweaty husband? Certainly nothing wrong with that.

A pounding on the front door had Logan's forehead wrinkling. "I'll go see who it is."

The sound increased in volume and intensity. I followed him down the hallway. Logan mumbled something under his breath, and I had a feeling it included lots of four-letter words.

"Logan, I know you're here," Nick yelled from the other side of the door.

"Ooh, methinks someone heard about our nuptials," I whispered when Logan paused in front of me on the steps.

"Shit. I really don't feel like dealing with him."

"Wait," I told him. "Take off your shirt."

His head whipped around. "What? No way."

"Trust me." I yanked my ponytail down and dug my fingers into my hair, fluffing into a wild mess. As I tried to twist it over one shoulder, very "unintentional intentional mess," Logan sighed and did as I asked. My eyes didn't even attempt to go anywhere except the stretch of his abs when he peeled that shirt off. Oh, there was peeling, and I was here for it.

"Coming," I yelled, slipping past Logan to skip down the rest of the steps. I pinched my cheeks, then my lips as I approached the massive door.

"What are you doing?" he hissed from behind me. I took one precious second to study his bare chest.

Ohhhkay then.

Endless stretches of tan skin, muscles upon muscles, all tightly stacked on top of each other. Veins popped happily under the curves on his arms, and I sighed. "It's not even right."

"Huh?" he asked, shaking his head and reaching past me to pull open the door. "What's gotten into you today?"

A retort was on the tip of my tongue to tell him what I wanted to get into me when the angry face of his brother came into view. At the sight of me, he glared.

"You've got to be kidding me," he spat. "You actually did it?"

I wound an arm around Logan's waist, his skin hot and smooth under my wandering hands. Sure hope he wasn't ticklish because I was going to stroke everything stroke-able within reach while I had the opportunity.

"Well, if it isn't my new brother-in-law," I said with a wide smile. "Sorry I ran out of invitations at the last minute. We would've loved to have you there."

Logan's big hand landed on my shoulder, and he gave me a short squeeze in warning. Right. Don't poke the angry bear.

Nick's face turned a mottled, unattractive red. "This is bullshit. You're committing fraud."

"Prove it," Logan said in a quiet, dangerous voice. His strong fingers curled around the edge of my shoulder, pulling me into his side.

Using the tip of my finger, I traced the muscle that started at the top of the V. You know the one. Immediately, Nick's eyes honed in on the small movement, and if it were possible, the color on his face deepened even further when he saw the gold band around my ring finger.

"I don't know what you think you're playing at, Logan," Nick said, "but it'll take a lot more than a blow-up doll of a wife to get me off your—"

Logan moved before I could blink. He grabbed Nick's shirt in two fists and yanked him up on his toes. "You ever say something like that about her again, and I'll wreck your pretty boy face, you got it?"

"Get your hands off me, or I'll come after you for assault too," Nick hissed. He shoved Logan's hands away, but the growled warning effectively made him step backward.

It was pretty damn effective for me too. No shit, I felt my thighs squeeze together at the sight of him ready to beat the shit out of his brother, simply because of some empty words tossed in my direction.

I'd heard worse over the years. Modeling wasn't exactly a highly respected vocation, no matter how revered we seemed among pop culture, and definitely not for a misogynistic a-hole like Nick. A lot of men did view us like blow-up dolls. Empty vessels created for their own pleasure to be looked at and dissected and judged for the things they could see.

Some people thought I was a giant, raging bitch for the way I expected men to talk to me. Thought I was "too much" because I lost my filter completely when they acted like I didn't have the right to be treated with respect, like an actual human being.

If everyone had a trigger, that sure as hell was mine.

And watching Logan risk retaliation from his brother, simply to defend me, triggered another reaction entirely.

I stepped forward and lifted my chin. "How about you get the hell off our property before my *husband* is forced to remove you from it."

Nick sniffed, straightening the wrinkled front of his dress shirt. "You're both insane."

Logan said nothing, simply pulled me back into his side when I tried to take a step forward.

"If you don't mind," I told Nick with a sickly sweet smile, "we only have about thirty minutes until the girls get home from school, and I've got *big* plans for every single one of them."

When he opened his mouth to say something, I slammed the door in his face.

Logan and I stood there while he cursed on the other side of the door, then while got in his car, until the door snapped shut, and the engine roared down the street like we didn't dare talk until he was truly gone.

"He's a real peach," I mumbled.

Logan turned to me, which meant his hand slid off my shoulder and back to his side. "I'm sorry he spoke to you like that."

I tilted my head to the side. "You don't have to apologize for your brother. It's not your fault."

His face was flushed, his eyes tight. Logan's fists curled up, and the veins in his arms rippled in response. He was angry. Really, actually angry.

My mouth fell open. "That wasn't just for show, was it? I thought maybe it was."

He sighed heavily and looked away. "Any time … any time I hear a man talk like that, I want to break him in half, no matter who he is. Because in a few years, the girls will be old enough that they'll have to deal with it too. Makes me insane."

"I have to tell you, Logan," I said quietly, stepping up to him and carefully placing my hands on his bare, heaving chest. "I really feel like I want to consummate something when I hear you talk like that."

He pinched his eyes shut and gently grabbed my hands in his. To my utter dismay, he pulled them off his skin before he took a step away from me.

"I don't think that's a good idea, Paige."

Don't pout, don't pout, don't pout.

When I thought I could speak intelligently, I cleared my throat. "Why not? If we're stuck together for the next two years, why can't we enjoy each other? You know, if the urge strikes."

Logan opened his eyes again, and the heat simmering behind the green had my skin going hot and prickly and all the kinds of things I wanted to feel when a man like him looked at me the way he was looking at me.

"Because it would complicate an already complicated situation," he said. "There are too many risks. Too many ways it could go wrong."

Immediately, I latched onto the things I didn't hear him say. He didn't say that he didn't want me. Desire wasn't the issue. I doubted Logan would argue with me if I told him he wanted me as much as I wanted him right now. I could hear it in his tone. He wasn't willing to budge, no matter how hot it was the two times we'd kissed. There was no way that man could look me in the eye and say we weren't complete fire together.

It had been so long since I'd felt this kind of attraction, and the thought of not acting on it, of not sinking deeper into something so decadent made my soul shrivel up and weep a little bit.

I took a deep breath and blew it out slowly.

"If you say so," I said.

"Celibacy won't kill you," he said ruefully.

He walked past me.

"Wanna bet?" I tossed over my shoulder.

"I'm going to take a shower before the girls get home. Takeout menus are on the top of the fridge if you want to pick something to order for dinner. Nothing fried for me."

I sank down onto the bottom step, resting my head in my hands, trying to breathe away from the mental image of him naked in the shower.

It was official—I'd married an evil, evil man. And I still had to survive our first night sleeping in the same room.

With a dramatic groan that made him chuckle as he walked down the upstairs hallway, I stood from the step to go find the stupid takeout menus.

CHAPTER 10
PAIGE

"Careful, Lia," Molly said, casually spooning curried rice onto her little sister's plate. "Curry will stain your hair yellow if it touches a single strand."

Lia's eyes widened in horror as her plate slowly filled with the offending side dish.

Logan shook his head and kept eating.

I sat back in my chair, the one just to the right of his. If I moved forward too much, our knees brushed underneath the long dining room table.

Using my elbow to nudge Claire, I nodded at the rice. "Actually, it won't stain your hair, but turmeric makes an excellent face mask."

Her lips peeled back in a disgusted curl. "Gross. You've put that on your face?"

Lia shuddered, poking at the food on her plate. "Nasty," she whispered. "What's turmersick?"

Isabel sighed. "Turmeric. It's a spice. And she's kidding."

"No, I'm not," I said. "I'll make you one if you want."

In answer, Isabel flicked her eyes away from mine and pulled her headphones from around her neck up over her head. Considering her phone was up on the kitchen counter, she was making it perfectly clear she just didn't want to hear me talk.

Logan reached forward and snatched them off. She sputtered, smoothing at the flyaway hairs lifting off her head.

"No headphones at the dinner table." He gave her a look. "Which you know perfectly well."

If my aunt Emma was disappointed by my marriage for monetary reasons, then she must've been throwing a party in heaven over my first full day as a brand new big sister.

I was being examined, no doubt about it. But so far, I felt like I was doing all right. Logan's mom and I made ice cream sundaes for the girls when they got home, and my addition of crumbled up cupcakes on top went over big.

Even with the unexpected addition of me, they all played a role and slipped easily into the rhythm of this little family that I'd suddenly inherited.

Molly, though she was the oldest among the girls, had true middle child tendencies. She was outgoing and carefree, she laughed easily, and moderated the bickering between the twins like a freaking pro. I was taking notes on how she handled them within an hour of them all piling through the door after school, harmless curry staining threat notwithstanding.

Isabel, though she was in the middle with Molly, sandwiched between an older, popular sister, two strapping big brothers who were currently engaged in a battle over who should have them, and the younger, insanely high energy twins, was quiet and watchful. More than once, I caught her eyes resting on me, her dark eyebrows (which I had massive envy of because women spent big bucks to have brows like hers) bent in a thoughtful V.

Anytime I'd tried to engage her in conversation, those headphones popped up like a jack-in-the-box.

And the twins? Okay, well, they were like trying to watch a wind-up toy that had been wound too many times. Just in the first hour that they got home, they'd sailed through the family room on scooters, whipped in circles around the large patio in the backyard on roller blades, and got into a wrestling match when Lia looked at Claire's iPad wrong. Apparently, it was a thing between them.

At the top of the chaos, like an unflappable stalwart, was Logan.

Not once had he raised his voice at any of them, but when the first scooter came zipping around the corner, he simply held his hand up, then pointed a finger at the large double slider that led outside.

Not only had he not raised his voice when they started acting up, but he was interested. He asked sincere, thoughtful questions about Molly's day. Got Isabel to talk in complete sentences. But only when she thought I wasn't listening. As soon as she caught sight of me around the corner, she snapped her mouth shut. But instead of chastising her, Logan laid a big hand on her shoulder and squeezed.

We finished dinner without any major incident, and as I started to clear the dishes, one of my jobs at Luke and Allie's place, Logan stayed me with warm fingers wrapped around my wrist.

"The girls clear the dishes."

When he dropped his hand as quickly as he'd touched it, I saw Isabel's eyes narrow in question.

"Ahh, okay," I said and handed my plate to Claire.

Molly shrugged. "I'm injured."

He raised his eyebrows. "You have one good hand, last time I checked."

Nancy smothered a smile, as did I, but Molly grabbed some silverware with a huff.

When the girls were in the kitchen, arguing over who had carried the most, I took a second to fully absorb the moment.

I was sitting next to a man I didn't know, who was my husband in the eyes of God and the state of Washington. In the kitchen were four young, impressionable girls who would look up to me as an authority figure. For the next two years, this was my place, and these were my people.

For the first time in my adult life, I was going into a new situation, living or otherwise, with a set amount of time stickered onto the front end.

Maybe knowing it would end, knowing that I'd be able to try something new once it was over, would keep the restlessness at bay. The curl of my toes and twitch in my fingers to move, go do something, go try something, go visit a place I'd never been.

To my complete surprise, I loved the energy barely contained inside the house. The walls and roof could scarcely hold it, but I loved how that felt. Like I was inside one of those wind chambers.

The rest of the evening passed in a strange, exhausting blur. I flipped channels on the TV while Logan studied film in his office—a room off the family room—and the girls spread out on the floor in front of the couch doing homework.

Logan's mom herded them toward their bedtime routine, which I observed from the end of the hallway, letting her have her time before she left us the next day. They adored her, and it was so obvious in the way they listened without argument and gave quick hugs and kisses when they were brushed, cleaned, and in pajamas.

Molly gave her a one-armed squeeze, and from where I was standing, it looked like her eyes were wet. Logan's mom whispered something into her hair, and Molly nodded, giving me a quick smile as she stood in the doorway to her bedroom.

"G'night, Paige," she said. "I'm glad you're here."

Something weird happened in my stomach when she said it, shy and sweet, looking much younger than her sixteen years once her face was scrubbed clean. It was sweet and snuggly as though she'd poured a warmed-up bottle of honey down my throat. "Night."

Nancy stood next to me and sighed. "They don't really need my help."

I glanced at her. "No?"

She shook her head. "I had two boys, so when I'm here, I feel like I get to indulge that part of me that always wanted a girl. Brush their hair out when it's still wet out of the shower. Help them pick what clothes to wear to school. Argue about whether they're too young for makeup."

I smiled at her. "My mom didn't even notice when I started wearing makeup. I think I was twelve when I walked out the door to school with her burgundy lipstick on."

Her eyes were a little sad when I said it. "That's awfully young."

"Trust me, the greater tragedy was how that color looked on me."

She rubbed a hand down my arm. "If you say so, honey."

The endearment made me blink. When was the last time someone called me anything like that in a loving, respectful way? Not a "hey honey, bring that ass over here" kind of way.

"I gave you my cell phone number, right?" Nancy asked.

I nodded. "Stored and saved in the number one favorite spot." She laughed, but I yanked my phone out and showed her. "No really, I have a feeling I'll talk to you more about those girls than I will with Logan over the next sixteen weeks, and that's if they *don't* make the playoffs."

She sighed heavily. "You may not be wrong about that. Once the season starts, they barely see him. He does his best to carve out time for the girls, but it's been tough on him. And every time a housekeeper quits, it gets worse."

"Yeah," I drawled. "What's up with that?"

Her eyes twinkled. "Let's just say that I wouldn't be surprised if the twins put you through the same hazing ritual that all the others got."

"Oh, great," I mumbled. A yawn took me by surprise, which triggered one on her own.

"You'll do fine, I think." She wrapped me in a quick hug, which was over before I could react to it. "I'm exhausted, and I should finishing packing tonight. I'll see you in the morning, okay?"

"G'night," I told her and watched as she made her way down the stairs to the guest room tucked beyond the kitchen.

Since Logan was still awake and working, I decided that going around the house to lock doors and turn off lights probably wasn't my responsibility. The girls' rooms were quiet when I walked past the closed doors. Only behind Molly's could I hear the low hum of some background music.

My fingers trailed along the wall as I walked into the master bedroom.

The couch, the one meant for one of the two bodies sharing the room, was fricken offensive if you asked me.

Like where did it get off hiding an entire bed in such a compact way?

If it offended me, I couldn't imagine what the gorgeous California King felt like. All big and beautiful and perfectly capable of holding two adult bodies that were, apparently, not consummating their marriage tonight.

I blew a raspberry out of my lips and stomped into the closet.

Who, exactly, would it complicate things for if we scratched an itch?

Sure as shit wasn't me.

It would be very uncomplicated. Very simple.

Him and me, in a bed, no clothes, orgasms for everyone. There were literally no losers in that scenario.

But as I stared across the closet at the perfectly organized clothes belonging to my brand new hubby, I had a feeling he'd always look at it differently than I did.

Impatiently, I shucked the leggings down my legs and kicked them toward the large white basket in the corner. I reached underneath my tank top and unhooked my bra, pulling the straps down my arms and the rest of it out from underneath my shirt.

As I was leaning over the bathroom sink that had been designated mine, I heard a door open and shut.

"Paige?" Logan called.

"In here." My voice was muffled behind the plush white towel that was pressed against my face.

"What'd you—?"

At the sudden pause in his words, I dropped the towel to see what happened. He was frozen in the doorway of the bathroom, staring at the bare length of my legs.

His green eyes, normally so bright, darkened as his jaw clenched visibly.

Leg man. Got it.

"Done working?" I asked casually. I plucked my brush off the counter and pulled the bulk of my hair over the front of my shoulder so I could start working through the tangles.

"What do you think you're doing?"

"Getting ready for bed? It's exhausting work to get married."

He gave me a long look, then his eyes trailed down the front of my body. Really, really slowly, stopping briefly on the very best parts.

And did my body perk up underneath the white tank top? Sure did. The girls wanted to get to know Logan better too.

"You know what I mean," he said tersely.

I propped my hands on my hips and faced him. "Actually, no, I don't. I didn't know how long you were going to be at work. For all I knew, by the time you finished, I'd be fast asleep right smack dab in the middle of my brand new bed, since you have no plans of sharing it with me."

The unhappy tightening of his lips was about as much of a victory as I'd get. Add it to the list of Logan Ward facial clues when he doesn't want to admit I was right. "And that's what you sleep in?"

I took a step toward him, insanely gratified when he tightened his fists at his side and his chest heaved on a deep breath.

"Normally, I sleep naked." I swept my hands down my body. "This is me making a concession for your comfort."

"How kind of you," he said, eyes searching my face.

"What do you sleep in, husband?"

He blew out a slow, controlled breath at the husky pitch of my voice, but he didn't answer.

"Regret marrying me yet?"

The line of Logan's throat worked on a swallow, and his eyes stopped heavy on my mouth. "You have no idea," he murmured.

The slight creak on the floor outside the bedroom door was as much warning as we had. Someone was trying to catch us with that kind of entrance, so catch us they would.

Just before the door flew open and banged against the wall behind it, I grabbed Logan's hands with mine, wrapped them around my waist and lifted up on tiptoes. He jerked back at the last second, my lips grazing the edge of his.

Our eyes held as Isabel stormed into the room, hair flying out behind her like a flag. My heart thundered wildly in my chest at the way she barged in.

Or how he was holding me. How he smelled. Pick one, really.

"Iz," Logan said patiently, dropping my hands and turning toward his sister. "You should know better than to barge into this room."

She sniffed, appraising our body language with unconcealed suspicion. "It's never been a problem before."

"It is our wedding night, though," I said, sliding my arm around Logan's waist and plastering my chest to his side. When I started to play with the edge of his gym shorts, he snatched my hand, lifting it to his mouth for a quick kiss. "This would probably be a good night for a little bit of privacy."

Oh, she didn't like me stepping in, judging by the darkening of her face, the pink spots that popped on her fair cheeks.

Logan sighed and let go of me, walking toward his sister, who so, so clearly didn't want to believe this was real. Or maybe she did want to believe it and proving that it wasn't was the easiest way to protect herself.

The thought had me tilting my head to watch her. Had me imagining Faith in her shoes.

He leaned down and took hold of her slim shoulders, so gently that I almost wanted to look away because I felt like I was intruding.

Whatever he said to her was too quiet for me to hear, but she mumbled a sorry in my direction before she left. Once the door was closed behind her, Logan hung a hand from the back of his neck.

When his head swung to the couch, and he frowned, a smile spread immediately over my lips. Bingo. In her own little way, Isabel just inadvertently helped my "sleep with my hot husband" cause.

Logan swung around and pointed at me when he saw my triumphant grin. "Fine. No fold-out couch because I can't have one of them barging in and wondering why we're not in the same bed. But if I have to line the middle of the bed with pillows or tie you down to keep your hands to yourself at night, don't think I won't."

With pursed lips, I walked over and tested the headboard. "Can't see myself breaking this if you tied me down, but I do love a good challenge." Dark, ominous thunderclouds gathered in his handsome face, and I laughed under my breath. "Kidding."

"I'm going to go work some more," he ground out. Before he turned, I glanced down, and yup, I was not the only one who enjoyed the visual I'd just thrown out.

"Good night, honey bunch," I said. He paused with his hand on the door and sent me a dark look over his shoulder.

"Three days until the season starts," I heard him mutter. "*Three* days."

I was still smiling when I slid between the cool sheets on the big, big bed and fell asleep with the smell of Logan all around me.

CHAPTER 11
PAIGE

WASHINGTON WOLVES

Me: OMG Am I supposed to talk to them about birth control???

Me: LOGAN. This was not something we discussed! Lia was going through my purse looking for gum, and she found my birth control, and now she's ASKING QUESTIONS.

Me: HELLO ARE YOU DEAD WHY AREN'T YOU ANSWERING ME

"It's so small, though," she said, turning the plastic circle one way and then the next. "How is that supposed to stop you from getting pregnant? Claire! Look at her anti-baby pills! They're tiny."

Her twin raced around the kitchen island, snatching the pills and holding them up to her face. "Isn't that what condoms are for?"

My eyes widened in my face. "What do *you* know about condoms? You're like eight years old."

They scoffed, identical sounds, identical eye rolls, and identical horrified expressions. "We're twelve, Paige. Not even close to eight," Claire said. I think it was Claire.

Her fingernails winked purple at me from the back of the pill packet, which I snatched back. Yes, it was Claire because Lia had proclaimed purple "the ugliest color in existence" the night before, which caused World War III. AKA day two of married life.

Clearly, Logan would be no help, so I texted my next line of reinforcements.

Me: Football players SUCK. Why can't they check their phones during practice???

Allie: Awww, poor Paige. Motherhood not what you imagined?

Me: Did you know that 12 yo girls know about condoms??? And that they call birth control "anti-baby pills"????

Allie: I'm not laughing at you, I swear.

Me: *middle finger emoji* You're no help.

Once my birth control was safely zipped back into my purse, I sank my head into my hands and sighed. Logan's mom made this look so freaking easy, that bitch.

And honestly, it wasn't that it was hard. The girls were good kids, even when they were stealing people's prophylactics. The heart of it lay buried in the constant worry over what they were doing, what they were watching, did they finish their homework? How did parents do this all the time without completely losing their minds?

Living with Allie and Luke, Faith was my buddy. It was awesome. I got the perks of a little kid without any of the responsibilities.

Now I'd well and truly jumped into the deep end. It was almost impossible to remember a version of me who thought she couldn't be rattled by anything.

Enter the twins.

Or the fact that for the past two nights, I was asleep before Logan came to bed. And unfailingly, I woke to an empty bed. Curses for being such a deep, even sleeper. What would it hurt to suddenly develop insomnia? Curable only by a good, hard body over mine.

When someone entered the kitchen, I lifted my head. Isabel watched me curiously, her notebooks trapped tightly against her chest.

"Having a breakdown already?"

"Oh no, if I were having a meltdown, I'd be at least one bottle deep into the chardonnay right now."

By the sardonic lift of her eyebrow, she didn't appreciate my attempt at humor.

"Kidding," I said with a smile. "Whatcha working on?"

Isabel made a sharp pivot toward the fridge, opened it with a snap, then closed it just as quickly after she grabbed a bottle of water. "Homework."

"Yeah? Anything I can help you with?"

I saw her frame tighten up, but her eyes never left the front of the fridge. I couldn't tell if she was looking at the picture from our courthouse ceremony, or if they were pinned on the snapshot of them with their mother.

"No need," she said. "Homework is never hard."

Somewhere upstairs, one of the twins screamed, and I pinched my eyes shut, waiting for whatever would come next, but laughter followed. I breathed out. "That's good. Logan said you were smart."

There was no reaction to that except a mulish set to her jaw. At fourteen, I'd been nothing like Isabel. I didn't have to be. My parents might not have noticed me much, but that served me just fine. That meant they never told me no.

But this girl, she'd had a father pass away, and a mother walk off into the sunset. Yes, Logan loved them, but looking at that hardened, pretty little face of hers, I felt so much unexpected sadness. She'd hate it if she knew that I noticed it at all. The way she held herself together so tightly. The way she constantly kept both arms out toward me just in case I tried to engage with her.

"I'd say thank you, but it's not like I can help it. I was born with this brain, you know?"

I nodded. "True."

"Just like you were born pretty."

The way she said the word, like it was coated with acid, I couldn't stop my smile.

"You're pretty too, Isabel."

"Yeah, not everyone can have both, I guess," she snapped back with a pointed look at me.

I sat back against the island and crossed my arms over my chest. "Okay, I'll give you one free shot because that's the first genuinely bitchy thing you've said to me. Next time, there are consequences."

"You're calling me a bitch?" Her voice rose shrilly.

"Come on now, smart girl. You know the difference between saying something bitchy and being a bitch. I know I don't have to explain semantics to you."

She huffed, pivoting to leave the kitchen, and her lack of argument felt an awful lot like I'd won a small victory.

Lia ran around the corner, stuttering to a halt when she almost ran into Isabel.

"Hey, Paige!"

I narrowed my eyes at her huge smile. "Hey."

She held out her hand. "Oreo? I saved you the last two in the package."

Isabel's eyes darted between the two of us.

"That's very sweet of you, but I don't actually like Oreos."

To my utter surprise, her face morphed into a disappointed frown. "But … I only save the last two Oreos for my favorite people." She hung her head and started to turn, shoulders drooping and everything.

Isabel raised her eyebrow at me. I sighed.

"That's really sweet, Lia. I'd love an Oreo."

Grosssss. I hated the cream. Hated the weird cookie that didn't taste good by itself. She grinned widely and handed it to me.

"Mmm," I said, right before I crunched down on it.

Her smile tilted up at the exact moment I froze.

What the ever-loving hell?

"Oh, holy fuuuuu—" I turned and emptied my mouth into the sink. That little shit swapped the cream for toothpaste. I spit the remaining crumbs from my mouth, grabbing a glass so I could guzzle water.

She took off with a squeal when I whipped around.

Claire came in just after her. "Good cookie? I told her to use mayo instead of toothpaste, but she doesn't have the balls."

My eyes narrowed.

"Where's Molly? She's supposed to help me paint my nails."

I rubbed at my temples. "I thought she was upstairs reading?" I asked. Great, I lost a kid already.

Isabel waved a hand toward the slider. "She's out there in her bathing suit."

My mouth opened and closed. It was like, cloudy and windy, the threat of rain hanging over the house in the shape of fat, juicy gray clouds. "She's … what now?"

"Ooooh, is the neighbor boy home?" Claire asked. "That's probably why."

"What neighbor boy?" I asked as I straightened.

Isabel sighed, actually loosening the arms that still clasped her notebooks to her chest. "She's got a stupid crush on this boy. He's too old for her, and Logan would flip out if he knew. He already caught Molly flirting with him once, and I thought his head was going to explode."

Even leaning over, I couldn't see where Molly was lying. *Lord save me*, I thought. A sixteen-year-old sunbathing in an almost rainstorm. "How old is he?"

"Like I pay attention to how old the neighbor is." Isabel kept talking when I didn't say anything. Apparently, the key to removing the padlock she kept on her vocabulary was the possibility of trouble for her sister. "He plays football at U-Dub," she said, referencing the University of Washington. "Logan hates him."

"How come?"

"Because he has a peeeeeenis," Claire sang.

"Claire," I admonished.

"What? That's what Logan said. He said boys that age only have one thing they worry about, and it's their penis, and Molly shouldn't go near him because she's too young."

As soon as I neared the shiny glass of the slider, I groaned, because I finally saw Molly. She was lying, oh so casually, in a teak lounger next to the in-ground hot tub. If she wasn't full-body shivering in that red bikini, I'd eat my freaking hat.

Then she arched her back and stretched one leg out. The only thing ruining the Kardashian-esque pose was the wrap around her injured wrist. Before I pulled the slider open, I reached over the back of the couch and grabbed a blanket.

"Lia, grab my phone, I want pictures of this," Isabel whispered.

"No way," I said. I pinned her with a look. "You listen to me, smart girl. It might be funny to watch your sisters get in trouble, but the four of you are a team, got it? You don't *ever* give outsiders a single piece of ammunition to use against your teammates."

Isabel's mouth fell open, maybe because she was surprised by my fierce tone. Then she nodded carefully.

Finally, I felt like I'd done something right.

But of course, I still had to deal with the underage display in front of me. I approached carefully.

"Got your SPF on?" I asked, wrapping my arms around my chest when a gust of wind made me shiver. A cold front had moved through the day before, dropping the temperature about twenty degrees below the normal August temps.

"I'm f-fine," Molly answered through clenched teeth.

Pinching one eye shut, I glanced over at the house next door. The second level was plainly visible above the fencing that separated Logan and neighbor boy's house. Through a large window, I could see the outline of a male playing a video game or watching a movie or something. Not once did he glance down at Molly.

"Come on, I'll make you some tea or hot chocolate." I held out my hand, which she looked at stubbornly.

Lord, what *was* it with these Ward women?

"Molly," I said gently, moving to sit on the edge of the lounger. Her body and all its goose bumps were on full display. "He's not looking. And trust me when I say that you don't want to have to pull stuff like this to get a guy's attention anyway."

"He's perfect, though," Molly gushed, sitting up with wide eyes and all that black hair spilling over her shoulders.

"No such animal, honey."

Her eyes got all big and Disney princess on me. "Not even Logan?"

My eyebrows popped up. "Not even Logan. He snores." Maybe he snored. It was as good of a guess as any.

It did the trick because she smiled. "Hot chocolate sounds okay."

I wrapped the blanket around her shoulder, and she gripped the edges together with her good hand.

"I may need to borrow that suit sometime," I said with a lift of my chin. "It's cute."

We walked inside with my arm tight around her. Thankfully, the peanut gallery had dispersed.

Just as I was locking the slider behind me, I heard Logan walk into the kitchen. He'd showered after practice, a plain white tee stretched over his chest and those long legs encased in dark denim, ending with black, scuffed-up boots.

Yes. Please.

"Are you in your bathing suit?" he asked Molly with a tilt of his head.

She gave me a panicked look over her shoulder.

"I asked her to model it for me," I said smoothly. "Don't guys ever do random fashion shows?"

His lips quirked in a reluctant smile. "Not that I can remember."

I walked up to him, aware that Molly was watching us with a grin. With a gentle hand on his chest, I lifted up on tiptoe and kissed the edge of his mouth. "Have a good day, honey?"

One of his dark eyebrows rose slowly. "Did you? You smell like chocolate and toothpaste."

"I taste like it too, I'm sure," I said, lifting my chin in a blatant taunt.

Molly giggled.

Logan blinked and backed away. "Right. Sorry, I'm late. Practice ran over."

"It's okay. We'll have to get used to it just being the girls when the season starts this weekend."

Molly's answering nod was so enthusiastic that Logan gave her a dry look. "Ready to be rid of me this year, are you?"

She smiled at me. "I think we'll do okay without you, Logan."

I crossed my arms and gave him a wide smile.

Totally rocking the big sister thing.

Until he lifted up his phone. "Want to tell me what happened with the birth control?"

CHAPTER 12
LOGAN

The locker room was a powder keg ready to blow. One spark, and we'd ignite. The moments before a game were my favorite. The energy rushed and rolled through everyone while we taped up fingers, smeared black on our face, and used the flat of our hand to slap the pads protecting our bodies. A brief burst that did nothing to feed the beast that we all waited to unleash on the field.

It was my twelfth season opener. The twelfth time I'd stood in this tunnel with high hopes for the season; sixteen games stretched out in front of us that were ours for the taking. The only thing standing between us and the reality of how those games would turn out was the clock ticking down to kickoff, and it never got old.

This year, I was even more amped up than normal, jumping up and down on the balls of my feet while we waited to take the field. The roar of our fans was audible as we left the locker room, bouncing off the concrete walls painted black and red.

The last time we played, we lost. Lost the conference championship that would've brought us to the Super Bowl. And none of us wanted to feel that again. I looked to my left and saw Matthew

Hawkins grinning behind his helmet. It was his first official game wearing a Wolves jersey.

If we won this year, it'd be because he was here to help us, the best defensive end in the league. He and I had come a long way since he joined the team after a small, teeny tiny misunderstanding where I asked out his girlfriend, not knowing she was his girlfriend.

It hadn't been pretty at the time, but it was amazing how one almost fight in the weight room could turn everything around for two teammates. I grinned back at him.

Like his body couldn't contain the same excitement I felt zipping under my skin, he tilted his head back and let out a roar. The rest of the defense shifted, jumped, and smacked fists against each other's helmets. The players lined up in front of us took off onto the field, and the crowd took to their feet, a wave of unstoppable anticipation greeting me as my cleats clawed up the turf.

Cheerleaders waved black and red pompoms, and our mascot ran in front of us, waving the massive flag with the howling wolf's head. Music poured thick and heavy with bass from all around, but that was usually easy for me to tune out.

Like I always did, I took a moment to stand in the end zone, and breathe in for four, hold for four, breathe out for four. The fans jumped and screamed, pounding their feet and hands to a beat that I couldn't hear.

When the screens lit up with a view of the owner's box, Allie's smiling face made the fans scream louder again. She wore a Pierson jersey, as she always did, same as Faith standing next to her. And just to the right, I caught a glimpse, just a flash, of red hair.

For a moment, I held my breath and prayed that the camera would pan over so I could see Paige. She came to most games, so that was nothing new. No one would pay extra attention to her presence, but I did. Suddenly, I wanted to know if she was wearing a jersey with my name on it. Every day, I'd come home to her pressing a kiss on the right edge of my lips. Never in the center. Not on the left. Like she knew that someday, I'd turn and meet her exactly where she wanted me to. So far, though I don't know how, I'd resisted. Every night this week, I'd crept quietly into the bedroom I now shared with her and took a few selfish moments to stare at her sleeping form.

She slept curled up on her side, one hand shoved under the pillow and the other up against her chest. As far as I knew, she barely moved in her sleep because each of those mornings, when my eyes popped open at five a.m. like they always did, she was usually in the same position. But in the daylight, the red was brighter, her dark, curled lashes visible, and the pink of her slightly pursed lips more apparent.

And every morning, I struggled with the same thing. I wanted to slide my hand up the impossible length of her legs, always bare and aimed toward me. Wanted to see if that touch would cause her back to arch, or her lips to curl up in a victorious smile before her eyes opened.

She'd gloat if I ever caved to her. And I'd have to swallow it with my lips and tongue and teeth, devour and use it as fuel to stoke the fire that was already kindling between us. And I wanted to, even if I knew I shouldn't.

Wanted to wedge one of my legs between hers to test if our bodies locked together like I imagined they would.

I'd imagined plenty in all the cold showers I was taking.

Long, toned legs.

Wavy red hair that almost reached the small of her back.

High, firm breasts.

Lips that smiled easily and a tongue that had as much snap and snark as I expected from her.

Someone ran past and smacked my ass, pulling my brain from an uncharacteristic distraction once I was on the field. I blew out a hard breath and ran to midfield, where I waited with the rest of the captains for the coin toss to take place.

When we won the toss, Luke chose to defer receiving the ball until kickoff at the beginning of the second half. He hit the side of my helmet.

"Sit 'em down, Ward," he yelled in my face. I hit his helmet back, a player's version of a high five if there ever was one.

I jogged back to the line with the rest of the special team's players. My skin hummed and snapped while I watched the kicker pull in a breath and take off toward the ball waiting against the small piece of plastic that kept it from the other team.

With one snap of his foot, it was in the air, and we were off, running full tilt toward whoever would be catching the ball. I saw a receiver step forward, saw the way his eyes and feet shifted. No wave of his arms to signal a fair catch, so I dipped my head and ran faster.

He caught it with a sharp twist of his hands and made a neat pivot around one of my defensive backs. I turned around one of his blockers and leaped forward, wrapping an arm around his chest and knocking us both to the ground.

The fans roared because he hadn't even made it five yards before I tackled him.

With a pump of my arms, their volume ticked higher. It was the start we wanted.

Snap after snap, we stopped them. On each third down, they were forced to punt.

Luke drove the offense down the field, first for a touchdown, then a field goal.

I held my chin up while someone squirted Gatorade into my mouth when I caught my first glimpse of Paige on the jumbotron. Allie was waving her giant red foam finger after the field goal, and Paige was doing the same. But it only showed their faces, and I desperately wanted to go up to the camera and use my bare hands to yank the angle so I could see what she was wearing. Her hair was tied up in a messy bun, her lips the same bright red as the shirt Allie wore.

I found myself smiling, then I blinked hard.

"Focus, asshole," I said under my breath.

"You all right, old man?" Robinson asked, giving me a strange look. Compared to him, I *was* old. Thirty-six to his twenty-three. And I could still keep up.

"Yeah. Come on, time to get back out there." I hit him on the back, and we snagged our helmets from the ground, ready to start another defensive series.

Their offense lined up like it would be a draw, but I kept my eyes on the QB. He licked the tips of his fingers, then yelled out his play as he lifted his right knee, the same strange rituals we all had to varying degrees. The linemen shifted just before the play, and the quarterback took the snap, faking a handoff to the running back who came up quick. He tucked his hands like he had the ball, but I sprinted to the left, where the halfback took off on a post route. I was step for step with him, breath sawing in and out my lungs as our feet pounded in perfect rhythm down the turf.

His eyes found the ball in the air, and I saw him arch his body to the side, an adjustment I wasn't expecting. Just as the ball came down in a perfect spiral, I pulled my hand back to knock it away from him, but he pivoted again, and our feet tangled. One of his teammates knocked into us, his shoulders ramming into both of us as he tripped. My left leg wrenched backward as I fell.

Pop.

I felt a bright, coppery snap in my knee, a flash of pain that had me hissing in a breath before I hit the ground.

In for four, hold for four, out for four.

Again and again and again.

I laid on the training table in the locker room, now still and silent as a tomb. A trainer poked and prodded at my knee, and I had to grit my teeth not to unleash a multitude of curse words from my raw, straining throat.

If it was my ACL, I was fucked for the rest of the season.

I'd made it four seasons without any sort of injury, and now, in game one, my knee was already jacked.

"Let's do an X-ray, Logan," she said, wiping her hands down the front of her pants as she stepped back from the table.

My answer came through a tense jaw. "Let's, Maggie."

If she noticed my sarcasm, she ignored it. That was how you knew someone was used to work with grumpy-ass injured professional athletes. She patted me on the shoulder as she walked back to get the mobile machine. I covered my eyes with one hand and focused solely on keeping my breathing even. Not allowing any rage or useless frustration to swamp me.

It wouldn't help. Not in the slightest. Best-case scenario, it was a grade one tear, and I could rest for a couple of weeks and jump back in before midseason hit.

Worst case?

I was out. For the rest of the year. Beyond that, I was a thirty-six-year-old player with only one year left on my contract after this one. It would be well within Allie's rights to release me because of an injury like I might have sustained. I might be out for good. An unwilling retiree.

I'd be stuck home, gardening or buying a car dealership or a pizza franchise or whatever the hell guys did when they were done playing football. Stuck home with my brand-new wife.

A laugh started deep in my chest because I'd married Paige since I wasn't home during the season. Not enough, at least. Now I'd be home all the time. The sound of my building hysteria echoed through the room.

The trainer rolled the machine back toward me with her face scrunched in confusion. "You losing it, Ward?"

I swiped a hand under my eyes as my laughter ebbed. "I think I am."

She aimed the machine over my leg with efficient movements. "Not used to guys laughing when they're lying here."

That sobered me because, over the years, I'd seen enough teammates benched, those whose names slid over to the Injured

Reserve List with little ceremony. I'd be a scrolling ticker along the bottom of SportsCenter. *Logan Ward (WA) out for the season with an ACL tear.*

I took another deep breath as I imagined it.

"Please, just tell me it's not the ACL."

Just as I thought she would, Maggie kept her mouth shut, clicking away on the screen that I couldn't see.

The locker room door pushed open, and Allie's voice called out from the other side. "Everyone decent?"

"Come on in," the trainer said.

I closed my eyes when I heard Paige say something beyond the door.

Was it less than twenty minutes ago that I'd wondered if she was wearing my jersey, staring up at the jumbotron like it was the most important thing I could've paid attention to?

What an idiot.

Maybe if I'd paid as much attention to the game as I was her, I wouldn't be in this mess.

"What's the damage?" I heard her ask, a light touch landing on my chest.

My eyes closed even more tightly, and I couldn't bring myself to speak.

She kept speaking when I didn't say anything. "The girls are up in the box. Luke's mom is staying with them. I didn't know if you wanted them down here."

In for five. Hold for six. Out for seven.

Not even that worked, and I finally pried my eyes open.

Above me, Paige was ringed with a bright halo over her head, a simple byproduct of the lights in the ceiling above her. Simple it might have been, the resulting effect was almost blinding. There was so much worry on her face that I almost looked away, but that was too easy.

If she wanted to marry a football player because it seemed fun and exciting, a quick route to a big payday, well, this was the fucking reality.

Injuries and losses and disappointments. Hard work, violent games, and even more violent effects on our bodies.

The big names in the league made it seem like it was all parties and glamour, living on the fringes of popular culture, but for most of us, the majority of us, it wasn't like that.

Hell, half the guys I knew worked random jobs in the off-season because only a handful of players got endorsements. Paige was seeing the other side now, and I waited for her to say it was too much, that she'd catch me at home, and breeze on out.

Except she simply stared at me with concern stamped all over her face.

Around Paige's neck was a VIP pass, probably something Allie had procured for her to be able to be in here. It laid gently against the shirt she was wearing.

Not my jersey.

I opened my mouth to say something, I didn't even know, when Maggie piped up.

"Not the ACL."

A massive gust of air deflated my lungs. "Thank God."

"No kidding."

Paige smiled, her hand smoothing up my chest to the curve of my shoulder. I'd stripped off my jersey and pads, so her fingers touched sweat-cooled skin at the edge of my typical undershirt. It wasn't anything fancy, just a white t-shirt with the sleeves ripped off.

"What is it?" I asked Maggie. She moved the arm of the X-ray machine so I could sit up on the table. Paige's hand fell off when I did, but she stayed close.

Maggie kept her eyes trained on the screen as she answered. "I'll show it to Doc, but it looks like either a grade two or grade three MCL."

"Shit," I said under my breath. It wasn't worst case, but it definitely wasn't the best, either.

"What does that mean?" Paige asked.

Maggie blinked, like she was just noticing Paige for the first time. She'd worked for Washington for a couple of years, and she had the same tendency as the players to block out anything non-essential when she was in the thick of her job. "Hi, who are you?"

Paige and I shared a glance. Hers questioning, mine more than likely full of grim resignation.

I gave her a slight nod, and Paige hitched a thumb at me. "His wife."

Maggie's eyebrows popped up in clear surprise. "Ah, okay, then. Congratulations?"

"Thanks," I mumbled. "You can send us a wedding gift later. How long are we talking, Maggie?"

She grimaced. "You know you need to let Doc look at it before I can answer that."

"Yeah, where is Doc, by the way?" I asked. "Shouldn't he be down here?"

Maggie slipped her phone out of her pocket and checked the screen. "He'll be here any minute. Concussion protocol on the sidelines."

My head snapped up. "Who?"

"One of the rookies. Sounds like he's fine. Idiot led with his helmet, so he's lucky he's not ejected for targeting right now too."

I blew out a breath. As much as this sucked, being benched for who the hell knew how long because of an injury to my knee, concussions were much scarier than that. At least to me. I didn't need someone knocking my brain around in my skull like a ping-pong ball.

"I'm going to go grab him," Maggie said. She pinned me with a warning look. "Don't move that leg."

Maggie excused herself, but it was clear she wanted to give me and Paige some privacy. I very much wanted to tell her that was the last thing I wanted with my very beautiful wife, looking at me with all too much concern in her very beautiful blue eyes.

I dropped back onto the table and closed my eyes again.

Without the sense of sight, without the red hair and black shirt, red lips and blue eyes, I could smell her, even among the strong scents of the locker room.

It was lemon and lavender. Clean and fresh and sweet. I didn't expect it of Paige. Never would've imagined that she smelled so sweet. One look at her, and I imagined musk and something dark and mysterious, something just spicy enough that you weren't sure if it was meant for her or someone else.

"Girls okay?" I asked.

"Isabel was freaked out when you went down." She exhaled. "The other three were okay. I mean, they were worried, but okay."

Isabel would be freaked out. She hid it well, but anytime something happened that even hinted at an unexpected health issue or the possibility of a massive life change, she shut down, not sure how to handle what might happen. Her emotions were so big for her little body, but she had them so locked down that even I struggled to help her untangle them. Again, it made me thankful that it was just my knee, and she hadn't seen me lights out, lying still and unmoving on the field.

"I'm glad they were up in the box," I admitted. "If they'd been in their usual seats, it would've probably been scarier for them."

That had been Paige's idea. Normally, they sat about five rows up near the fifty-yard line.

There was a pause, and I was glad I couldn't see her face. "Why don't they sit up there? I know Allie would love to get to know them better. A lot of people would."

My chest expanded on a large inhale before I answered. "The more people they get to know, the more likely it is that everyone will know I'm their guardian. And there's no reason for anyone to know they live with me. I don't want them used as some social media attraction or spotlight magnet. That's the last thing they need."

Paige hummed. "I guess that makes sense." She cleared her throat. "I was texting with your mom. Told her I'd let her know what you heard from the team doctor."

My eyes stayed purposely closed because it felt far too big that she was here, soothing my sisters, and communicating with my mom before I'd had a chance to grab my phone from my locker. There was no counting to be done right now, no breathing exercises to try to stem whatever feelings were building to a rolling boil inside me.

"Are you okay?" Paige asked.

I opened my eyes and stared up at her. Besides my mom, it had been years since anyone wondered how I was doing. The girls were too young to really think about what any of this felt like from my perspective. The tightness in my chest loosened, just a little, even though my brain was still buzzing angrily at the possibilities of what might unroll in front of me in terms of recovery and therapy and conditioning.

"I don't know," I told her. The words were out before I could consider what the naked honesty might mean between the two of us. "I really don't fucking know."

CHAPTER 13
PAIGE

"Are you sure you don't need anything?" I asked, my shoulder leaning up against the frame of the guest bedroom door.

Logan was lying in the middle of the bed, his leg immobilized with the brace that Maggie had put on him before she sent us home with strict instructions to move it as little as possible for the first couple of days. Only a few hours ago, when we were still at the arena, the team physician did indeed confirm that it was a grade three MCL tear, which would have him out for at least four weeks, possibly up to eight, depending on how his PT progressed once he'd adequately rested the injury.

And let me tell you, an injured Logan reminded me an awful lot of what I imagined a bear was like when his paw was stuck in a rusty trap.

Not that the constant glower wasn't attractive on his stupid face because it really, really was. It did something to the already hard edge of his jaw that made my tummy quiver. Especially now that he was a solid twenty-four hours overdue for a shave. Rawr.

"Paige," he said wearily. "You've asked me that five times in the last hour that I've been in this bed."

On the bedside table were his iPad, headphones, three books, purple glittery nail polish (he didn't so much as blink when Claire brought it to him), a bottle of water, four energy bars, two apples, and a bottle of ibuprofen.

Fine, okay, so apparently, I went a little overkill when faced with being an unexpected caregiver. I'd never experienced anything like this before.

Seeing him the way he was tapped into some strange part of me that wanted to help, do something, make him feel better, provide him with anything he might need. Like a vein I didn't know existed had been split open, contaminating the rest of the blood flow in my body with some insatiable desire to make sure he was okay and settled and fine. Not wanting.

So weird.

"Okay." I sighed. "I'm going to go change. Do you need anything from our room?"

His brow lowered, and I held my hands up. I'd already brought him a clean change of clothes, which he didn't need because someone had helped him at the arena before we left. Not that he needed help, he'd insisted.

"Right, sorry, sorry," I said quickly.

He pulled the headphones up over his head and picked up the iPad. Before we'd left the arena, he'd loaded it up with game film to keep him occupied.

The girls were cuddled on the couch, still wearing their various Washington Wolves gear, munching on popcorn and watching some random Netflix movie. A jailbait type cute boy grinned on the screen, and I swear, all four girls sighed in tandem, even Isabel.

I perched on the edge of the couch and leaned down by Molly. "What are we watching?"

"To All the Boys I've Loved Before," she whispered. "That's *Noah Centineo."*

"Uh-huh."

She gave me a dirty look at my unimpressed answer.

"Geez, no one wants me around right now." I wandered into the kitchen and stacked papers into a neat pile, then opened and closed the fridge when I realized everything else was in order. No lunches to be made because the girls always ate hot lunch at school.

Even though it was early, I made my way upstairs and stood in the middle of the dark bedroom where I'd be sleeping by myself for the next two nights until Logan could manage the steps. The bed seemed huge, which was ridiculous, because as far as I knew, we hadn't had a single instance of nocturnal touching. But something was to be said about the fact that every night when I slipped between the covers, I knew he'd join me at some point. That maybe I'd super accidentally end up tangled up in his heavily muscled arms, one of his big hands on my ass and one of my own down the front of his boxer briefs or whatever he slept in.

I didn't know what he slept in because he was a bed ninja.

In the closet, I peeled off the Wolves shirt and tossed it into the laundry basket, replacing it with something clean. When I'd entered the locker room, my shirt was the first thing he'd zeroed in on. It was one of the multitudes I owned since Allie took over the team. In fact, my collection of Washington clothes almost rivaled Logan's when I took in the entire closet. Sure, he had jerseys with his name on it, something I'd constantly hinted to Allie that I deserved, given my permanent fixture within the team.

Laughable now because in the most legal, technical sense, I did have a jersey with my last name on it. I pulled one of his off its hanger and traced the letters with the tip of my finger. Ward.

I hadn't changed my name on my license or anything, but I still felt a little bit like I really was Paige Ward.

"Stupid," I said under my breath and put the jersey back. The man wouldn't even sleep with me, a hilarious turn of events considering that men had tried with me for the past two years in the exact same way I was now trying with Logan.

It was clear enough what I wanted, but still waiting for the other person to give the official green light.

In the bathroom, I splashed cold water on my face and let out a deep breath. I washed my face with brisk movements and felt some of the tension in my shoulders melt away as I rubbed the night cream into my cheeks with small circles. I brushed out my hair and then grabbed the bottle of leave-in conditioner, spraying it onto the strands. My eyes narrowed when I saw a strange color.

I sniffed, my nose wrinkling instantly.

Yanking the bottle up to my face, I almost gagged at the smell of garlic and onions and something a little sour.

"Those little assholes," I whispered.

Molly choked on a laugh behind me, and I spun around.

"Okay, you weren't supposed to overhear that."

She smiled and then hopped up onto the bathroom counter. "What'd they do now?"

Carefully, I uncapped the bottle and sniffed. "They must have dumped ... holy shit ... I think they mixed ranch dressing in with my serum."

"Ewwww."

"Blech." With the faucet turned all the way to hot, I dumped the contents of the bottle down the drain, my mind spinning as it disappeared.

"Are you going to..." Her voice trailed off as she motioned to the section of my hair now covered in dressing and Lord knows what else.

Instead of hopping in the shower, I leaned over and ran the section of hair under the water, making sure everything was out of it before I grabbed a towel to soak up the wetness. "Do they do this with everyone?"

Molly nodded. "They've let you off pretty easy so far, but I think it's because they actually like you. You don't treat them like a nuisance."

"I didn't up until today," I muttered, which made her laugh.

"One of the counselors Logan made us talk to after Mom left said it was something about testing people. Seeing how far they could take it before everyone left."

I turned that over in my head, adding it to the list of rapidly growing information to be banked and processed.

"But they don't test Logan like that?"

She shook her head. "He's never allowed anything to separate us. My earliest memories have Logan in them. Even if he didn't get along with our dad, he was at every birthday and every holiday. Going on school field trips during his off-season. Every T-ball game in the summer, every soccer game in the spring."

Well damn, if he was gonna go and be perfect then. That didn't help my desire to strip him naked, gimpy leg or not. Hell, I liked being on top as much as the rest of the female population.

"It's really amazing what he's done for you guys," I told her.

Molly smiled. "Isn't it stupid that he doesn't see it that way? He deserves every award in the world for the brother he is to us, no matter what he does for a job. I wouldn't care if he was a janitor. We all feel that way."

I nodded. "I can see that." My lips screwed up as I thought about something she'd just said. "Wait. What makes you say the twins are letting me off easy?"

"How much time do you have?" she asked dryly.

I laughed.

"Our last housekeeper got locked in the bathroom." She lifted up her wrist, still wrapped. "That's how this happened."

One of my eyebrows rose, and it made Molly blush prettily.

"Okay," she hedged, "it's how I snuck out. Hurting my wrist was my own fault."

I turned to hitch my butt onto the counter next to her. "Promise me something, okay?"

Her eyes were so wide and worshipful when she nodded that I felt a quick tinge of guilt that I was here for less than selfless reasons.

"If you unlock me from whatever room they inevitably lock me in, then I won't judge if you promise to tell me why is it you want to leave, so I can make sure whatever it is you're doing is done safely and legally."

She chewed on the bottom of her lip. "Logan wouldn't say something like that. He'd ground me until I was twenty."

Setting the towel behind me on the counter, I nodded slowly. "Logan has to make decisions like he's your parent even though he's your brother."

Like marry a virtual stranger.

"And you don't?"

I blew out a slow breath. "Let's think of it as, I don't know, parenting light. I'm your sister-in-law, but I'm still new, and I'm trying to figure out exactly what my place is."

Molly smiled. "I like having you here, Paige. None of my friends have a supermodel for a big sister."

I groaned. "Oh, those days are far behind me. Didn't you see how much pizza I ate for dinner?"

She stood with a laugh. "I guess. Plus, you dipped it in the..." Her voice trailed off, eyes dawning with understanding when she looked at the bottle. "The ranch," she finished.

"Ohhh, they messed with the wrong woman," I whispered.

"Are you going to tell Logan?"

With a grin, I shook my head. "Hell no. They just started a war, and they have no idea."

Molly and I kept our lips sealed as the girls got ready for bed, not a word was spoken about the ranch hair serum. A few times, I caught the twins give me curious looks, but I simply smiled while herding them toward bed.

Once the house was quiet, I changed into soft sleep pants and another tank, bra discarded into the top drawer. When I walked to the guest room, I was knotting my hair on top of my head. The light from the end table cast Logan in a small circle of warm light. The headphones had been removed when the girls went to say good night, but his face was still lit blue from the screen of his iPad.

"Need more ice for your knee?" I asked.

His eyes tracked down the length of my body before he answered. "Sure, thanks."

I grabbed a pack from the freezer, along with a thin towel to wrap it in, and contemplated pressing it against my hot cheeks before going back into the bedroom. Why did helping him feel like the most intimate thing we'd done since I kissed him?

Logan was quiet when I entered the room, his iPad dark on the bed next to him. The black T-shirt he wore stretched tight across his chest, and with each deep breath, I saw the outline of muscles underneath the cotton.

Only a sheet covered the lower half of his body, and I couldn't bring myself to look at him when I pulled it back.

"I can do that, you know," he said gruffly.

"What kind of wife would I be if I didn't help?" I teased. Carefully, I set the ice pack on top of his knee, eliciting a hiss from his lips. "Sorry."

"The fake kind," he answered.

I blinked up at him. Those three words felt harsh, but I could see how aware of it he was, so I didn't call him on it. The twins got it from somewhere, so did Isabel, that desire to shove people backward and see the amount of force they could use before the person toppled.

Logan had made it perfectly clear, from day one, what this was to him and what it wasn't. I was the one trying to blur out the lines with the sheer force of my lust-crazed will. Like I could scrub those boundaries into something faded and crossable because I wanted to know what his skin tasted like under my mouth.

"You hate that I'm helping you," I guessed. "It makes you uncomfortable."

Even saying it, I was trying to spur him into a reaction. See what it did to him when I pegged him correctly. See if I could draw out some sort of reflex that he was desperately shoving down. Tap on the right spot, and he'd kick out at me. Or if I was lucky, kiss.

Lord knows he could use the distraction as much as I could.

As he watched me, I remembered the line from a song that Allie liked, one that made my skin itch because it felt like someone was shining a harsh spotlight on me. Something about not kicking up the dust around me just because I was lonely.

Except I didn't feel all that lonely. I felt restless. The chaos of the home during the day kept it strangely at bay, but at night, when it was quiet and he looked at me like that, I felt an edgy coiling under my skin that I wanted to let out.

"I hate when anyone has to help me," he admitted, shifting on the bed with a wince. "Nothing personal."

"Liar."

His eyes snapped to mine.

"You were fine when Maggie was helping you. When Doc was helping you."

"Trying to make yourself feel more important?"

"Oooh, you've got sharp teeth when you're cranky." I propped my knee on the edge of the bed near his hip, and he clenched his teeth. His eyes glinted dangerously. "You remind me of myself."

Logan snorted. "Don't do this, Paige. Just because I didn't imagine you being the perfect domestic helper doesn't mean I'm having an internal panic attack at needing your help."

His hackles were raised, and if he'd been an animal backed into a corner, I imagined a big tiger, pacing and panting, baring his teeth because he didn't like what I was doing.

"So it's not me," I repeated.

Logan sank his head back against the bed frame and closed his eyes impatiently. "Nope."

With a quick smile that he couldn't see, I shifted my weight onto the knee that was already on the bed and swung my other leg over to straddle his lap.

His eyes flung open wide. "What the hell are you doing?"

"Proving a point." I set my hands on his chest, looking over my back to make sure I was well clear of his knee. Logan moved to remove my hands, but when I made a small swivel of my hips, he hissed again.

It was not a hiss of pain.

And judging by what happened underneath my ass, it was the kind of hiss I wanted to hear from him every single day.

It was torture. Longing. Unwilling desire that had been wrenched from his body. By me.

Logan held my eyes and moved his hands from mine, a slow trek up the length of my arms, over my shoulders and down the curve of my back.

Like a cat, I arched into the surety of his touch, practically purring as he did. I moved my hands to the sides of his head, lowering my mouth to his.

"I think," I said against his lips, and closed my eyes when his hands closed around on my hips, "that you're lying to me."

Still, he admitted nothing. His fingers flexed, hard enough to make me inhale sharply.

"It would be so good, wouldn't it?" I whispered. The shaky exhale from his lips had me achy and wanting, my breasts sensitive under the thin cotton of my shirt. "Just think about how we could spend this little pocket of time we've got together. So *many* ways to make it fun."

"Paige," he said, the edges of his lips brushing mine.

"Yeah?" I rocked my hips forward again, smiling when his fingers tightened to the point of pain.

That was when he lifted me off him, dumping me unceremoniously onto the bed next to him.

His jaw was clenched tight, eyes shut, chest heaving on deep breaths. "You need to go."

I might have been embarrassed, but under his black athletic shorts, he was as hard as a rock and big enough to have me licking my lips.

Sighing heavily where I sat on the mattress, I gave his lap a loaded look. Logan's eyes opened just as I did. He grimaced, pulling the sheet back up over him, which didn't help in the slightest.

"Okay, Logan." I stood and raked shaky hands through my hair. "Text me if you need … *anything*."

"Good night, Paige," he said firmly.

"Could've been a better one," I told him with a raised eyebrow.

"It's not a smart idea, so it's not happening."

Oh, the people in this family had no idea who they were dealing with, I thought with a grin. Right in front of my face, he'd just waved a scarlet flag.

CHAPTER 14
LOGAN

I woke up cranky and edgy. And turned the hell on.

Two nights in a row, I'd dreamed of her while I slept on the too-soft mattress of the guest room.

If I'd closed my eyes after I woke, I probably could have slid back into the dream that I'd been having about Paige. No surprise, the dream version of her rose over me, skin bare, hair tangled in my hands and curling over her shoulders.

While the thoughts I had of her while I was awake were faster, harder, and designed to quiet her smart mouth—except for moaned words and pleas for more—my subconscious lingered over her body.

Probably because ever since she settled her weight onto my lap, all I could think about was how good it had felt and how I wanted more. I wanted to lean forward and see what the skin between her breasts smelled like, tasted like.

The gasp that came out of my mouth when I woke was loud enough that I was afraid someone heard me even though I knew I was the first awake. I always was. Before Paige or the girls got moving that morning, I hobbled to the bathroom and back into bed, popping two ibuprofens to alleviate the ache in my knee.

Robinson had called me old man, and hell, I felt like I was a hundred as I lowered my body back into bed.

And hundred-year-old me had a wife who was driving me slowly into sexual tension-induced madness.

Wouldn't it be easy? one side of me asked. We were married. The relationship was supposed to be real, for all intents and purposes.

The girls thought it was, that was for sure. If Isabel thought it was fake, she might have actually given Paige a chance because it meant Paige was no emotional risk.

That's why, a sneaky, snake-like voice hissed in the back of my head.

That's why you think you can't touch her, it said as it grew even louder. *You know the risk if you allow her in. You can't love people in halves, and going all in with her would leave you with nothing because she'll be gone as soon as the time is up.*

I dropped my head back, hitting it a couple of times to knock that voice right out. It was stubbornness. That was all. She was so sure that I'd cave that I felt the need to dig my heels in even further.

It had nothing to do with the fact that Paige was the riskiest bet I could've taken. Nothing. Even as she straddled me, pouring lurid images in my head of how it would be between us, she managed to remind me that this was temporary.

This was a payday to her, and to me, it was everything that mattered in my life. That fundamental difference in how we were looking at a finite amount of time was enough to keep my hands off her, no matter how she felt sitting astride me. How tempting it would be to unleash all the things building inside me.

I sighed as I scrubbed a hand down my face.

The sounds of the four women I shared a roof with trickled into the room as they woke, started breakfast, and got ready for school.

The day before, my first day post-injury, Paige had been gone most of the time that the girls were at school, texting me throughout the day to make sure I didn't need anything.

Paige: Going to Allie's to do some foundation work. Need me to grab anything?

Me: No thanks.

Paige: Done at Allie's. Have kickboxing at noon. Want me to pick up a late lunch? I'm always starving when I'm done.

Me: Just had a shake. Thanks, though.

I'd locked the damn door when I knew she was getting home because the thought of her sweaty from the class she was taking was almost more than I could handle.

That was probably where the dream from night number two had come from. The one I still couldn't get out of my head. A soft knock sounded on the door. One of the girls. Because Paige would've just walked in, as I'd learned.

"I'm up," I said.

Molly poked her head in with a broad smile. "Need anything?"

"I'm not completely helpless, you know."

She rolled her eyes and opened the door wider. "I know. Paige is helping the twins pick clothes. Or trying, at least. If she can get Claire to stay away from another all-purple ensemble, I think she might earn a Pulitzer or something."

"That's for writers," I pointed out.

"Whatever. You get my point." Molly leaned her back against the doorframe. "She's cool."

"Twins leaving her alone?"

"Erm, you know, it's getting late. I should go. I still need to drop the twins off."

Her avoidance was obvious, but I could ask Paige easily enough after the girls left for school. Now that Molly had been cleared to drive, she was back to dropping the twins off at their middle school, just down the road from the school that she and Isabel attended.

I glanced at the bedside clock. "You have at least twenty minutes before you need to leave."

She sighed. "Do you want some coffee or not?"

I swung my legs carefully to the edge of the bed and stood stiffly. I grabbed the crutches and wedged them under my armpits. I hated the damn things, but I was stuck with them for at least one more day until Maggie cleared me to switch over to a hinged brace.

"I'll come with you. I could do with a change of scenery."

I was just hobbling into the kitchen when an ear-splitting scream came from the twins' bedroom. Molly glanced up the stairway, rolling her eyes when I started swinging my crutches in that direction.

"Is everyone okay?" I yelled, cursing the fact that I couldn't move quickly or easily.

There was quiet, and then I heard the low tones of Paige's voice. When one of the twins replied to her, every word spoken too far away for me to discern, I cocked my head to the side.

"Fine," Lia called down. "I just … it was nothing. I thought I saw a spider, but it was lint or something."

I narrowed my eyes, but nothing else happened, so I turned back to get my coffee.

The girls were uncharacteristically quiet when they came downstairs, followed by a peacefully smiling Paige still clad in the same soft gray pajama pants and tank she'd been wearing the other night.

"Everyone okay?" I asked again as they loaded up backpacks and laptops for school.

"Fine," Claire said quickly. "You know how Lia is about spiders."

I accepted hugs and kisses before they all filed out to the garage, Molly shouting at them not to touch anything in her car.

Paige was shaking her head when the door finally slammed shut behind them.

"What was that?" I asked.

"Nothing." Paige sipped her coffee, eyeing me over the rim of the mug. "How'd you sleep?"

Unable to stop myself, I glanced at what she was wearing, those stupid tank tops that hugged her body and hinted not so subtly at all the things I wanted desperately to uncover and the pants that hung off her hips, showing a sliver of her toned stomach.

"Like a baby," I lied smoothly, pivoting on the base of my crutch so I could fill my own cup.

"Moving back upstairs tonight?" She hitched a hip on the counter and watched me.

"Most likely."

Her eyes glowed at my answer.

The entire day stretched out in front of me when she looked at me like that. No girls to interrupt us, no reason for me to sleep downstairs anymore now that the constant pain was subsiding.

Forty-eight hours of keeping my knee as immobile as possible, Maggie had said. After that, early movement is better for recovery. Paige heard her say it. There were no more excuses, no reason for me to sleep separately from her. Except now, I wasn't leaving for work at dawn every morning. Wasn't practicing all day every day, watching film late into the evenings to prepare for Sunday.

I'd help my team where I could, be on the sidelines once cleared to, and help the coaches and players win. Even if it meant I held a clipboard, called plays, or as the fucking water boy if necessary.

But I had no reason to be there for twelve hours like I normally would during the season. No hiding from the redhead currently staring at me like she wanted to eat me for breakfast. I turned away from her because if I closed my eyes, I'd think about how easy it would be to slip my hands under her ass, boost her up onto the counter, and do some feasting of my own.

My phone rang from the guest bedroom, and I went to answer it as her low, amused laughter followed me like the hounds of hell licked fire at my heels.

Surviving the day had been easy enough. I spoke to Allie. Spoke to Coach and Doc Hendricks and had a plan laid out with Maggie for my recovery. The aim was for me to return to the field six weeks later. Eight, if the tear healed slower than anticipated.

I'd only miss half a season.

And in those eight weeks, I'd make damn sure that the entire defense played their asses off, even if I had to shove a bullhorn in their faces during practice.

Paige came and went. While I sat on the back patio talking to Maggie figuring out my game plan for when I was able to come to the facilities the next day, Paige walked into the kitchen with bags of groceries, unloading them like she'd been living in my home for months and not a mere matter of weeks. When she pulled a massive squeeze bottle of mayo out, I narrowed my eyes because it wasn't something I usually kept in the house.

She left again shortly after that, waving at me through the slider while I watched film. Beneath a see-through black shirt, I caught a glimpse of an electric blue sports bra. High-waisted black leggings with a sheer panel running down the sides of her legs covered her bottom half. Her hair was pulled back tight from her makeup-free face.

I pinched the bridge of my nose when she walked away because a host of images bombarded me in the wake of her exit.

The girls came home from school while she was at her class, and listening to their happy chatter, something I usually only got to witness in the winter and spring, was the only positive side effect of my injury. If my impromptu marriage hadn't forced Nick off my back, then me being home due to my knee wouldn't have hurt.

I was sitting at the island with Isabel, working on her math homework, when Paige got home.

"Hey," she said. Her face was flushed and damp, the front of her sports bra soaked through, sheer shirt nowhere to be found.

My mouth went dry as she wet some paper towel to wipe her forehead.

"You're all sweaty," Isabel said with disdain.

I almost chastised her, but Paige laughed. "Hell yeah, I am. If you got your ass kicked like I did for the past hour, you'd be sweaty too."

Isabel set her jaw, and even though I saw the carefully hidden spark of interest in her eyes, she didn't comment.

"When did you start doing that?" I asked when she pulled matte black boxing gloves out of her gym bag. I motioned for them, and she passed them over. My eyebrows popped briefly at the beat-up state of the gloves.

"A while ago. It's not new." Her mouth curled in a smile.

"You haven't seen her gloves before?" Isabel questioned immediately; suspicion evident in her eyes.

I shrugged. "Nope."

"We didn't live together before we got married," Paige said smoothly. "Lots of things go unseen."

She worked her jaw back and forth. "If you get your ass kicked so bad, why do it?" Isabel asked.

Paige searched my sister's face, and I wondered if she saw Iz the same way I did. If she saw through the prickly questions and blank face, the ironed-out control that she had over herself like a sheet of armor.

"Because it always makes me feel better when I'm done. Anything hanging over my head, anything I'm worried about, stressing over, that's eating away at precious brain space, I leave it on that bag. I never, ever regret going, no matter how much it hurts. How many things in life can you say that about?"

She scoffed. "Lots of things."

"Yeah?" Paige leaned forward, body language open and her face carefully casual. "What always makes you feel better?"

Isabel opened her mouth to answer, and I held my breath to see how she'd answer, but she caught herself too quickly. My glance at Paige didn't go unnoticed, and it seemed she was holding herself as still as I was.

"Finishing my homework without interruptions," Isabel muttered.

Undeterred by the moody teenage response, Paige shrugged. "You should come with me sometime. I think you'd like it."

The huff of air that came out of my sister's mouth was half laugh, half scoff.

Shaking my head, I handed the gloves back to Paige. "Did you do this when you lived in Europe?"

Now it was Paige's turn to scoff. "Hell no."

The pencil scratching across the notebook paused, hovering over the paper while Isabel pretended she didn't care what we were talking about.

Paige saw it too.

"Why not?" I asked.

Before she answered, Paige pulled a tangled pile out of her bag, black hand wraps that held the distinct smell of physical exertion. I knew that smell—it was in every locker room I'd ever played in—and damn if I didn't find it hot as hell that Paige appreciated it as much as I did. She separated the length of the wraps, wrapping them up loosely. "The fashion industry—especially when you're dealing with high fashion, the elite designers, photographers, and editors—has a very narrow window of what they're looking for physically." The wraps went back in her bag as did the beat-up gloves. Isabel's pencil still wasn't moving, but her eyes stayed trained on her paper. "Skinny is important to them. Strong isn't."

I nodded.

Paige shrugged. "Anytime I exercised, the photographers freaked out. *Can't look athletic. Too much muscle,*" she mimicked in a snide tone.

Apparently, that was the line where my sister stopped pretending to pay attention. The pencil dropped, and Isabel crossed her arms. "What's wrong with looking athletic?"

"An excellent question," Paige said. "Absolutely nothing, if you ask me. And I got really sick of these scrawny old men telling me that I wasn't allowed to do something that made me healthy and made me strong, simply because they wanted me to look better in a sample size."

Iz wanted to say something else, but she picked up her pencil and hunched back over the paper in front of her. Paige shook her head. "I'm going to go hop in the shower."

I nodded.

One minute after she walked upstairs, I let out a slow breath. I heard the water turn on, and my fingers started twitching on my leg.

That was when she screamed.

Isabel's head snapped up.

"I got it," I said, grimacing at how slow my progress would be walking up the stairs. I was huffing by the time I made it to the hallway and imagined all the ways Maggie would murder me for taking them faster than I should have.

Molly yanked her door open when I passed, headphones pulled off her head. "What happened?"

I barreled past to the bedroom. "Are you okay?" I yelled when I whipped the door open.

"Ohhhhh my gosh, get it, get it, get it," she said from the bathroom door, pointing toward the shower. She had a white towel wrapped around her wet body, and her hair hung in red, ropy strands down her back. I blinked away from the gap in the towel where I could see the flash of her hip bone and swell of her ass.

"Get what?"

"The snake!"

"What?" I bellowed. "Where?"

I hobbled into the bathroom and saw it.

It was tiny, green, and slithering happily along the tile. "*That* little thing is what made you scream?"

"If you found it behind your shampoo bottle, you'd scream too," she snapped. Her eyes were bright blue in her face and her cheeks still pink from exercise and snake-induced terror. "Ohh, they are gonna get it now."

I leaned over, snatching the snake off the ground. The garter snake, still a baby, wiggled in my hand.

"Who's going to?"

Her eyes narrowed dangerously now that the threat had been eliminated. "The twins."

"They did this?" My head started shaking immediately. "No way."

Even as I said it, I knew she was right. I'd have to have a serious talk with them.

"Yes way." Paige turned, dropping the towel before she entered the closet. I would've closed my eyes, but her body was too … naked for me to have the slightest chance in hell of that.

I blew out a slow, controlled breath, then frowned at the snake. "This is all your fault," I whispered.

She was yanking on pants when she came back out, a T-shirt hanging off her shoulder.

"What are you doing?"

Quite inexplicably, she ripped open the dresser drawer and pulled out a squeeze bottle of mayo and a jar of Vaseline.

"Paige," I said slowly. "Seriously, what are you doing?"

She grinned. "It's called payback, Logan. Keep up."

"What in the hell is going on in this house?" I yelled.

CHAPTER 15
PAIGE

Behind me, Logan yelled something, but I was too distracted by the *snake in the effing shower* to hear a word he said. I'm sure whatever he was thinking was mature and logical and blah-di-blah, but I marched into the girls' bathroom and glanced around until I found the messy-capped toothpaste shoved into the toothbrush holder.

I snatched it up, not really caring they were upstairs, because I had a sneaking suspicion that they'd locked their bedroom door as soon as they heard me get in the shower. Leaning over the trash, I rolled the tube until a healthy amount had slid out.

"What are you *doing*?" Logan asked, appearing behind me.

"So help me, if you've walked into this room with a snake still in your hand, I'll lose my shit."

"I'm not going anywhere until you tell me what is going on."

I straightened and whirled around to face him. "Right now, I'm replacing their toothpaste with mayo and then their hair gel with Vaseline, if you're going to be nosy about it."

His face turned stormy. "The hell you are."

My eyebrows popped up. "You think you're going to stop me? Ha. Think again, buddy. They've more than earned some retaliation. I went easy on them this morning."

That knocked him back visibly. "This … what?"

Well, look at that, the nozzle of the mayo bottle fit perfectly into the mouth of the toothpaste. I squeezed, a vicious streak of happiness going through me as I imagined them filling their toothbrushes with it.

"Paige," he said in a low voice.

"You know, it's amazing how I can't hear a word you're saying as long as you're holding that *freaking snake* in your hands."

He pulled in a deep, slow breath. "We're the adults in this house, Paige. We don't sink to their level."

"Maybe you don't," I mumbled as I recapped the toothpaste and popped it back into the toothbrush holder. Before I could grab the gel, he reached forward and snatched the jar of Vaseline from the counter.

"Hey!" I swiped for it, but he held his hand out of my reach.

"That's enough." He stuck his head out into the hallway. "Lia! Claire! Out of your bedroom *now*."

"Oh no, you better stay in there if you value your precious little lives," I yelled just as loudly.

From her bedroom doorway, Molly watched all of this unfold with eyes taking up half her face. Even Isabel peered carefully around the top of the stairs. From the twins' room, I heard rustling and whispering. My eyes narrowed in the direction of the sounds, and Logan exhaled noisily.

"Iz, come take this." He stuck his hand out, and the wriggling, wiggling snake made me shudder.

Isabel grimaced but did as she was asked. The handoff was careful, and she glared at the door containing her little sisters much in the same way I did. When she disappeared downstairs, I breathed a sigh of relief.

Logan gave me a hard look. "Bedroom. Now."

Molly wisely snapped her door shut.

I lifted my chin and propped my hands on my hips. "Why don't you try talking to me like I'm not your paid subordinate."

His chest heaved like he was a bull about to charge, and a

muscle popped in his jaw. "Paige, if you don't get your ass in that bedroom so we can talk in private, I will carry you in there myself."

"Try it," I whispered, stepping up into his chest. "I dare you."

The way he looked at me was an insanely potent mix of *I want to strangle you* and *I'm going to rip your clothes off if you say one more word*. A grenade dropped between us wouldn't have done shit to dispel the sexual tension that pulsed between us in waves.

Logan slicked a tongue over his bottom lip and tilted his head to the side. "Paige," he said softly.

"Yes, dear?" Kiss me, kiss me, kiss me.

"I would be eternally grateful if you would please join me in our bedroom."

Right fucking now. Those were the words he'd not said out loud, but they were in his eyes and the set of his jaw.

"Of course, husband." I breezed past him, purposely brushing my chest against his arm as I did. It took him a second to join me, so I made myself comfortable on the edge of the bed, legs crossed, and my hands braced behind me.

Logan paused in the doorway, giving me a pretty epic stare-down before he took a slow, stiff-legged step into the room. The door snicked shut, and I felt a pretty epic moment of guilt at the fact that he'd stormed upstairs with an injured knee when he heard me scream.

But *snake in the shower*. Come on. Anyone would scream.

Maybe I could buy the sweet, pretty team trainer a giant bottle of wine or something as an apology when she wanted to know why Logan's knee was even more jacked up than it had been on Sunday.

"Care to explain what you've been keeping from me?" he asked carefully.

"You mean when I put a fake spider in Lia's backpack?"

"Yeah," he ground out. "Like that."

"Or when they mixed ranch dressing in my fifty-dollar bottle of hair serum?"

He dropped his chin to his chest.

"Or when Lia just *had* to give me the last Oreo, and I took it, even though I hate Oreos, and that little punk swapped out the cream for toothpaste? You mean those things?"

Logan's head lifted, and his eyes were fire. "Yeah, like those things."

"I was dealing with it, Logan." I spread my arms out and stood off the bed. "What else was I supposed to do?"

"Discipline them," he said. "Give them boundaries. Consequences."

"What do you think I was doing?" I jabbed a finger into his chest. "You tossed me into this house and bounced off to practice without so much as a single shred of guidance when it came to four girls in an age bracket that can be really freaking tough to deal with. I'm dealing with them the best way I know how, considering I've got three out of the four testing me in all these fun and exciting ways."

My sarcasm was not lost on him, but he didn't bend in the slightest. If anything, he inhaled so deeply, like he was pulling in his arguments from the air around us, and a sick thrill slid hot up my spine from the way we almost, almost touched when he did it.

"Exactly. They're testing you, and what lesson are you teaching them, exactly?"

"I'm teaching them exactly what I would've needed to be taught when I was their age. That if you're going to dish it, you damn well better be able to take it. That if you're going to try to bend someone to your will with bad behavior, they may not react in the way you expect them to."

His eyes narrowed, and to my utter surprise, he said nothing.

And that was fine by me because I was nowhere near done. "Unlike you, I've been a teenage girl. I know what it's like to want to sneak out of the house because I have a crush on a boy, or what it's like to want to be seen as older, smarter, or more mature than I really was, or desperately want to know that anyone saw me for who I was, even if I wouldn't have admitted it with a gun to my head."

Logan slicked his tongue over his teeth.

"You've been in charge of them for years. Good for you. They're great kids, pranks and attitude aside. But they've been shoving at every person who walks in this door who isn't you or your mom." I poked him again, and his eyes flared dangerously. "I'm not their mother, nor should I try to be. And if you expect me to have any impact in this family, you won't try to force me into some pre-defined role. You deal with them in your way, and I'll deal with them in mine. For the next two years, at least. Then you can go back and do things your way."

He propped his hands on his hips and studied me. The quiet way he processed freaked me out, not that I'd ever admit it. I almost preferred it when he flipped out, when his emotions got so big that he acted without thinking everything through first.

When he let go.

He'd only done it once. In the bathroom before we got married. The moment overwhelmed even his careful thoughts, the resulting kiss something I thought about often when I laid in that big ass bed by myself. That kiss was better than the last two rounds of sex I'd had, which should tell you something about the last two rounds of sex I'd had, if one brief kiss swamped them in my memory. And that was what I needed to tap into because Logan unleashed was the side of him I wanted most.

"I'm still going to talk to them about the pranks." He lifted his own finger, and so help me, if he poked *me* in the chest, it was fricken on. "It needs to stop, and I can't have you trying to one-up everything they do because, believe me, they'll meet you step for step every single time."

I crossed my arms and considered what he said. "Fine. But I'll talk to them. If you want to institute some arbitrary consequence, I want them to know it's coming from you, not me."

One eyebrow lifted slowly over those burning eyes. "Now

you're bargaining for how I should discipline. Aren't you the little hypocrite?"

"I'm doing no such thing, Logan Ward." I stepped closer, and he held his ground. "And if you keep standing there giving me hot sex eyes because I'm pissing you off, you better be prepared to do something about it."

He swallowed. "I'm not giving you hot sex eyes."

I gave him a meaningful glance, and his face shuttered in an instant. He stepped backward a moment later.

"You drive me insane, Paige McKinney," he said quietly.

"Yeah, well, so does half the population of Seattle, or so I've been told. Is that supposed to make me feel special?"

Logan breathed out a laugh, shaking his head a little. He turned and walked stiffly to the door, favoring his right leg as he did. Before he walked out, he paused and gave me a loaded look over his shoulder. "Yeah, it should."

I practically fell backward on the mattress as my heart thrashed wildly in the cage of my chest. I was going to die if he didn't touch me soon. Combust. Explode. Skin split open from the sexual energy trying to claw through my body into his.

"He is the worst," I whispered.

A small person—definitely not my reluctant husband—cleared their throat from the doorway. One of the twins, I could tell instantly from the sound of it.

"Whose idea was the snake?" I asked without sitting up.

"Mine." They said at the same time.

"It was not," one said.

"Yes, it was! You could barely pick it up without screaming. It was totally my idea."

"Oh my gosh, you two," Molly said. "You came in here to apologize, not to argue about who had the crappy idea in the first place."

"It wasn't crappy; it was awesome. Did you hear her scream?"

"Lia," Claire hissed.

"*Ouch*, keep your pointy elbow off me."

I couldn't help it, I started laughing. It was the rib-creaking, bone-stretching kind of laugh, and it felt really good. I sat up and eyed the gathering of girls in the doorway, motioning them in once I'd wiped tears of mirth from under my eyes.

Molly shoved her sisters forward. They tried very hard to look apologetic, but they failed. Miserably.

"I hate snakes, you know." I crossed my legs and swung my top foot while I stared them down. I gave them my very best pissed-off-model-but-still-so-fierce look. I'd perfected it at the age of twenty before my first spread in *Vogue* UK. "I'll have nightmares for weeks about that little thing."

Lia bit down on her smile. "Sorry, Paige."

"Sorry, Paige," Claire added after Molly nudged her.

"Your brother seems to think that I shouldn't have pranked you back."

They shared a look, clearly unsure of what the correct response was.

I shrugged. "Now, I'm of a mind to disagree with him because I think you two are way too smart for your own good. I also think that if someone had given you a taste of your own medicine a while ago, it wouldn't be as fun as it is now."

Neither one of them answered me.

I stood from the bed and walked slowly in their direction. Both pairs of big dark eyes looked up at me, and with their older sister behind them, they had nowhere to go.

"So are we, like, grounded forever?" Claire asked.

I shook my head. "Nope."

"No iPads?"

Shook my head again.

"What's our punishment then?" Lia asked, visibly out of patience.

"Number one, careful with your tone, I'm still one of two adults running this household, okay?" I waited for them to nod before continuing. "Two, I suggest a truce. The house will be a demilitarized zone for both sides unless we can find a common enemy."

Lia's eyes widened. "Who's the enemy?"

I tapped my chin. "Well, who's the one person in this house who needs to lighten up a little bit?"

"Isabel," Claire said immediately.

I smiled. "I was thinking someone a little taller, a little more facial hair."

Molly gaped at me. "You'd seriously let them play a prank on Logan?"

Lia and Claire mirrored identical evil smiles, and I could practically see the wheels turning in their heads.

"Even better. Let's make it a competition. The first person who can pull one off on him wins."

I held out my hand to Lia because if there was a ringleader, it was her.

The girls looked at each other, then Claire nodded at her twin. Lia stuck her hand in mine.

"You've got yourself a deal."

CHAPTER 16
LOGAN

The night Paige had the reptilian shower guest, I moved back into our bedroom. Just … not in the bed. She gave me an incredulous look when I joined her in the room, got ready for bed, and then pulled out the sleeper sofa with a vicious yank.

"You cannot be serious." She set her book down and watched me rip back the top sheet. "You'll barely fit on that thing."

She wasn't wrong. I gave it a skeptical look and tried not to think about what was in store for me. But anything would be better than sliding into bed next to Paige. I thought about how close I'd been to snapping earlier, how close I'd been to shoving her up against the bathroom door, shoving my hands into her hair, and shoving my tongue into her mouth and my hands down her pants.

If I was within reaching distance of her tonight, I'd cave.

Hence the small, shitty bed.

"You offering to take it?"

She shook her head sadly. "I know I probably should, but I think my decision-making ability is skewed because I'm trying to process the fact that I've scared you straight onto the sleeper sofa."

Scared. Yeah, right. That was Paige dangling the bloody chum, waiting for the shark to break the smooth surface of the water.

I smiled. "You've scared me, all right."

"Most men wouldn't admit it. Look how self-aware you are, Logan."

I turned my back to her, unwilling to engage. "Scared that your subconscious is stuck at kickboxing and I'd wake up to you practicing your roundhouse on my knee."

She snorted. "If you say so."

It had nothing to do with fear, not that I'd admit that to her. Or not the kind of fear she was talking about, at least.

I didn't fear how it would feel if I gave in. The pleasure we'd find together didn't scare me in the slightest. I'd spent far too much time thinking about how it would feel to be even remotely scared by it.

I didn't fear that Paige, just by her own nature, would overwhelm me. That she would be too much for me to handle, in or out of bed.

Paige wasn't too much. She was just right.

Her personality, strong and brash and unafraid, slipped right into an unnoticed opening in our family. There were cracks I hadn't noticed before. The way she handled the twins. The way Molly latched onto her. Even in the way Isabel was resisting Paige so stubbornly.

All of it was because she fit.

Fit me.

Fit the girls.

Knowing that, or being willing to admit it, was what had me on the too small bed with a creaky frame and a bar wedged in my back, listening to the sound of her deep, even breathing as she slept. What had me leaving for the training facility the next morning before anyone else in the house had woken.

The highways were fairly quiet as I made my way out to the Wolves' training facility, the sun rising brightly from the east. Maggie wasn't expecting me for another hour or so, so I took my time and walked slowly through the parking lot with the crutches braced under my arms.

A rookie from the offense was leaving the weight room, and he stopped to chat with me as I wound through the hallways to find Maggie.

"You'll be back in what, six weeks?" he asked.

I nodded. "That's the goal. Eight, at most."

He slapped my shoulder. "Good luck, man. We'll miss you out there." He started walking away when he paused and looked back at me. "Oh, and congrats, by the way."

That drew my head up, but he was gone before I could respond. My eyes narrowed on his retreating back, but then he turned a corner.

My grimacing face had Maggie laughing when I entered the PT room.

"That good, huh?"

"Hurts like a bitch," I admitted, sitting with a wince on one of the tables. "I tried to keep it immobile, but …" I shrugged. "Didn't necessarily go according to plan."

If I wanted to, I could explain about the snake and the shower and my sisters. But it was always that invisible line I worried about. If I told one person, and she told someone else, who would end up knowing about my role in my sisters' lives?

"It never does," she murmured, poking around my kneecap until I cursed. "Sorry."

As I laid back on the table, we talked through what the next week would look like, stretches I could do at home, things I could do at the facility—because any work she gave me that would keep me away from being alone with Paige in that house was good—and what progress I should expect.

A few teammates filtered in and out of the room to work on the various aches and pains and twinges that came with the regular season. By week sixteen, every single one of them would be beat the hell up to varying degrees, but that was part of the job. You taped yourself up, took the ice baths, jumped into the cryo chamber, and let a masseuse abuse every single muscle in your body to be able to do what needed to be done on the field.

And if I was lucky, in six to eight weeks, I'd be able to do those things again too. Last season, we ended one game away from the Super Bowl. One game. And this year, our roster was sharper, faster, with a good balance of young talent and seasoned veterans.

"Aw, man, I forgot your gift at home," Robinson said to me as he passed my table.

I blinked up at him. "What are you talking about?"

He simply grinned and punched me in the shoulder. "You haven't been in the locker room yet, have you?"

"No. Why?"

Maggie cleared her throat, and I gave her a suspicious look.

"It wasn't me," she said.

"What wasn't you?" I started to get off the table, wincing slightly when my foot hit the ground, and I put too much weight on my knee.

Robinson started laughing. "Hang on, hang on, lemme grab my phone first."

They trailed after me, Robinson filming the entire way.

"If that ends up on Twitter or Facebook or whatever, I'll punch you in the nutsack, Robinson."

He simply cackled.

What the *hell* was going on?

We passed two defensive players, and they whistled and clapped as I walked toward the locker room.

"Wait, wait, hold up," Robinson darted in front of me. "I need better light for my video."

I pinched the bridge of my nose and tried to center my breathing before I walked in. The door swung open, and my mouth hit the floor.

Pictures of Paige. Everywhere.

My locker was wallpapered with shots of her from *Sports Illustrated*. Hanging from the ceiling were posters, complete with a photoshopped pic from some cheesy wedding shot. My scowling face, and her puckering her lips in a kiss.

Someone tossed gold glitter into the air. Strung along the painted logo was a gold and ivory banner that said *Congratulations*.

My teammates whistled and cheered, some approaching me with the wedding poster and asking for my autograph.

"Can you sign it with her last name, though?" Gomez asked. "If I got to marry her, I'd take her last name in a second. I'd take anything she asked me to."

"Oooooohhh," was the resounding answer, guys shoving at each other over the jibe.

I glared mightily in his direction, which had him roaring.

"Who told you?" I asked. Luke stood by his locker with a broad grin on his face. "Was it you?"

He held up his hands. "I told one person. That was it."

"You married *Paige McKinney*?" Robinson asked. "You dog. How come we didn't know?"

I shoved at him. "Because it's none of your business, asshole."

Hobbling over to my locker, I propped my hands on my hips and stared at the pictures of her. My hands itched to rip them down, which was ridiculous, because her image had been seen by millions over the years that she spent in front of the camera.

And there was a good reason for that.

My wife was insanely beautiful.

Emphasis on insane because that was the direction she was driving me. Straight to insanity.

Someone nudged me in the shoulder, and Colt's face blanched when I lifted my face to his. My irritation must have been clear in my eyes. I felt like it was clear in my eyes.

"I had no idea she was like, with you, when I hit on her at the party. I'm so sorry, man."

I took a deep breath and clapped a hard hand over his shoulder, then squeezed. Maybe harder than I needed to. "No worries, Colt. The thing about my wife is that she can handle herself. She doesn't need me stepping in to help her."

He nodded. "I could tell. It was hot."

I lifted my eyebrows, and his face lost even more color.

"I mean, you know what I mean."

"Uh-huh." I looked around the room. The crowd had started to dissipate because they needed to get out to practice. "I know how you can make it up to me."

"Yeah?"

"Yeah. Take all the pictures down."

He sighed. "Sure thing."

I watched with a small grin on my face when he carefully pulled one picture at a time down off the walls of the locker room. "And hey, Colt?"

"Yeah?"

"You were slow off the line on Sunday, and your ball handling needs work. I'll be watching you next week. Got it?"

"Got it."

He continued pulling down the pictures, not arguing with me even though it would make him late to practice, and I went back to my locker. They'd spent the most time here, plastering her image everywhere.

With careful hands, I peeled back the tape of a glossy page. In the shot, she was lying on her stomach on the sand. No top, only a small bathing suit bottom. Her finger was in her mouth, and she was smiling coyly up at the camera.

She had the ability to destroy me without even realizing it.

Spending time with her, especially early on without the girls as a buffer, would only up those chances.

That was why I'd let the guys hassle me and let Maggie wreak havoc on my knee every day because it was safer for me to be here than anywhere around Paige.

So that was what I did. Every day for the next week.

If football was off the table, the place where I honed my body and mind into the fastest, sharpest version of myself, then channeling the effort into shoring up my defenses against Paige seemed like a worthy cause.

My knee improved every day. That was good.

There were no more pranks. Also good.

Molly only got caught trying to sneak over to the neighbor's house once, which I'd add to the win column, because her crush on that punk ass, football playing wannabe was enough to drive me insane. Fine, fine, I had to admit that he was a fricken phenomenal cornerback, one of the best defensive players in the country, and I'd probably like him just fine if my underage sister wasn't mooning over him.

There was no screaming at random times of the day.

In its place were *Chopped* and *Queer Eye* bingeing once homework was done.

"Logan?" Maggie said, snapping my mind back to the present. "Come on, you're not finished."

Gritting my teeth, lying flat on my back in the training room, I lifted my left leg for six more reps.

"Now on your stomach," she said, watching my movements with clinical eyes. "When you're done with these, I want to wrap it and try some simple range of motion stretches."

"Simple," I mumbled. "My ass."

"You're wearing the brace all the time, right?" she asked, eyeing my leg suspiciously.

"You'd think I'd be used to women nagging me about everything," I muttered as I pulled myself up to sitting on the table. The room was full of activity, guys coming in for treatment based on whatever hell their body had gone through the week before. We'd had a tough loss to Green Bay, but every week was a new shot. A new chance to focus on what we needed to do. My knee wasn't at the level yet where it was safe for me to watch from the sidelines with the team, but I'd stayed in the locker room and watched on the wall-mounted screens.

"Yeah, speaking of which," Maggie said. "When were you going to tell me you got *married?*"

I grimaced. "Never."

She clucked her tongue, making quick work of the black tape

she wound around the bottom half of my knee, making it tight enough that I hissed in a breath. "Exactly what I hope my future husband does someday, make it a point not to share his sublime bliss at work."

It was laughable, but I swallowed that. My sublime bliss laid in my ability to avoid said wife because she was hell-bent on breaking me down.

Maggie motioned for me to lie back on my hip with my left leg on the bottom. When I was in position, she stretched my leg out, sweat popping along my forehead as she did.

"Shit," I said under my breath. "If you make me cry in front of the guys, I'll never forgive you."

She chuckled. "Yes, you will. Who else can fix your knee and put up with your grumpy ass?"

My eyes pinched shut when she hit an angle that knocked my breath away. "I gotta tap out there, Sanders."

"Wuss." She brought my leg in and then pulled it back out again. "So how'd you two meet?"

"Who?"

"Seriously?"

I sighed, focusing my thoughts on Paige. It was a welcome relief from the burning pain she was inflicting on my helpless, old man knee. "Through Allie."

"Ahh. Makes sense." She pulled her bottom lip in, glancing at me for a second before she spoke again. "It might have surprised me, but she seems nice."

I started laughing. I couldn't help it. "Paige is a lot of things, but most people don't call her nice when they've only met her once. If you saw that in her, then it's because she allowed you to."

The observation came out so easily, something I'd never pieced together before, not consciously. It stunned me into silence. I'd always been the guy who paid attention to the people around me, silently absorbing the energy in the room.

But with Paige, I'd erected a barrier so I wouldn't go to her, but it wasn't solid. It was permeable, so permeable that I stopped thinking about the things that were filtering back to me.

Without realizing it, I'd been consuming bits and pieces about Paige, things that made her uniquely her.

And that was dangerous because those bits and pieces were what had the capacity to break down the barrier separating us.

It was the thing about me that almost no one knew. I had no ability to be invested in someone halfway. If you were a friend, I'd step in front of a bullet for you, but if you weren't, I could ignore you without guilt. It was why some of the new guys on the team thought I was a dick. Why a handful of my longtime teammates *didn't* think I was a dick. They understood to a point.

There was no way for me to edge my toe over the line of a relationship. I didn't operate that way.

And Paige was methodically, without me realizing it, tugging my entire body over that border. She was slowly pulling on a string that she'd hooked somewhere inside me.

With that permeating at the back of my head, I finished up with Maggie, spoke with Coach and the orthopedist on staff, then made my way home. A quick glance at my watch told me it was almost dinnertime.

For some reason, I was nervous to walk through the door for the first time since I'd slipped that simple gold ring onto her finger. Our neighborhood was quiet as people inside their large homes ate supper or finished homework or sat in their perfectly manicured backyards with their families.

My own house was closer to the street than a lot of our neighbors because I'd wanted the house with the larger yard. Surrounded by fences and mature trees and shrubs, the girls had been able to run free and crazy back there without having to worry about people staring or watching.

Just one of a thousand decisions I'd made because I knew it was best for them. My job had faults—the hours and the toll it took on my body—but I'd been able to afford this life for them. But despite that, the only reason I wasn't fighting desperately in a courtroom to keep it was because of Paige.

Yes, she'd banked a big check, and because she was smart, that check was probably sitting somewhere accruing interest for her. As I approached the door, I caught a glimpse of them through the sidelights in the kitchen. She was sitting on the kitchen island, Lia and Claire in front of her, performing some weird dance move that was making her laugh.

There was so much more to her than the world knew.

I'd written her off more than once.

Pretty face.

Insane body.

Rich girl with rich friends, who had no idea what real problems were like.

And she was making our life better, happier, because she knew it was the right thing to do.

Not only that, but she'd shown herself to us. The real her. The Paige that I suspected very few people saw.

The one I hadn't wanted to see. Because if I thought sex was the thing that would complicate things, I was sorely mistaken. What would complicate my life even more than that would be letting her sneak into the one place I couldn't afford for her to be.

My heart.

Because when she left, and she'd reminded me more than once that she would, she'd take it with her.

When I let myself in the door, the twins bum-rushed me with an endless litany of rushed words and stories about their day. Paige shook her head and smiled at me as I tried to calm them down.

Finally, I set a hand on each of other their rapidly moving mouths. "Stop. Breathe."

Lia rolled her eyes. Claire knocked my hand away.

"Did you finish your homework?" I asked in the blissful silence.

"Yes," they both said.

"We made homemade pizza crust for dinner. Paige showed us how to roll out the dough. She learned in Italy."

My eyes lifted to Paige, who was still on the island, long legs crossed and a slight smile on her face.

"Fancy," I said.

"And," Claire interjected, "she said I could make my own and put whatever I want on it. So I'm doing apples and pepperoni."

"Gross," Lia said.

"Why is it gross? People do pineapple and ham. That's basically the same thing."

I pinched the bridge of my nose. "As long as no one else has to try it, Claire."

"Okay, girls," Paige said, hopping down off the counter. "Go grab your sisters and tell them we're going to assemble the pizzas. If you want to eat one, you have to make one. I'll put the pepperoni and sausage in now, so we have something to eat while the smaller ones bake."

They bounded off, racing up the stairs to see who could make it to the top first.

"My kingdom for a tenth of their energy," I mused.

Paige laughed. "How was your day?"

I grimaced. "Painful."

She walked over to me, stopping an arm's length away. "They must be working you really hard."

"Why do you say that?"

Her eyes tracked my face. "No reason."

If she hadn't looked so amused before she turned away, I might have pressed, might have made her finish, even though the unspoken truth between both of us was that I was avoiding her.

She knew it. I knew it.

It was why I was careful not to brush up against her while we made pizzas. Why I chose a seat across from her at the table and not next to her as we ate.

During the meal, I stayed quiet. Not upset. Just watching.

Molly tried a bite of the apple pepperoni pizza before spitting it into her napkin.

Isabel smiled more than once.

The twins created a game out of who could chew a single bite the longest before it disintegrated in their mouth. Where the joy was in that competition, I had no idea.

More than once, Paige gave me a curious look over the rim of her wine glass, a red she'd bought from the store earlier and opened about halfway through the meal.

"You sure you don't want your own glass?" she asked. "Because if you keep staring at my wine like that, I'll have to fight you for it."

I laughed. "Fight you? Yeah, right. I'm injured. You'd wipe the floor with me."

She leaned forward, eyes sparkling. "I bet I could hold my own even if you weren't."

"I'd put my money on Paige," Lia piped up. Claire giggled.

Isabel rolled her eyes. "That's ridiculous. Logan has more body mass. It's almost impossible that she'd beat him."

Paige pursed her lips and stared at my little sister. "It doesn't surprise me that you'd say that."

"Why, because it's logical?"

"No, because you have no idea what you're talking about. The person who wins a fight isn't always the biggest." Paige lifted her chin at Lia. "Why would you put your money on me?"

She looked at Paige with nothing short of adoration on her face. "Because you'd fight *dirty*."

Paige threw her head back and laughed. Her whole body shook from the force of it, and she looked so full of joy, so thrilled at Lia's answer, that I felt my heart churn slowly in my chest. Molly and Claire joined in, and I had to cover my mouth not to do the same.

That joy was contagious, loud and full and bright.

The mood was light after that as the girls cleared the table. Paige took her spot on the couch, and Molly plopped down on the floor in front of her so that Paige could practice some braid tutorial she'd seen on YouTube.

I watched film on my iPad, but instead of going into my office, I found a spot on the opposite end of the couch from Paige. Only Iz didn't join us, saying she had reading to do, and she escaped up to her room.

About halfway through the series I was watching, I stretched my leg out, and the hinge on the brace squeaked. Paige glanced over at me. "You okay?"

"Just sore. Maggie wasn't holding back on me today, that's for sure."

"Want some ice?"

Something in her eyes made me breathe more deeply, like my muscles were screaming for more oxygen like they did when I ran drills. It was real enough, raw enough, that I found myself standing.

"Uhh, no, it's fine. I'm pretty beat, actually. Might go upstairs."

She glanced at the big face of her watch and gave me a wry look. "It's like … seven thirty."

"He's old," Molly said by way of explanation, face glued to the TV.

I tossed a pillow at my sister's face, and she gripped it tightly to her chest with a broad smile.

"I'm just going to take a shower," I mumbled. Paige grinned like she'd won another skirmish, and for the life of me, I couldn't figure out what it would take for her to feel like she'd lost a round.

Were we at war, though?

Everything we'd done and all the things we'd agreed to should have had us on the same team. But suddenly, I found myself in a defensive position, just like I was used to on the field.

Protect the asset. Defend the goal. Take away their weapons, in any way possible, while following the rules.

Paige might play dirty, but I didn't know how.

Upstairs in the master bathroom shower, I stood with my hands braced on the tile and let the invigorating cold water beat down on my back. I hung my head even though water ran over my face. Paige's weapons were nothing I could neutralize because she was her own weapon. Her smile, something sharp and slick, she wielded like a knife. Her eyes could slice through me, and she knew it.

All of it, each separate part of her, the physical and everything else about Paige, was dangerous.

That was the last thought I had when I shoved viciously at the handle to turn off the shower. The sound of the water dripping off me and onto the tile floor was the only sound in the bathroom as I took a careful step to the fogged-up glass door.

My hand reached out, only to find the towel bar on the wall next to the shower empty.

"Shit," I whispered. I swiped water away from my face and peered out into the bathroom. Not a single bath towel to be seen. There was a neat stack of hand towels on the counter, and I rolled my eyes as I limped over to grab one.

Amazing how you didn't realize exactly how small your hand towels were until you were trying to wipe down your six-four frame, and the door to the bathroom swings open.

"Whoa, privacy," I yelled, cupping myself with the tiniest ass hand towel in the entire Pacific Northwest.

"My eyes are covered," Paige said. "Just realized I didn't bring the folded towels back up here."

"You did the laundry?"

Even with a hand clapped over her eyes, I could feel the eye roll. "Who did you think did it? The laundry fairy? That bitch doesn't exist, much to my chagrin. And I'm too cheap to pay someone to do something that I'm perfectly capable of doing myself."

I snatched a towel off the top of the stack that she held out. "You can go now."

Just as I was tightening my hold on the edge of the towel, wrapped tightly around my waist, I felt her gaze on my skin.

Somehow, without looking, I felt it.

My hands slowed, and I lifted my head. Paige was studying my chest and arms, and there were delicious pink spots on her cheeks.

"Blushing," I murmured. "That's new."

She blinked guiltily, then hitched a hip on the counter. "So if I whipped my top off right now, you're saying you wouldn't physically react in some way?" She smirked. "I'd call you a liar."

There would be no need for Paige to call me a liar because if she stood there long enough, watched me long enough, she'd see the physical reaction just fine.

"Thanks for the towel," I said. I turned my back, hoping she'd get the hint.

She got the hint. She just chose to ignore it.

One of her fingers, just the tip of it, landed in the middle of my back. I froze, and my eyes fell shut.

"Missed a spot," she said quietly. "Left some soap right there."

Her finger swiped at the spot of skin, and my chest heaved on a deep breath.

Don't turn around, don't turn around, don't turn around.

Except then her finger followed the line of my backbone, slow and deliberate. My hands clenched into fists when she hummed.

"I've seen a lot of hard bodies in my day, but yours is ..."

I whirled around, and she jumped but still held her ground. "New rule," I told her in a gruff voice, "I don't give a shit about what other hard bodies you've seen."

"So very alpha of you," she whispered, her lips curling up into a satisfied smile.

I wanted to inhale her, snort her, stick her directly into my veins until she was part of me in a violent, visceral way.

They don't matter anymore. Anyone you've seen or touched or admired in the past, they don't matter anymore. The words hovered on the edge of my tongue, but I swallowed them down. There was a time limit to this. A ticking clock that I could practically see hanging over Paige's stunning face. Once the clock struck zero, the days and hours, minutes and seconds ran dry, she'd find some new adventure to make her blood race. Some new thing to make her senses hum.

The moment I forgot that was the moment I'd laid the last vital thing on the line. Not just my future happiness, but the girls' too. They'd be able to move on when Paige's role in our life was done, but I wouldn't.

Paige had no desire to settle down, she'd said so herself. This was an itch that she wanted to be rid of. A craving she wanted to feel melt away on her tongue.

Her eyes glowed unholy blue when she stepped closer, and I couldn't stop the hiss. The tether holding me back frayed more and more each day, to the point where each sliver that cracked and broke felt like a bang in the back of my head.

Her hands hovered over my chest, and just before she set them down, my free hand shot out and gripped the back of her neck. My thumb tilted her chin up with gentle pressure. Her mouth opened, and a sound escaped that I'd never heard from her.

It was lust-heavy submission. It was mindless urging.

Urging me to take what she clearly knew I wanted. What I knew I wanted to.

"I swear, if you don't kiss me, I will die," she pleaded, settling her fingers on my skin in curved claws.

I swallowed roughly and laid my forehead against hers. "Don't be so dramatic."

Paige's fingernails were short and rounded, but the way they pricked my skin, I felt them like they were sweetly coated needles. I wanted them on my ass. Along the backs of my thighs.

Her mouth opened, and she tilted her chin up.

"You cannot lie to me and tell me you don't want this, Logan." Her hips pressed against me, my hardness trapped between us with only the flimsy towel and her thin sleep pants as a barrier. "Seriously, what would it hurt?"

That was the crux of it.

I filled my lungs with her scent, let my fingers stay tangled in the hairs that had escaped her ponytail and fell down the back of her neck.

It could hurt everything. And damned if I begged her to stay at the end of all this, if I'd feel like we were an anchor keeping her down.

My hand slid from the back of her neck, and I watched as my thumb traced the curve of her full bottom lip as if I wasn't making the decision for it to do so.

Her tongue darted out to catch my skin. That slip of her tongue, wet against the pad of my thumb, tugged on something inside me, pulled me closer, reeled me in. All Paige had to do was curl her little finger around the line and tug.

I took a step backward.

"Logan," she said.

I held up a hand. "I can't."

"No, you *can,*" Paige said just before I walked out of the bathroom. Her tone had me pausing in the doorway. "You just won't. Don't confuse the two."

I took a deep breath, then walked away.

CHAPTER 17
PAIGE

WASHINGTON WOLVES

"All I'm saying is, I think you should think about it."

I jammed the phone between my shoulder and my ear while I unlocked the garage door into the kitchen.

"Allie, you know a thousand other people who are far more capable of doing this."

Even over the crinkle of the paper grocery bag in my arms, I heard her sigh. "You're not wrong."

"Thanks a lot. You're not supposed to agree so readily."

She laughed. "You're qualified because you're you, Paige. That's all the girls need."

The bags fell onto the counter with a plop, and I peered cautiously inside the first one to make sure I didn't crack the eggs. "How big is the event?"

Put me in front of a camera, and it was second nature for me. Posing came without a single thought, awkward hunches of my shoulder, the pop of a hip, the bend of an elbow. Toss my hair or stick out my butt if it was a bathing suit shoot. Take my cue from Tyra and smize the hell out of the camera. But the simple addition of a microphone had my body crawling with the heebie-jeebies. Especially when that mic would be facing row upon row upon row of young girls, all attending the first annual Team Sutton event that Allie was organizing.

Her foundation, the one she'd established after she took ownership of the team, had done a lot of smaller events. She went to schools and spoke about finding your place, encouraging leadership opportunities, and educating girls that a successful woman doesn't fit one mold or have one background. But this new event, one she wanted to use as her crowning jewel each year, was going to be on the fifty-yard line of the Washington Wolves field because, in her mind, she wanted these girls to see exactly what they were capable of. The sheer scale and size of what they could achieve.

Yes, Allie owned a professional football team because her dad gave it to her. But in less than two years, she'd made it soar. She'd increased profit margins, made changes in the arena that boosted season ticket package sales, and employee/player morale had never been higher in the history of the entire organization.

Gawd, I was so freaking proud of her. I could cry just thinking about it, if that was something I was capable of. But being proud of what she'd achieved on the stage she'd been given didn't mean I wanted to have that particular spotlight shining in my face.

"I need to check how many we have right now," she said, and I heard the rustle of paper. "But we've already got commitments from a few area schools. They're busing girls into the arena for this and giving them class credit."

"Shit," I said under my breath.

That made her laugh again. "You'd be amazing."

My lip pushed out in a petulant pout. "Why don't you call Ashley Graham's people? Now she's a model who can rock a motivational speech. I'd ask for class credit if I could come to that too."

"She was busy," Allie replied smoothly.

After a laugh burst out of my mouth, I sighed. "Let me check my very busy calendar. I'm a household CEO now, if you weren't aware."

As I put my almond milk on the top shelf, she hummed in my ear, but there was so much self-satisfaction in that sound that I almost hung up on her ass. "I thought you were going to hire a part-time housekeeper."

"Because, I don't know, my hands and arms work just fine? Besides, keeping those girls grounded is the best thing we can do for them. Keeping household staff at a minimum certainly helps. How many little snots did you and I know back in the day?"

"Way too many."

"Exactly," I said, lifting the avocado in my hand up like a battle flag. "It will be good for them to know how to do their own laundry."

Allie made a hesitant sound. "Just … be careful."

I paused by the open fridge door. "What do you mean?"

"Be careful they don't come to rely on you too much."

"Aww, are you guys missing me at Casa de Football Empire?" I teased, but I wasn't completely successful in taking the bite out of my tone.

"You know what I mean. This is a temporary solution, not a long-term commitment. It's great to help, and it's even better to be able to make an impact while you're there, but at some point, you won't be. Right?"

I was quiet because, as crazy as it sounded, I spent about zero time thinking about my end date. Logan's injury made it even more likely that this year could be his last, depending on what happened the latter half of the season.

If he wasn't playing anymore, his brother wouldn't have much of a case.

When I didn't speak, Allie kept going. "Because, unless I'm mistaken, you and Logan have not enjoyed any marital bliss, coital, postcoital, or otherwise, and he has not professed any undying love and asked you to stay forever, right?"

"Obviously not," I drawled. "Like I'd even want him to."

"Mmmkay."

"Don't come at me with that judgey humming thing, Sutton. He is hot, and I would love to climb him like a ladder at the first available opportunity." So what if I slammed a drawer a bit too forcefully as I finished that sentence. "But that doesn't mean I'm looking for some sticky sweet cotton candy happily ever after as a shiny prize at the end of this."

"It's amazing, truly."

If she thought she could bait me into asking, she didn't know me at all. I rolled eyes and pushed my tongue into the side of my cheek.

"And since you won't ask because you're as stubborn as Logan is, it's amazing how well you're able to mask what you want with unbridled cynicism."

I snorted. "You're so full of horseshit, Allie."

"I'll translate that to, I hate when you're right, Allie." Before I could respond, she muffled the speaker on her phone and spoke to someone else. "I've got to go, meeting with the players union rep in five! Love you."

There was a click before I could say I loved her too, and I shook my head. Such was life when your best friend was a freaking mogul.

I was putting the last of the groceries away when I heard a loud clang come from the weight room that I'd yet to see Logan use. He was too busy escaping to the Wolves' facility every day to even contemplate working out at home. My forehead bent in concern because I was pretty damn sure he was supposed to be taking it easy on his knee.

I shoved the grocery bags into their spot in the pantry and attempted to fix my ponytail before I walked past his office to the space at the back of the house.

With my shoulder against the frame of the door, I watched Logan on the weight bench. Glory hallelujah, he had small white earbuds in, which was why he didn't realize I was home. The reason this was so glorious was that he was shirtless. A shirtless, bench pressing Logan was my absolute new favorite look.

I kept myself perfectly still while he shuffled his butt and back on the black bench, then blew out a hard puff of air as he shifted the grip he had on the metal bar. I'd always had a firm appreciation for the professional athlete. Someone who was so disciplined that they crafted their body into a machine, fast and strong and dangerous to the person who would come up against them in competition.

As I watched him, seeing the shift of muscles under all the golden, smooth skin only interrupted by those few tattoos that I wanted to trace with my tongue, my appreciation changed into something else entirely.

Appreciation was a hop, skip, and a jump away from obsession, I realized. All it took was the right person, and appreciation became awareness, a hum under the skin. Awareness slid right into focus. Noticing things you didn't notice before. Like the way his triceps moved when he lowered the bar over that sweaty, slick chest.

Focus rolled naturally to fixation.

And I was fixating so hard.

I'd fixate all damn day if he'd let me.

Logan gritted his teeth, letting loose a grunt as he did another rep.

My thighs rubbed together because if I closed my eyes, I could perfectly imagine him making that sound as he lowered himself over me. Again, and again, and again. But like, harder. And faster.

I fanned my face, and the movement must have been just enough to catch his attention as he slid the bar back into place on the rack.

"You're home early," he said, breath heaving in and out as he punched a thumb against the screen of his phone. That heaving did marvelous things to his pecs.

"Uh-huh." My eyes hovered in the region of his abs, the flex and pull of each little square.

"Paige."

I snapped my gaze up. "What?"

He shook his head, but he was smiling.

"Are you allowed to be doing this?" I asked breathlessly. Why was I breathless?

One eyebrow rose slowly. "Doing what?"

"Umm." I waved a hand toward the weight bench. How rude of him to require actual words and actual sentences to understand me. It was his fault I was like this. If he'd been a good husband and screwed me on our wedding day, I wouldn't have been reduced to this stuttering, fumbling version of myself.

"Lifting weights?" he supplied.

So helpful, he was.

I shook my head, trying to break up the lust fog coating my normally very capable brain. "Yeah, that. Won't what's-her-name be pissed at you?"

Logan picked up a towel hanging over the edge of the weight bench. "Maggie said working my upper body was fine as long as I wasn't putting weight on my left knee."

I nodded.

"And it helps, so I think I'd do it even if she said not to."

I snorted. "Typical man."

Logan shrugged. He swept the towel over his chest and neck, and my mouth went dry. *Fluffy cotton, Sahara Desert, sand poured down my throat* dry. "If I don't give myself some sort of physical outlet, it makes it hard to keep my head steady."

Oh, that was something I could focus in on. "Like me with kickboxing."

"Yeah." He gave me a wry smile. "If you hadn't noticed, I'm not much of a talker. This is my way of getting everything in my head out without needing to say a word."

Huh.

I still said all the words.

But not everyone did. I thought of all the emotionally mute people in my life, not that there were many people in my life as it was, but maybe they just needed a good sweat.

A thought tickled at the back of my head, if I could just snatch it with my fingers and pull it forward.

"What?" Logan asked, regarding me curiously.

I blinked. "What?"

He breathed a laugh. "You look like your wheels are turning pretty hard."

I gave him a droll look. "That happens on occasion."

"I don't doubt it."

Oh, gracious. He was potent, wasn't he? A shirtless Logan, dark hair sweaty and messy, eyes warm and lips slightly curved was just about enough to make me spontaneously orgasm. If that wasn't a sad reflection on my state of physical needs, I didn't know what was.

But Logan's potency was not the current issue. *Or not the most pressing one,* I thought as the idea rolled around in my head.

"Just thinking about Isabel, actually."

His chin lifted. "What do you mean?"

I drummed my fingers on the top of my thigh. "Nothing. Or maybe it's nothing." I smiled. "Ignore me."

Logan sighed. "Wouldn't my life be easier if that were possible."

"Hey." I laughed.

He really was more mellow after working out. It wasn't a side of him I was used to because this emotional outlet happened at the training facility, not at home, given my presence.

Logan went to grab the bottle of water from the floor next to the weight bench. I didn't want Logan to ignore me, so I loved when he admitted he couldn't.

I backed up toward the door as he approached, knowing full well that I should just leave the room. Naturally, I decided to wait exactly where I was, in the small amount of space that he'd need to pass through in order to exit.

Instead of chastising me as I expected, he ambled closer and gave his stomach a lazy scratch.

I pressed my back against the door. From there, everything happened in slow-mo.

When the airhorn went off, I screamed and leaped forward, smack into Logan's chest. He caught me with an *oof,* one arm tight around my waist.

The sound cut off as soon as my weight left the door, but I swear, my ears kept ringing from the violent blast of sound.

"What the hell," Logan groaned. "I think I'm deaf."

I dropped my forehead to his shoulder and burst out laughing. My entire frame shook.

"The-" I gasped, "the twins. Oh my gosh, I think my heart just stopped."

His eyes narrowed. "I thought you guys were done playing pranks on each other."

We were still standing chest to chest, my hips lined up precisely perfect with his, and as long as he wasn't setting me back, there was no way I was going to move.

I grinned up at him. "We are."

Logan looked meaningfully past the door, eyebrows raised. "So the air horn duct taped *itself* to the wall?"

Helpless laughter spilled out of my lips. It was so good. I couldn't even be upset that they beat me thoroughly.

"We called a truce under the banner of mutually beneficial competition."

Carefully, I laid my hands on the upper part of his chest, and his eyes flickered hot in response.

"Care to define that further for me?"

"You," I said around my wide grin.

His gaze flicked to my mouth. "Me what?"

My fingers trekked slowly up the side of his neck until I could feel the damp line of his hair. "First team to pull off a prank on you wins."

Logan's mouth fell open in shock.

"I like this look on you," I whispered as I lifted up on the balls of my feet.

Surprised, post-workout Logan didn't have nearly as many defenses up, and it worked for me. I knew this because his hand tightened on my waist, and he didn't push my hands off him. Just one little nudge, and we'd topple into something excellent.

"Let me get this straight," he said evenly. I smiled and lifted my chin another fraction of an inch. My entire body was primed to explode if we stayed hovering over this precipice of a kiss. "My sisters, who have never played a prank on me in their entire life, joined forces against me because you asked them to?"

One.

Little.

Nudge.

The tip of my pointer finger traced the velvety edge of his ear, and he closed his eyes. "Yup."

"And you didn't worry about retribution?" he asked in a rough voice.

"Oh," I cooed, "I counted on it."

That was when I kissed him.

No more waiting, no more tiptoeing around it. I, literally and figuratively, took the bull by the horns.

My arms wrapped around his neck as he devoured my mouth. His tongue was sure and slick as it pushed and pulled with mine. Our teeth clacked when I angled my head and pushed even higher on the balls of my feet. I wanted to mount him.

His strong arms held me steadily in place, but his lips, they launched me into star-riddled skies.

Everything about it was perfect, hot and searching, no part of my lips untouched, no inch of my mouth unexplored. Logan might not have initiated the kiss, but he sure as hell took it over the moment I scraped my teeth along his bottom lip in a soft nip.

His hand slid up my back, and he fisted his hand in my hair. The sharp pinch of pain had me groaning into his mouth. That hand directed my head, moving me into exactly the place that he wanted me. We shuffled backward, my hands gripping tightly to his back until I was against the flat expanse of wall just to the side of the door. He rolled his hips when I hitched my leg up his side.

My head dropped back onto the wall.

This.

This was what I'd wanted.

I scraped my hands down the front of his chest, greedy and

demanding and not getting nearly enough of what I needed from him. This was a nibble of something delicious, and I wanted to devour the entire freaking meal.

He hissed in a breath, and I froze.

"Your knee," I said on a gasp.

"Fuck my knee," Logan groaned into the curve of my throat.

I exhaled a shaky laugh when his mouth sought mine again, our tongues tangling, lips nipping and sucking, teeth dragging, hands gripping.

It was so, so good. And I wanted so, so much more.

Judging by what I felt pressed against my belly, and by the strength with which he held me, Logan did too.

Acquiescence had never felt so decadent, neither had submission.

He was submitting, no matter how much he was dominating me with his kiss.

"Oh my *gosh,* PDA much?" A young voice had us freezing in place just as his hand reached down to palm my ass.

Logan exhaled heavily, and I might have whimpered. Visions of him screwing me on the gym floor went poof! In an instant.

"Molly," I said, my eyes closed and my leg dropping slowly to the floor. Logan lifted his weight off me. "We weren't expecting you home this early."

She snorted. "Obviously. Iz and I had a half day. You didn't remember?"

That snapped Logan and me into motion. He shifted behind me because of big, hard reasons that showed pretty clearly beneath mesh gym shorts. Isabel was standing next to Molly, just outside the weight room. Her arms were crossed over her chest, and she was watching us with narrowed, thoughtful eyes.

"Uh, no." I ran a hand through my hair, which felt like a hot mess. I cleared my throat. "Sorry, guys."

Isabel rolled her eyes and pivoted on her heel.

Molly grinned. "We can pick up the twins later, if, umm, you guys need some more alone time."

Logan stepped out from behind me, the situation clearly under control. "It's fine. I can pick them up."

I allowed myself one teeny, tiny pout. His shoulder brushed mine as he passed, and just that one slide of contact between us had me sucking in a breath.

See? Potent.

But I saw the tightness in his jaw and the stern set of his mouth. When I sucked in that breath, there was no hot look in answer, and I could practically feel him talking himself out of whatever we'd just experienced.

If there was smoke coming out of my ears in bright red frustrated puffs, I wouldn't be surprised.

"Men," I said under my breath as I walked into the kitchen.

"I know," Molly commiserated.

I closed and opened a drawer with a loud smack, just for an outlet to the sexual energy crawling angrily through my body. "They're like cattle, you know? Big dumb cattle who can see exactly where the river is when they're dying of thirst, and still—*still!*—we have to drag them over to drink."

She nodded, eyes wide and mouth open at my vehement tone. "Totally."

My hands slapped onto the counter as I steadied my breathing. "It's ridiculous. We shouldn't have to do this, Molly. But we do. We have to force their hand because we know what they want, don't we?"

"We do," she answered feelingly. "Man, if it's still frustrating for women like you, I don't stand a chance."

I grabbed her face, her beautiful face, and shook my head. "You stand a chance, young lady, because you're beautiful and smart and kind and anyone would be lucky to have you. Do you understand me?"

Molly nodded frantically, and I finally felt my hormones ebb to a more manageable level.

"Sorry," I told her, wrapping her in a quick hug. "Got a little carried away there."

"'S okay," she said into my shoulder. "I liked it."

I pulled back with a laugh. "If you say so."

Molly held out a fist for me, and I reluctantly bumped it with my own.

"We're fighting, young lady," I said. "I would've had a really good afternoon without your interruption."

"You'll forgive me," she said cheerfully, winding her arm through mine. "It's not like you can't kiss him anytime you want."

Right.

CHAPTER 18
PAIGE

WASHINGTON WOLVES

"Nope."

"Oh come on, Paige," my former agent begged. "They're going to pay you a stupid amount of money."

I rolled my eyes and kept typing. I'd been sitting at the kitchen counter, trying to focus on getting some work done before Logan came home with the twins.

No surprise, but he disappeared within ten minutes of the hottest make-out session of my twenty-nine years, mumbling something about needing to run some errands after he got them from school.

My ass. He was hiding.

On my laptop screen was a blinking cursor on a blank document. The title was the cleverly thought out "Allie's stupid talk that she wants me to do." It was as far as I'd gotten before my agent called with an offer for a cover, but they wanted me in New York in seventy-two hours.

"I already have a stupid amount of money, Carol."

I hit the backspace with a vengeance until the title disappeared.

"Hear me out," she said.

I rolled my head on my neck until I heard a few pops. "Like I could stop you. I haven't figured out how in the last decade."

She chuckled, and vaguely, I wondered how many more packs of cigarettes she'd smoked in the year since I'd seen her. Probably a few hundred.

I heard her typing, those harsh chicken pecks on her keyboard that I was so used to, given I'd known her since I was eighteen. "It's for *Bazaar*," she said, pausing meaningfully.

My eyebrows popped up in surprise. "You're kidding."

Carol coughed. It was gross enough to make me push my cell phone farther away than where it sat on the counter. "Why would I? If you don't get paid, I don't get paid."

"Yes, I remember." I drummed my fingers on the edge of my laptop. "Why would *Bazaar* want me? I haven't modeled in forever. A year for the fashion industry is like five years in the real world. For all they know, I've gained fifty pounds and grew a wart on my chin."

"That's what photoshop is for, sweet cheeks." She sighed. "It's some theme cover, the passing of the guard within high fashion. You'd be posing with a few newcomers. Kendall might do it, but they can't guarantee it, and they've got two older than you already signed on."

"You're shitting me," I said, sitting up in my stool. Isabel walked into the kitchen, set a jar in front of me, and kept going to the pantry.

A swear jar. Of course.

It was loaded with change and some wadded-up bills. Honestly, it was a miracle I'd evaded this tax thus far.

"Come on, Paige," Carol said. "This is a huge opportunity. Just because you've been quiet for the last year doesn't mean people don't remember you. Aren't you going crazy staying in one place and not working?"

I laughed. "Who says I'm not working? Just because I don't have any assholes telling me to starve myself doesn't mean I'm bored, Carol."

Isabel had her back to me after she pulled some food from the pantry, but she'd stopped moving while I talked.

"Yeah, but I know you. You went through this phase about five years after I signed you. Remember? No fashion shows for about eight months. Then you said no swim shoots. Doesn't mean any of those assholes forgot you or didn't want to work with you. They just waited you out until you got antsy for something new again."

Isabel's shoulders dropped, and I saw it happen. My heart clenched at how that must sound to her, the one in the house who was still looking at me like I was going to dart out the door. Allie's words from earlier rang through my head, to be careful with them. Logan's words about why he worked out did too.

"Carol, I said no, and I meant it. They can find someone else." On the speaker, her voice sputtered incredulously, but I hung up before she could try to argue with me.

Isabel started making a sandwich as though she hadn't been eavesdropping.

"Hey, go get changed," I told her. "I'm taking you somewhere."

"Can't. I've got homework."

I hopped off the stool. "Good thing you had a half day and have allll this extra time, huh?"

She spun and settled her back against the counter. "Where are we going?"

"You'll see when we get there. Come on, wear something you can sweat in."

Isabel snorted. "No way."

I crossed my arms over my chest and gave her a level look. "I'm asking for one hour, Isabel. That's all."

"Why would I?"

"Hey, if you don't think you can handle it, that's fine," I said smoothly. "I won't judge you."

She lifted her chin. "I can handle it. I just don't want to."

"If you say so." I started out of the kitchen. "I'm leaving in fifteen if you feel like proving me wrong. I doubt you will, though."

Twenty minutes later, she sat next to me in the passenger seat of my car wearing a mulish expression on her pretty face. It was so hard not to smile as we drove to my gym. I'd sent a text to the owner, begging her to do a session with just the two of us because I had a feeling Iz would get overwhelmed by a full class of people who'd been doing this a long time.

When we got to the nondescript building just outside downtown Seattle, Isabel gave it an unimpressed lift of one dark eyebrow.

"I already feel more empowered."

I laughed at her droll tone. "As you should. Just wait."

Inside, music pounded over the speakers, and out of the corner of my eye, I saw her take everything in.

In the middle of the huge room was the boxing ring, and lining the edge of the room were heavy black bags chained to the iron structure above them. The office in the back was bright, reds and blues adorning the wall. I tossed my bag onto the rubberized floor and pulled out a pair of wraps for her, and then myself.

She stared at the pink polka dot material.

"I can do the first one, if you want," I told her. I hooked the top of my wrap over my thumb and started the process to protect my hands. Three circles around my wrist, three around my knuckles before I started looping them between my fingers. She was watching avidly.

"No, I think I can do it."

"'Kay." I kept my tone light, but I slowed my movements so she could pay better attention. Once I had the Velcro fastening closed around my wrist, I unrolled the second wrap. She did the same, and even though her movements were tentative, and she spent more time than necessary smoothing out the material, she did great for her first time.

I saw her make a fist when she was done, and I almost screamed in triumph when her lips curved up in a tiny smile.

When my second hand was wrapped, I did the same thing to make sure I didn't have them too tight. "The first time I did this, I remember feeling like I was the biggest badass in the world. And then they started class, and I realized how not true that was."

I saw Amy stand from her desk in the office, but I held up my hand to give us a minute. She nodded.

"Why not?" she asked, still not looking at me as she studiously wrapped her second hand.

It was the first honest question Isabel had asked me since the moment she met me. I had to breathe out a slow breath to temper my excitement.

"I was really, really out of shape. I almost fell over when I tried my first side kick. And my jab cross looked like I was shooing flies, not throwing a punch."

She smiled again; I saw it in the lift of her cheeks.

"Laugh it up now, Ward," I told her and gave her shoulder a slight shove. "You'll see soon enough."

Amy came out, a pair of gloves tucked under her arm for Isabel. Isabel looked at her, awe clear in her big blue eyes.

Amy had that effect; she was tall and striking with arms I'd forever be envious of. Her black hair was done in thin braids, which she had wound up on the top of her head, and had a red bandana across her forehead. Her teeth gleamed white when she smiled, and it made the flawless golden color of her skin look even deeper.

"This is our new fighter?" she asked.

I set my hand on Isabel's shoulder, unbearably proud of her when she stood straight and held out a hand for Amy. "I'm Isabel, and Paige doesn't think I can handle doing this for an hour."

We both laughed.

"Well, then let's prove her wrong, shall we?" Amy handed her the gloves, which were black and purple.

I stretched by one of the bags while Amy showed Iz all the basics.

She was naturally athletic, which shouldn't have surprised me. Logan had the same DNA, after all.

And she was focused, which definitely didn't surprise me. She'd certainly harnessed all that focus in my direction for the past few weeks.

Amy gave her a small correction on her foot placement when Isabel didn't pull her hips around correctly for a roundhouse.

"Paige, why don't you show her?"

I nodded and felt Isabel's shy glance in my direction. "Just the kick?"

"Why don't you do a combo, so she can watch the flow from the upper body strikes into the kick." Amy stood next to Isabel and crouched so she was closer to Iz's height. "Watch how she uses her lower body for the strikes. It's not just about her arms. Then she'll plant her feet for the roundhouse."

Isabel nodded.

Since my gloves were still off, I kept my strikes light, a quick jab cross, a hook to the side of the bag, a drop of my shoulder for an uppercut, then I stepped out and snapped my hips around and felt the satisfying smack of my shin on the bag.

"Great," Amy said. "Did you see how she pointed her foot?"

But Isabel didn't answer because she was too busy gaping at me. "That was awesome," she breathed.

I smiled. "Let's see what you've got, Iz."

Amy started us off, and after only fifteen minutes, my heart was pounding, my face was hot, and sweat dripped down my spine. Isabel was hesitant at first, but she caught on so quickly, I couldn't believe it.

Soon she was jab cross hooking like a freaking pro.

"Nice," Amy shouted from behind her bag. She smacked it. "Come on, drop those shoulders, Iz. Leave it all here, baby girl."

She yelled out another combo, and I hissed out with each strike, blood flowing and body hot.

We worked our asses off, and Isabel kept up every step of the way. I braced my gloves on my knees and hung my head. "Holy crap, Amy, did you take speed before we got here?"

She laughed and stepped up to the bag next to me. "No slacking now, McKinney. Little girl there is showing you up."

Isabel grinned at her bag, then her face turned fierce, and she leaned back for a front kick that sent the bag swinging impressively, considering how slender she was.

"My ass, she is," I shouted.

When Isabel laughed, I felt like I was flying.

As we started the last stretch of work, Amy pushed us up another level. Isabel's face was bright red, the front of her shirt dark with sweat, as was mine.

Amy braced herself behind Isabel's bag and held it. "Come on, baby, whatever you've got for the next thirty seconds. You put everything right here. All of it."

From the corner of my eye, I saw her movements pick up speed, and she lost just a bit of technique in the process, but that was understandable. Her little fists pounded the bag.

"That's it, get it out, Iz," Amy yelled. "Whatever pissed you off, you leave it right here."

The first sound out of her mouth didn't register. But when she did it again, my head snapped in her direction.

Amy's face dropped in surprise when Isabel let out another sob.

Her arms flailed wildly at the bag, not even punching anymore. She pushed with both hands and stepped back, then did it again, throwing the entirety of her weight into it when she pushed once more. Amy braced her hands on the bag.

"That's it, baby," she said, not yelling anymore.

I approached slowly because I definitely didn't want to catch a hook to my chin. I yanked my gloves off and tossed them behind me.

Tears streamed down Isabel's face, and my heart broke with every single one. When she stopped to suck in a breath, I laid my hands on her shoulder.

She whipped around and threw her arms around my waist. I clutched her to me and sank to the floor when her weight all but collapsed from the force of her sobbing.

I didn't even remember what I said to her or the words I tried to use to soothe her wild outlet of all the things that had been building up inside her for who knew how long. I smoothed my hands down her hair and her back, rocking us a little while she shook in my arms.

"It's okay," I whispered into the crown of her hair, sweat-soaked, just like mine. "It's gonna be okay, honey."

Her hands tightened around my back, and I felt split apart inside. My eyes burned, my nose tingled, and when she pulled in a shuddering breath, I felt a tear slide down my chin and onto my neck.

"I- I don't know why I'm crying," she said in a watery, hoarse voice.

I braced myself for her to pull away, but she didn't. Isabel kept her forehead against my shoulder and her arms around me. I laid my chin on the top of her head.

There was nothing about this that I felt qualified for, but I thought about what Allie or Luke might say to Faith. Or if Logan was here, what he'd say to his sister.

But they weren't here.

She came with me, and maybe whatever words she needed to hear were the ones I would say. Not someone else.

"If I had to hazard a guess," I said carefully, smoothing my hand down her ponytail again, "I'd say it's because your mom is a selfish bitch who gave you trust issues, and you've had to deal with way more than your fair share in your very short life. Those big emotions had to go somewhere."

Isabel sniffed and pulled back. "You shouldn't call my mom a bitch."

I thought about myself at her age and how I'd want someone to speak to me. I'd want honesty. No sugarcoating the reality of their life. "She's not my mom, so I can call her whatever I want. I think what she did was selfish. And I can call her a bitch because I'm old enough to have excellent bitch radar."

"Bu-but she's still my mom," she said, voice hiccupping around her tears. "I-I think that about her too sometimes, and it feels like I'm doing something wrong."

I cupped the side of her face and waited until she was looking at me. My heart could barely handle what I saw there. "I heard a smart person say that if you're not willing to fight the devil himself for your children, then you don't deserve to be their mother."

Her eyes filled up again, her little lips quivered, and dammit, I felt mine fill up too.

"Isabel, you deserve someone who'll take on the devil for you. And you know that's your brother."

She sniffed. "I know. He doesn't even let anyone know how much he's done for us. But he would. He'd fight for us."

"Every day," I said quietly.

"And you too?" she whispered.

I swiped under my eye, and my sweaty wraps caught the tears. Yup. There went my heart, right out the flipping window. Here Allie thought that Logan was going to make a play for that feeble organ inside my chest, but she never expected that a fourteen-year-old girl would steal it first.

I blinked a few times until my eyesight cleared, then held her face in my hands. "He doesn't stand a fucking chance against me. You understand?"

She nodded, tears spilling over her cheeks again. I wiped them away with my thumbs.

"Want to go home?" I asked.

Isabel exhaled slowly. "I think I want to finish if that's okay."

I smiled at her. It felt impossible, how much I loved her at that moment. "Yeah, that's okay."

So we stood, bumped fists, and finished.

CHAPTER 19
LOGAN

WASHINGTON WOLVES

"Whoa," Lia said from the back seat of my truck.

"What?"

"She's like, smiling at Paige."

We pulled into the driveway just as Isabel and Paige were walking out of the garage.

"I'll be damned," I whispered.

"Swear jar!" the twins yelled happily.

I sat up and pulled my wallet out from the back pocket of my shorts. Without glancing in their direction, I tossed it to Lia to pull out whatever the hell she wanted.

She tore into it with glee. "I'll take a twenty, so you're prepaid for the next week."

"Sounds good," I said, eyes unable to move from where Isabel said something that made Paige tip her head back and laugh loudly.

They were both sweaty and disheveled, and Paige had her gym bag slung over her shoulder. The leggings she was wearing hit high on her waist, and it made her legs look like they were two miles long, especially with the cropped T-shirt she had over it. All I got was a glimpse of toned stomach and the naked skin on her arms. Strands of red hair had fallen out of her ponytail, framing her face and lining the back of her neck.

I slid the truck into park and got out, not as quickly as the twins, who instantly bombarded the two with their after-school chatter.

"Where did you guys go?"

"Did you go kickboxing?"

"Why can't you take us?"

"Did you hit anyone?"

Paige held up a hand, and they fell silent. "Take a breath, ladies." Then she grinned at Iz. "Why don't you tell them what we did?"

The look Isabel gave Paige was nothing short of adoring, and it about knocked the breath from my body.

"Paige took me to her gym." Iz glanced at me, and her cheeks flushed an even deeper pink than they already were.

"You liked it?" I asked.

She grinned, nodding. She walked over and hugged me, wrapping her thin arms around my waist. I leaned down to drop a kiss on the top of her head.

"Everything okay?" I asked Iz quietly.

Her chin lifted, and she rested it on my stomach as she peered up at me. "Perfect."

"Tell me later?"

Isabel nodded again, then started inside.

"Girl is a natural," Paige told me when the twins sprinted to the door.

Her hand brushed against mine while we walked, and my entire body wanted to pitch in her direction from just that one small touch. The afternoon away from her hadn't lessened the impact of our kiss. Not nearly enough.

"I can't believe she agreed to go," I admitted.

Paige shrugged. "She's as competitive as her brother. It was pretty easy once I told her it was fine if she couldn't handle it."

I exhaled an incredulous laugh. "I can't tell whether you're insane or a genius."

She turned and grinned up at me. "I'd like to think it's a little bit of both."

My hand almost lifted to cup the side of her face, simply because I wanted to. It was exactly what I was afraid of when it came to Paige. That uncorking everything inside me would cause an explosion, the pressure of what had been building up between us too great to keep contained.

I'd touch her because I couldn't not touch her.

I'd kiss her because I couldn't not kiss her.

And if we'd stood there for another three seconds, I would've done it. I would've dropped my chin and touched my mouth to her upturned lips. I would've slid my tongue against the opening of her mouth until she let me in.

Paige knew it.

She was a mess, her hair was a disaster, and there wasn't a stitch of makeup on her face. But I wanted to kiss her as badly as I ever had.

That was when the door opened, and Lia popped her head out. "Logan, Nick is here!"

Our heads snapped in her direction. "What?"

"He always ruins the best moments," Paige grumbled, striding toward the house.

And sure enough, seated at the kitchen island was my asshole brother, smiling like he was actually welcome in my home.

"What are you doing here?" I asked, striving desperately for a civil tone.

The girls knew we weren't close, but so far, we'd managed to keep any outright arguments away from them. Nick's eyes took in Paige's state of dishevelment, and he grimaced.

"Haven't seen my sisters in a couple of weeks," he said, leaning back and crossing his arms over his chest. "I missed them."

Molly rolled her eyes. "He was grilling me about you two."

Paige stood next to me. "Was he now?"

Nick smiled, but it didn't reach his eyes. "Just curious about my new sister-in-law. Told Molly that we should have everyone over for dinner at our place. Cora makes a mean brisket."

"Sounds delicious," Paige answered politely.

I clamped my jaw together. "We need to get homework started, Nick. If you want to visit the girls, call ahead next time."

"It's almost like you don't want me here," he said, standing from his stool. "Why would that be?"

The words were heavily laced with suspicion, and Isabel glanced uncomfortably between us. Molly sensed his change too, and she huffed. "Come on, Nick, don't be a jerk."

"I'm not being a jerk." His eyes tracked over Paige's body. "Just wondering if she'd be gone already, given the injury."

I breathed in for four, held for four, out for four.

Molly's brows bent in confusion. "Why would she be gone because he hurt his knee?"

Isabel frowned, and she watched Nick steadily.

"Girls, why don't you give us some privacy?" Paige asked. She set her hand on my back, maybe because the tension rolling through me was starting to show.

Neither of them moved. Thank goodness the twins were playing in the backyard.

"Or not, whatever," she muttered under breath.

Nick smiled at Molly. "Just waiting for the missing piece to reveal itself. Everyone's got reasons for doing what they do."

Paige's chest rose on an inhale.

"We're not doing this here, Nick," I said. "You've got nothing you can use against me, and it's time for you to admit that. The girls stay right where they are."

"For now," Nick said.

Isabel's face tightened, and I saw the way her breathing increased. She was terrified.

"Time for you to go," I said, taking a step toward him. I'd drag his ass out of the door if I had to.

"What does that mean?" Molly asked, her eyes bouncing back

and forth between me and Nick, then me and Paige. "He can't actually take us from you, can he?"

"Not just for now," Paige snapped, taking a step forward. "Where do you get off, dude? You're not welcome in this house, not just because you're a disrespectful asshole to me, but you've got no right to talk about this in front of the girls when your only reason for doing it is to piss off Logan."

Nick pointed his finger at me when I came within arm's reach. "You lay a single hand on me, and I'll get you for assault."

"That threat is getting really old, Nick."

He lifted his chin. "Then how about you stop threatening me."

"Nick, come on," Molly pleaded. "This isn't funny. We want to stay here."

"You girls would be so much better off with me and Cora," he said, barely even sparing her a glance. "We'd have you in better schools, a bigger house, all the right people in your life." He tilted his head at me. "And the kind of woman you should have looking out for you. One who hasn't basically sold her body for the masses to consume."

I sucked in a breath and stepped forward; I was over him using this as his spiel. Paige was his easiest target because all of his other options were dead-ends. I was ready to risk the assault charge when Isabel stormed forward.

"Shut up, Nick," she said, all fierce eyes and balled-up fists. "You don't even know her."

My brother was just as shocked as the rest of us at Isabel's outburst. She was always the quiet watcher, just like me.

"And you do?" he asked. "Let the adults discuss this, Iz. You have no idea what you're talking about."

Isabel's face flattened out, and she stopped when she was in front of Paige. "*You* don't know what you're talking about. I know that Paige listens to us. That she makes Logan laugh. She got the twins to stop playing their stupid pranks, and Molly to quit sneaking outside to show off for the neighbor boy." She jabbed a finger in the air, and I curled a hand around her shoulder. I could barely risk a glance at Paige because I didn't want to tear my eyes away from my sister. "So what if she doesn't wear pearls and lace and belong to some stupid club." Her voice wavered, and I had to swallow past a lump in my throat. "That bullshit isn't important. She'd fight the devil for us, she told me so, and that's what matters. Our own mom wouldn't even do that, and if you try to take us, she'll fight you too."

My mouth hung open, my chest cracked in half, and my eyes swept behind Isabel to Paige, who looked just as stunned as I felt.

Her skin was pale, and her eyes took up half her face, glistening dangerously until she blinked.

Nick's jaw worked back and forth, his eyes flat and his mouth tight.

"You ready to leave now?" I asked calmly.

"He better be," Isabel said. Molly laughed in delight, but when I glanced at Paige, she looked terrified.

"For now," my brother repeated even though he knew that for the moment, he had nothing he could say or do. When he walked out, Isabel turned around and buried her face against Paige, hugging her fiercely. Paige smiled and curled her hand around the back of Iz's head.

"Geez," she said lightly, "one kickboxing class and look at you being all badass."

"He shouldn't talk about you like that," Isabel said, her voice muffled. "I don't like it. It's not your fault you're so pretty."

I closed my eyes as I exhaled a laugh because all of this was almost too much. In a good way but still so big and unexpected. Paige must have felt the same way because I saw her hand shake when she lifted it from Isabel's back to smooth some of the stray hairs back on top of her head.

I cleared my throat. "Hey, Iz, why don't you go tell the twins to come inside, okay?"

She disentangled herself from Paige and did as I asked.

Almost immediately, Paige mumbled something about a shower and bolted upstairs.

"I'm, uhh," I said to Molly, then gestured toward the stairs.

She nodded. "Yeah, I'd check on her if I were you. I'll keep everyone corralled down here."

I gave her a quick hug. "I don't deserve you guys, you know that?"

"We sure do."

I was laughing as I climbed the stairs. I was faster than I had been a week ago but still not as fast as I wanted to be. The bedroom door was closed, and when I walked in, she was standing next to the bed with her hands speared into her hair.

"I hate your brother," she said.

I laughed as I closed the door, then locked it for good measure. "Yeah, me too."

She started pacing. "No, seriously, like, I could break something right now because he pisses me off so bad."

"You should."

"I wanted to grab a lamp or a vase or something and heave it at his tiny pinprick head," she hissed.

I approached slowly even though she wasn't paying the slightest attention to where I was standing.

"Just make sure it's an old lamp. Or one of the pink ones."

"Where does he get off, you know?" She whipped in my direction, and her eyes were blazing. "I've heard so much worse from bigger assholes than him, but there's something about the way he says it." She fisted her hands in the air in front of her, like she was choking an imaginary version of my brother.

But as much as she wanted to pretend it, this wasn't just about Nick.

And it shouldn't have slayed me like it did, that she was this emotional about my tough-as-nails little sister sticking up for her, but I was slayed nonetheless.

"What happened between you and Isabel?"

Her pulse fluttered rapidly at the base of her throat. "Seriously, I'm talking about throwing lamps right now, Logan."

What she was doing was holding onto anger because it was

easier to process than the raw emotion of what Isabel had revealed to us.

I walked over to the bedside table, yanked the cord of the lamp and handed it to her.

She blinked.

"Do it," I told her. "We can replace it."

Paige scoffed. "No."

"He all but called you a prostitute in front of the girls," I said, pushing just a little harder.

If anger was what she needed to grasp onto, clutch to her chest like a life preserver, then I'd shove her into the water if it helped push her past this.

Something happened between her and Isabel. Something important. Important enough that Paige was on the verge of a breakdown, that Isabel just stepped in front of Paige to defend her, and it had my head spinning with the possibilities of what it meant.

If this was what I had to do to get to the bottom of it, I would.

Paige's blue eyes flared hot. "I'm not a fucking prostitute, and he knows it."

I held my ground even though she looked like a Valkyrie bearing down at me. "He does. He puts you in his crosshairs because he thinks you're the easiest target for the fact that he can't have them. He doesn't even really want them; he just thinks he does."

"Ho"—she laughed harshly—"easy target, my ass."

"He has no idea who he pissed off, does he?" I marveled.

She snatched the lamp and hefted it in her hand, testing the weight. As much as I'd love to kick my brother's ass, the thought of Paige doing it had lust ripping through my body.

"No idea," she said quietly.

"He looks at you, and he thinks he knows you, but this"—I motioned to her face, her body—"is only the shell. It's not who you are."

Paige glared at the lamp, one that I actually did like very much, and pulled in a deep breath.

"Everyone thinks that, Logan," she said in a low voice. "It's what I made my money on for years, that all of this is the most important part of me, and it's not." Her hand shook. "And I hate the fact that, in front of those girls, he'd fucking shame me for it."

Paige turned around and paced, lamp hanging by her side, the cord dragging behind her.

"Do something about it," I whispered fiercely. "Like he was right here, do something about it. Whatever you want."

Show me the things you won't show anyone else, my brain, my heart, everything inside me begged. That was what I wanted from her.

"I'm not ashamed of what I did," she snapped, but she wasn't talking to me. "I never have been. But I … I didn't expect that, that assholes like your brother would love to remind me of the worst parts of the job. Like it's their job to shove me down into my place because I make them uncomfortable, and I intimidate them."

Her voice didn't waver, but it thickened, and I wished I could see her face.

"That's exactly it," I said.

She turned and heaved the lamp.

At my head.

"Holy shit," I yelled, ducking before it clocked me in the face. It shattered against the wall behind me, and I gaped at her. "You weren't supposed to throw it at *me*."

She had her hands clapped over her mouth, eyes wide in horror. "I almost hit you. I almost hit you!"

I wasn't sure whether I was supposed to laugh or be pissed, but I didn't have time to decide, because that was when Paige burst into tears.

CHAPTER 20
LOGAN

"Hey, hey," I soothed, "come here."

I approached her with a slight limp because the sudden ducking movement wasn't the best thing I could've done for my knee.

"I threw a lamp at your head," she cried, tears spilling over her cheeks. "What is *wrong* with me?"

"Nothing," I promised as I folded her in my arms. She clutched at my back and tucked her face into the side of my neck. "There's nothing wrong with you."

"Entirely not true," she sobbed. "I don't even know why I'm crying."

I rubbed a hand slowly over her back. "I basically goaded you into it."

She pulled back and looked at me. "You really did. What's wrong with you?"

Her face was a mess, and I laughed under my breath. I brushed some hair off her forehead and tucked it behind her ear. "Good question."

Paige sniffed, and as her tears slowed, she played with the neck of my T-shirt with absent touches of her fingers. "That felt really good."

I smiled. "Yeah?"

She nodded. "Now we need a new lamp, though."

"I think we can afford it."

Paige dropped her forehead onto my chest and took a shuddering breath.

My chin set perfectly on the top of her head when she stood like that, and I closed my eyes against how she fit in my arms.

"What happened with Isabel?" I asked quietly, brushing my mouth against her temple.

Paige blew out a breath against my throat, and that warm air from her lips lifted the hairs on the back of my neck. "We had an exercise-induced emotional breakthrough."

I tightened my hold on her and smiled. "Yeah?"

She nodded, and when she did, I felt the edge of her bottom lip against my skin.

"I should've warned you; the Wards don't do anything halfway."

"So much crying," Paige whispered. "Let's not repeat this tomorrow."

Everything I was trying to avoid was right here. I knew how she felt against me, how she looked when she dropped her mask. When she didn't hide the emotions that seemed to terrify her, she was the most beautiful woman I'd ever seen in my entire fucking life.

And if she walked away at the end of this, when her role in our life was fulfilled, I'd never be able to forget it. It was the knowledge that I'd crave this feeling until the day I died. Crave her.

There might be a hundred women who could manage in our life.

But she was the one who fit us perfectly.

As different as the two of us were, I had one big thing in common with Paige. For my own sanity, I kept the dam closed on certain feelings because when it came to this, to her, to what I could feel for her, it felt like I'd drown if I allowed myself everything I was capable of feeling for her.

I wouldn't just love her. I'd worship her.

I wouldn't just feel possessive. I'd slit someone's throat if they hurt her, and I'd do it without blinking.

It was something primal that I wasn't sure I could control, and something about that scared me.

But, I thought, it seemed like Paige would understand that. Like she had that inside her too.

I drew back and cupped the side of her face.

Her tongue darted out to wet her lips, and I rubbed my thumb against her bottom lip, rougher than I should have, but it wasn't hard enough.

The way her eyes burned and her cheeks flushed, she felt the same.

That was the piece I'd been missing all along.

Paige and I were the same.

Whatever fire burned inside her, I had it in me too. I'd just never met anyone who made me want to let the flames consume me. Who made me want to see how hot they could burn, what heights they could reach, what we could reach together.

"Logan," she whispered, arching into me as she fisted my shirt in her hands. "If you're going to hit the brakes again, tell me now, because I'm feeling like I'll start throwing more than lamps if you get me primed and then walk away."

My head was spinning. My hand slid up her back, and slowly, I wound the end of her ponytail around my fist. It tugged her chin up, her mouth in perfect reach of mine. She hissed out a breath when I tightened my fingers in her hair.

"If we do this," I told her, "you're mine. Do you understand?"

Paige held my eyes with hers, and she nodded. "Yeah."

"I mean it," I growled. I dipped and ran my nose under the delicate edge of her chin, spoke the words into her silky skin like a brand. "I don't do casual, and the second you bare your body to me, the second I get my hands on you like I've imagined a thousand times, the second you take me in, it's you and me, you got it?"

Paige arched her back, and the soft weight of her breasts against my chest had my heart slamming against my ribs. "Got it. Holy shit, I've got it. Please, please, please let's do all those things you imagined."

I laughed huskily, lightly biting down on the side her neck. She started walking us backward to the bed.

"If we did all of them …" I told her, lifting my head and speaking against her mouth. Just the slightest brush of lips against lips. "You wouldn't walk for a week. I'd break you."

She tilted her chin to the ceiling and exhaled slowly, like something I'd said was already bringing her to the cusp, the razor-sharp edge of pleasure that I couldn't wait to find with her. When she looked at me again, she looked half-drugged and heavy-lidded. "Promises, promises, Ward."

I let go of her hair and found the seam of her T-shirt. I fisted the edge of it with both hands and ripped it in two, tearing it off her shoulders, and she threw her head back and laughed.

"You don't think I can?" I asked her as I started pulling down the front zipper of her black sports bra.

Paige lifted up on tiptoe and bit down lightly on my bottom lip. "I *dare* you to try to break me."

Our mouths clashed, tongues immediately slipping and sliding and swirling. Paige was wound around me so tight, hands and fingers digging into any flesh she could find, and I did the same. One hand stayed anchored in her hair, and I dug underneath her leggings until my hand was filled with the firm flesh of her ass.

Everything before Paige, anything I thought I might have wanted from a partner was tepid and bland and safe.

This was the most unsafe thing I'd ever experienced, and when she tilted her head to deepen a kiss that was already impossibly deep, I groaned into her mouth and knew I'd take it even further, fling us high enough that unsafe wouldn't even be the right word for whatever it was we were doing to each other.

And she'd be with me every step of the way. Every touch and taste and everything we'd take would be done together.

Her hands started tugging on my shirt, and I let go of her long enough to tug it over my head and whip it away from us. Greedy eyes devoured my naked chest, and her fingers followed, dragging roughly over my stomach until they found the trail of hair that disappeared into my shorts.

With the sports bra half-unzipped, the soft mounds of her breasts were finally visible, and just the edge of her areolas was visible. A shadow, a hint that made my mouth water.

The effort to pull the zipper down slowly made my hands shake, and her chest heaved as I did. Each snick of the zipper snapped between us, like the click of an empty gun chamber when you didn't know which one held the last bullet. There was one that would pop, that would explode the action, but our eyes held while we waited for it.

Click.

Click.

Click.

Click. Boom.

I ducked, sucking one tip into my mouth, hands digging into her back as my tongue swirled around her warm skin.

She had her hand down the front of my shorts, and when I ripped off her bra, she tightened her grip, which made me hiss.

Paige abandoned the torture she'd been inflicting on me to clutch the back of my head, her breath escaping her in short, whimpering puffs. I licked across her chest to the other side, this time using my teeth. But only for a second, because she braced both hands on my shoulders and pushed me backward onto the bed.

I ripped at my shorts while she shoved her leggings down her legs. Because they were so tight, she almost fell over, and the resulting smile she sent to me—blinding and bright and beautiful—had my heart pinching tight behind the cage of my ribs.

Her naked body, which she showed me with zero shame, was long and lean, the lines of stomach and hips and shoulders strong and toned. I wanted to taste every inch, and I would.

Paige licked her lips when she watched my hand make the same movements that she'd been doing.

I jerked my chin. "Climb on up, cowgirl."

She set a knee on the bed and swung the other leg over my lap but didn't lower herself. She braced her hands on the headboard and worked her mouth over mine, the tips of her breasts brushing against my skin until she was whimpering.

"You could explode just from that, couldn't you?" I whispered, running my hands up her thighs and waist, digging my thumbs into the skin just below her hip bone.

"Later," she said on a rush. "Let's try that later. Please, Logan."

My hands dug into her flesh until she groaned, lining herself up over me as our eyes held. Paige lowered herself down, down, down, so slowly that my fingers curled from the need to shove her fully onto me, except harder, faster.

"Do it," she whispered, her lips curling into a sinful smile. "I know you want to."

I held her in place and snapped my hips up. She clapped a hand over her mouth to swallow the muffled scream, the other still holding tight to the headboard.

Paige worked her hips in tight circles, and I sat up to suck at her chest, use the soft, warm flesh to hide my groans of blinding pleasure that slipped slow and hot up my spine.

We were wound so tight around each other, and she threw her head back as she moved faster, the sweat-slicked skin of her chest sliding against my own.

My teeth found the edge of her collarbone as I felt her tighten around me.

White flashed bright behind my eyes as we threw each other over the edge at the same time. Her shuddering breaths hit my skin like strikes, and I tightened my hold around her back as we came back down to earth. She slumped against me and laughed incredulously.

"Good thing my ego can handle my wife laughing at me after

sex," I said into the curve of her shoulder. I traced my thumb over a mark I'd left there.

I wanted to tell her that I was falling in love with her, that the happiness she brought me was so acute, I could almost feel it slicing my skin open.

She looked drunk when she lifted her head. Her hair was wild around her face, half in, half out of the ponytail. Her lips were puffy and pink, the skin over her chest splotchy and marked from my teeth and lips.

"I'm laughing because if that's how it is between us when you're injured …" She stopped to hum. Then she slid up to kiss me again, soft and sweet and content. "You might break me after all."

I smiled against her lips, then raised my hips.

Her eyes widened when she felt me inside her. "How are you still …?"

"I told you," I said, "Wards don't do things halfway."

I smacked her ass, and she laughed.

"Hold on, wife," I instructed her. "We are nowhere near done."

CHAPTER 21
PAIGE

WASHINGTON WOLVES

I loved our bed.

I loved our bed even more with a naked Logan in it.

And for the last three days, there'd been a lot of nakedness happening.

He hadn't broken me yet, but oh, he was giving it his very best shot.

When I thought about him being fully healed, having full range of motion, my entire body almost seized up in orgasmic, anticipatory bliss. Never in my life did I think it was possible to meet someone who made me feel this way, sexy and powerful and addictive, but who, in his own right, was equally sexy and powerful and addictive.

He didn't ask me to dim who I was to appease his own ego; he simply matched me toe to toe.

"I think I'm going to send the guy who jacked up my knee a thank-you note," Logan said, stretching his arms over his head with a deep groan. The girls weren't awake yet for school, but once they were out the door, we'd probably end up back in bed. It was our fun new daily ritual.

Being married was awesome.

I hummed, kissing across the wide expanse of his chest, stopping to lick a tiny circle around the flat, bronze disk of his nipple. "Are you now?"

He dug his hands into my hair and tugged until I had no choice but to lift my head. "Would I be here right now if it hadn't happened?"

"I suppose not." I licked across the seam of his lips. He let me in, sucking on my tongue, making my toes curl up and my thighs clench. "Eventually, though," I said after I pulled back. "You would've given in."

He chuckled darkly, and that made my thighs clench too.

Who was I kidding? Everything he did made my thighs clench, a desperate attempt to ease the ache he set off inside me simply by breathing.

Logan touched me reverently, dragging his fingers down to the small of my back. "Eventually," he agreed quietly.

I set my chin on his chest and worked my hand down between his legs. His chin tilted up, and he swore under his breath, a string of dirty words that had me grinning.

He was so controlled, except with me.

The rest of the world got the quiet Logan.

They got disciplined Logan, who never lost his cool on the field. Who watched and observed and led with quiet strength.

I was the only one who knew the other side.

The fire in him wasn't lessened by the way he kept it contained. It just burned that much hotter when exposed.

All he'd been missing was someone to set off the reaction. I was the oxygen, and together, I found with incredible delight and many sore muscles, we burned the whole damn house down.

He turned me slowly onto my side with a gentle press of his hands on my hips, and I moaned into my pillow when his chest curved around my back. We'd gotten awfully creative with positions because of his knee, and this was a real crowd pleaser.

His fingers shackled my wrists, and he lifted them until my arms were stretched up over my head.

"Don't move those," he warned quietly. My fingers curled into the top of my pillow.

"If I do?" I asked. He liked it when I talked back. It usually ended in early orgasms for me, though I wasn't sure how he imagined that to be punishment.

Being with him, like we were now, felt differently than I thought it would.

A product of never meeting the right kind of man, I supposed.

Logan was strong enough not to be intimidated by me, and I felt safe enough with him to do things like throw lamps at his head or sob in his arms, something I'd never done with another human being. Not even Allie.

It was strange to be able to look at both of them and see how they filled the role of my best friend.

Logan was my best friend who I could easily see myself falling in love with. See it so clearly, that I knew I was halfway there already.

As he kissed the back of my neck, a spot he favored, I sighed happily. His hand swept down my side, stopping only when he cupped the back of my knee so he could hitch it higher on the bed.

That was when there was a tentative knock on your bedroom door.

"Noooo," I groaned.

Logan dropped his forehead onto my shoulder. He leaned over to the side of the bed and grabbed his boxer brief, sliding them up his legs while I tugged on my tank top.

"Come in," he said, rubbing his eyes with the heels of his hands.

Isabel poked her head around the corner. "Molly isn't in her room. I went to wake her up because I need to be at school early, and she's not in there. I can't find her anywhere."

I bolted up in bed as Logan strode quickly into our closet. "You looked downstairs?" I asked. "You know she can't hear anything if she's got her headphones on."

Iz shrugged. "If she's downstairs, then she's in a really good hiding spot."

Logan was pulling a T-shirt over his head. I grabbed my cotton robe from the chair in the corner.

"You call her cell phone?"

"I sent her a couple of texts, but no, I haven't tried to call her yet," Isabel answered.

"Her car's here?" Logan asked as he passed Isabel.

"Yeah."

I picked up my phone and tapped my screen until I pulled up her contact info. It rang and rang, her voicemail finally picking up. I ended the call and immediately called her again, shaking my head as her voicemail picked up even faster this time as if she'd sent me there.

"Molly, if you don't call us back in five minutes, you're grounded until you're twenty-five," I hissed into the phone.

Isabel sighed. "You shouldn't threaten punishment that you can't follow through on."

"I know," I said glumly. I flopped back onto the bed. "She can't have gone far."

There was something niggling, something whispery thin in the back of my head.

Isabel snorted. "She's probably modeling her underwear for the neighbor."

I bolted upright, and Isabel's eyes widened as we stared at each other.

"Holy shit, she's probably modeling her underwear for the neighbor," I whispered.

I scrambled out of bed so quickly that I almost face-planted on the floor. My cell phone was wedged between my shoulder and my cheek while it rang on the other end as I tugged my pants on with one hand. Not an easy thing to do.

"Logan is going to kill her."

Sighing, I yanked my hair into a ponytail. "Forget Logan, *I'm* going to kill her if that's where she is right now."

I flew down the stairs with Isabel behind me. "Logan, I think we know where she is."

He lifted his head from where he was tapping out a text. "Where?"

There was a knock on the door.

"If that's my brother, I don't care if he's got a cop standing behind him, I will kill him right now."

I could see two people standing by the door, the shadow of a third behind them.

"No murders today," I said. "Too tall to be Nick."

"Thank heaven for small favors," Logan mumbled. "I'll get it."

When he swung the door open, his face went slack with relief.

"Molly," he exhaled, "where *were* you?"

I hurried to his side with my arms crossed over my chest. Standing next to Molly was a giant of a man, a shock of white hair on his head and a stern look on his face. She was tight-lipped, her face drawn into a frown. Behind both of them was a tall, broad-shouldered kid. Dark hair and bright eyes with a sharp jawline that was tight with tension.

"Logan," the guy said with a nod. He gave me a pinched smile. "Sorry to meet you like this, ma'am. I'm Richard Griffin, your next-door neighbor. This is my son, Noah."

I attempted a smile. "Paige. Nice to meet you both."

"I'm returning your sister with a warning."

Logan watched Molly warily because she still hadn't moved. "What's the warning for?"

"Well, considering I just found her in my son's bedroom, the first one is to caution her against breaking and entering."

"Molly," I said on a gasp.

Molly pinched her eyes shut when Logan blew out a blistering curse word. The kid behind Molly hung his head and crossed his arms tightly over his chest. Logan pointed his finger inside our house in the direction of stairs. "Room. Now. I will be up to talk to you in a minute."

She swiped at a tear and hurried past us. I covered my mouth with one hand as the sounds of her pounding feet disappeared, and her bedroom door slammed shut.

Isabel was gaping up at her sister.

"Iz," I said quietly. "Why don't you give us some privacy?"

She nodded and ran up the stairs. I grabbed Logan's hand and twined my fingers through his. He squeezed but didn't look over at me. To be safe, I led us out onto the porch so we could talk privately and shut the door to the house behind us.

Richard propped his hands on his hips and shook his head. "She's not a bad kid, but come on, Logan. I've got a nineteen-year-old son on a football scholarship. If he got caught with a minor, his future is ruined. No judge in the world would care if she climbed through the window uninvited. That's statutory rape, especially if I'd walked in fifteen minutes later."

The son in question lifted his head and met Logan's quelling stare head on. "I'm sorry, sir. I didn't know how young she was. She told me she was almost eighteen when I met her. She looks … older."

I blew out a slow breath because if he kept talking about how Molly looked, Logan would probably lose it.

Logan slicked his tongue over his teeth and regarded our neighbor with a steady gaze, only a touch warmer than the one he'd given the son. "What were they doing in that bedroom, Richard?"

My eyes bounced back and forth between the two men standing in front of our house. The tension was so thick, I could taste it on my tongue when I worked to swallow.

"Everyone was clothed, for the most part," he admitted. "But your sister was on his lap, and they had their hands all over each other."

"Shit," I said under my breath. Dread pooled in my stomach as I thought back to my conversation with Molly.

Logan pinched the bridge of his nose. "I'll talk to her. But this isn't just on her."

Richard glanced back at his son, who had his eyes pinched shut, color high on his cheeks.

"He outweighs her by a few pounds," Logan in a dry tone. "He's more than capable of kicking her out of his bedroom. If Molly is being returned with a warning, then he's not walking away without one either." When Noah didn't open his eyes, Logan cleared his throat. "Kid, I'm talking to you."

He exhaled and opened his eyes. "Yes, sir."

"I catch you with your hands on my sister again, and the cops will be the least of your worries."

"Yes, sir," he said quietly.

Richard nodded stiffly. "Trust me, he's not getting off the hook for this with me and his mother, either."

"Good," Logan said.

"You plan on calling the authorities?" Richard asked, eyes carefully blank.

"Hell no," Logan answered. "That's the last thing I need right now."

"So this stays between us?"

"Absolutely," Logan said.

Visions of Nick hearing about it had my stomach roiling because he'd have a freaking heyday over something like this.

Logan pinned his glare on Noah again, the hardness in his eyes only softening the slightest bit. "One more thing, Noah."

Noah lifted his chin, and I had to give him credit for returning Logan's gaze as steadily as he was. "Yes, sir?"

"I've heard your name. I see it on the highlight reels, and the worst thing you could do for yourself, for your future as a player, is get into stupid, avoidable trouble when you're this young."

He sighed, nodding slightly.

"If you keep playing the way you're playing now, you'll have a lot of calls aimed in your direction leading up to draft day. And I'm a helluva neighbor to have as a resource when that time comes, if you catch my drift."

I glanced over at him curiously.

Noah's face smoothed over, and again, he nodded slowly. "You want me to stay away from her."

"You bet your ass I do," Logan said instantly.

Richard rubbed his lips together but didn't say anything, probably because, just like Logan did with Molly, he wanted the best for his son.

"Sounds like we're all in agreement then," I said.

Logan tightened his hand on mine and nodded to the two men.

Our neighbor smiled at me again and made a sharp pivot to leave. When they turned off our driveway and headed back to their house, Logan led us back into the house, closing the door so quietly, so slowly, that I was afraid to say anything.

"What the hell do I say to her?" he asked. He turned to me and held his arms out. "Seriously, what the *hell* do I say to her to make her understand that pulling shit like this is never acceptable. But it's even worse because of Nick sniffing around. How does she not understand that?"

I swallowed. "She's a kid, Logan. I didn't make the best choices when I was sixteen either."

"You're defending her right now?" He pointed up the stairs. "She broke into someone's house to try to seduce the neighbor kid. That's beyond *not making the best choices*. That's pure idiocy, and she is not the kind of kid who pulls stunts like that."

A sniff from the top of the stairs had me grimacing.

"I was just doing what Paige said," Molly said in a tiny voice.

"Whoa." I laughed uncomfortably. "I never told you to do what you just did."

Her eyebrows bent in confusion. "But what was that whole thing about leading the thirsty cow to water? How men know what they want but won't act on it unless we force their hand?"

With a muttered curse, I pinched my eyes shut again, and the excruciating pulse of silence had my stomach turning.

When I opened my eyes, Logan was glaring at me.

"Explain *now*."

CHAPTER 22
LOGAN

Paige opened her mouth, and immediately, I noticed she was wringing her fingers together.

"Molly, go back to your room," I snapped.

She stood slowly. "What about school?"

I cursed under my breath. "I'll bring the twins, and call your school to excuse you and Iz. But for now, go back to your room. I'm too furious to talk calmly with you right now."

Her nod was slow, her face sad. In the back of my head, it occurred to me that I should take a deep breath and try to lasso in the emotions stampeding through me.

I'd had moments over the past few days, now that I'd unlocked the iron chest that held me contained and steady, when I worried about what it might mean for the other aspects of my life.

With Paige, it was like being burned alive by pleasure, overtaken by a groundswell of happiness that I'd never experienced before. But that big, bright emotion had to have a ripple effect, and maybe this was it.

My cool was gone.

My ability to stay level was obliterated because I'd wanted to dive deep into this relationship.

Molly's bedroom door closed, and I tried for a steadying breath.

"What was she talking about?" I asked quietly.

Paige's face was bent in worry and apology, and that didn't bode well for this conversation. "So … the other day, I was kinda, umm, frustrated."

I crossed my arms over my chest and watched her.

"Right, stoic silence," she said. She licked her lips. "When I was talking out my frustration, I wasn't actually talking to her, or I didn't realize she was, like, taking notes or anything."

"What did you say?"

She grimaced. "Remember when they found us in the gym? After the air horn thing?"

I gave her a steady look.

"Of course you remember. Okay, so you ran, right? Disappeared. Poof. Gone in a blink and I was …"

"Frustrated," I supplied.

Judging by the way her eyes tightened, she didn't appreciate my attempt at being helpful. "Yes."

I nodded. "In your frustration, what, exactly, did you say?"

Her cheek bulged out like she'd pushed her tongue against it. "It's possible that I mentioned something about cows dying from thirst and taking things by the horns and idiot men."

I dropped my chin to my chest. In for four, hold for four, out for four.

I did it again.

"I need more information than that, Paige."

She mimicked my pose, which made me grit my teeth because the filter on her annoyance was starting to fray and snap.

"Sorry, Logan, I wasn't recording myself because I didn't realize that I'd be interrogated by my husband. How about you not make me the enemy right now?"

"You're not the enemy, Paige, but before I go upstairs and give my sister holy hell for what she just pulled, I need to know what you—one of two adults supposedly in charge of this household—said to her that would make her do something like this."

Her eyes narrowed. "I don't remember, Logan, I'm not lying. It just came out because if you recall, I was pretty tense after that encounter. I was pissed because you kept pulling away from me even though it was obvious how much you wanted me, so yes, I was fuming about how men hold back out of some misguided sense of blah, blah, blah whatever, and Molly was in the kitchen." Her voice rose with each word, and color crept up her chest and into her face. I felt my anger ratchet with each syllable, each defense. "I didn't think she was listening that carefully, Logan."

"Kinda how I ended up with a wife in the first place, wasn't it?"

She sucked in an angry breath and stepped up to me. "I think this has worked out pretty damn well for you, Ward, so I wouldn't go flipping out on the person who saved your ass."

"Ohhhh, yes," I drawled, good and angry now. It was easier, so much easier to lash out at Paige, even if I felt the dirt and grime of the words before I spat them out at her. "You did save my ass. Lucky for you that another instance of you running your mouth with a second thought bore positive consequences."

"Oh, go screw yourself," she bit out. "You're not perfect either."

No, I wasn't perfect. I was so far from it, it was laughable.

And having her fling those words at me like I'd ever think them about myself made me feel stupid. And feeling stupid made me even angrier.

I pointed up the stairs. "Tell me, tell me what the consequences were of you running your mouth without thought. Tell me, Paige. My sixteen-year-old sister, who already has a proclivity for not always thinking through what she does, took your words to heart because she idolizes you."

Her face lost some of its color, and she didn't argue.

"Seriously," I said, finger still pointed upstairs. "Did you think about that? Did you, for one fucking second, think that she'd listen to the woman who, for all intents and purposes, has stepped into the role of a mother for her? Of course, she's going to listen to you. Of course, she's going to heed your advice because, in her mind, you're the best thing to happen to them since Brooke walked out." I pointed that finger at my head and tapped it violently against my temple. "Use your head, Paige. This isn't a game, and you have to think about what you say and what they hear from you because they'll use it to shape their actions."

"I made a mistake," she said in a low, furious voice. "You're telling me you've never screwed up?"

"Don't do that." I shook my head. "Don't do that thing where you flip it on me because you're incapable of copping to what happened as a result of your actions."

Paige huffed, her shoulders rising and falling in a helpless shrug. "I'll never win, will I? Yeah, I screwed up with what I said to her. Fine, there you go. I messed up! But I also don't hear you even trying to balance it out with all the ways I've done stuff right." She poked me in the chest, and I had to grit my teeth not to smack her hand away. "You want to burn me at the stake because I vented, but you sure as hell won't let me know when I've done anything right. Look around, Logan, they're here because of me *running my mouth*."

I tipped my head back and laughed incredulously.

"It's not funny," she snapped. "God, you're so patronizing. Perfect Logan, who never messes up. Heaven forbid anyone around him makes a single fucking mistake. No wonder you've been alone. No one could measure up."

The simmering heat snapped into a roaring fire.

"Is this a joke?" I hissed. "How about Saint Paige, who lied at the hospital and banked a fat ass check to be here. Who runs away from all of her responsibilities when they get too hard. You're such a paragon of good decision-making."

Her hand cracked against my face before I even saw it coming.

"Stop!" Isabel sobbed from the top of the steps. Tears streamed down her face, Molly behind her, curling an arm around her sister's shoulders. "Just stop it!"

I touched my fingers to the burning skin on the cheek, shame coating my skin with sticky, oily tar. Paige covered her mouth with a shaking hand, her eyes welling instantly with tears.

"Isabel, please," she said as my sister flew down the stairs.

"Is that true?" she asked Paige. "You're here because you got paid to?"

Paige shook her head quickly, moving to crouch in front of Iz, but she stepped back so fast, she almost tripped. "No. I mean, not how you think." Over her shoulder, Paige gave me a desperate look.

"Iz," I said, reaching out to grab her shoulders. "It's so much more complicated than you know, but I'll explain all of it to you."

She knocked my hand away. "Don't touch me," she yelled, pushing against my stomach with balled-up fists. "You've never lied to us. Not until she showed up." Her fiery gaze pinned on Paige.

"Iz," Paige whispered, her voice shaky. "I'm so sorry. I'm so, so sorry you overheard that."

I swiped a hand over my mouth as Isabel looked at both of us with heartbreak stamped all over her tear-streaked face.

"Isabel," I said quietly. "Let's go …"

"No," she yelled. "No, I'm not going anywhere with you."

She turned, snatching her yellow purse off the floor by her backpack, which she grabbed with her other hand, and stomped toward the door.

"Hey, you're not allowed to leave," I said as she flung open the door.

"Watch me."

I started after her, but my knee twinged angrily from the way I'd stormed down the stairs earlier.

"Isabel, come on," Molly said from where she stood at the top of the steps. "Don't be stupid."

Her chin lifted, her jaw tight and angry. "I'm not staying here another second," she spat, slamming the door shut behind her.

"This is all my fault," Paige whispered. A single tear slipped down her face. "I'll go after her."

"No," I said firmly. "Isabel isn't your responsibility, Paige. She never has been. *I'll* go after her."

Her face froze with hurt at my tone, but I shook my head and went after Isabel.

My sister, she was what mattered. Not a fake wife who'd be out of my life as soon as she could manage it.

It would do me good to remember that.

CHAPTER 23
LOGAN

"Isabel, come on," I yelled, striding as fast as I could manage down the driveway.

Her dark ponytail swung angrily as she marched ahead of me down the sidewalk between the houses. One of our neighbors drove by as we turned the corner onto the next street, shamelessly staring as I limped after my little sister.

Great, just what I needed, someone snapping a pic and posting it to their Instagram. Logan Ward, injured safety, yells at little sister in public.

"You want me to injure my knee more than I already have?"

She didn't so much as slow. If anything, she pumped her arms and picked up the pace. How I ended up with such stubborn sisters was beyond me.

Suddenly, she stopped, whirled around, and pinned me with a glare so fierce, it took my breath away. "I'm so mad at you."

I propped my hands on my hips and exhaled roughly. "I know you are. And you have every right to be."

"Why shouldn't I go to Nick right now and tell him what I just heard?"

I dropped to my knee in front of her even though the pavement was hard and unforgiving. Much like the fourteen-year-old warrior in front of me, lashing out because her heart was hurt.

What I saw in her eyes gutted me. It absolutely gutted me.

"Please don't do that, Iz," I begged. "Look at me, okay? It's just you and me."

Her eyes darted over my shoulder, and she shook her head. "I don't want to live with Nick, you idiot."

I laughed under my breath. "I'm glad to hear that."

"But you lied to me," she yelled, a tear sliding down her cheek unchecked. It was followed by another. Then another. She swiped her cheek with the palm of her hand. Another car drove by, looking at us curiously.

"Shit," I said under my breath. "Can we please go back home and hash this out? I don't think either of us wants this out for public consumption."

Iz worked her jaw back and forth, probably trying to decide how pissed she was at me.

"Fine." She took off before I could push myself to stand.

"No, it's cool," I mumbled, "I don't need help standing up. Just the old cripple over here."

I groaned as I straightened my leg and followed her.

I walked slowly back to the house, which was good because we'd covered more ground than I thought when I was chasing after her. It also gave me a very necessary opportunity to breathe through … everything.

It had been years since I'd lost my temper like that, and it hurt down to my bones that Paige had been the recipient. *I deserved the slap,* I thought as I rubbed the spot on my cheek where she landed her hit. Honestly, knowing her, I was lucky all she'd done was slap me.

The downshift in emotions had been my undoing. The switch was clunky and awkward, like my brain didn't know how to keep up with it, the gears in desperate need of oil or something.

She'd brought me so much pleasure, in and out of bed.

She'd brought happiness to our house and to my sisters.

But she was impetuous.

She didn't think about the consequences of her actions, whereas I analyzed mine to death. I thought and thought and thought about how I said things to my sisters. Played through scenarios in my head and tried to figure out how I'd handle them. What was too firm, what was too lenient. How could I balance loving them with gaining their respect?

And I was furious with her for saying what she did in front of Molly, there was no doubt about that. But unclipping the leash on my anger wasn't fair either.

That made me slow my pace even more, even as Isabel kept going in front of me, because it was a direct contradiction to how I was with everyone else.

Even until I gave in and allowed myself to dive into my feelings with Paige, I took a fine-tooth comb to our interactions, to the way I acted around her. But not for the past few days.

I was me with her. The unfiltered me.

Today, that had gotten me in trouble. Apologizing to her was the first, most obvious step, but I also had to know exactly where she stood on things between us.

I knew I was falling in love with her, and if she wanted to make this real, make it something true, then I was right there. But if she had one foot out the door, I'd have to try my best to pick up the pieces.

There was no moving forward until I knew the answer to that.

I blew out a breath as I reached the door and braced myself for what might wait inside. Molly and Isabel were squared off in the kitchen, the twins eating cereal with wide eyes, like they were in the front row of a movie. Paige was nowhere to be seen.

"Guys, settle down," I said wearily as I joined them in the kitchen.

"She said she was going to tell Nick!" Molly yelled. "She can't do that, can she?"

"I said I thought about it. You're so dramatic."

I held up my hand. "Hey, that's enough."

"Who's telling Nick what?" Lia asked.

"Nothing," I insisted.

"I'm never sleeping in again," Claire said. "We miss everything."

Isabel turned to face the twins. "I'll fill you in. Molly broke into the neighbor's house. Logan got pissed. Paige gave terrible advice, and in the middle of their very loud argument, they admitted the entire marriage was a fake."

"What?" the twins screeched at the same time.

I tilted my chin up and stared at the ceiling for a second. Just breathe. Breathe through it.

"She's a liar," Isabel said. "And I want her gone."

"Okay, that's enough," I snapped. "You're entitled to be upset, but you'll still treat her with respect, and it's not your decision whether she stays or goes."

Isabel crossed her arms over her chest. "I have to respect her, but you don't?"

I tilted my head. "What?"

"I saw the way you talked to her. You were so respectful that she slapped you."

"Oooooh," the twins said.

"Would you two shut up," Molly said. "This isn't funny."

"All of you," I glared at each one of them, "let me talk." I sighed and faced Isabel. "Listen, I wish you hadn't heard what you did, but the truth is that I would do that and more if it would keep you four with me."

Her chin wavered. "You admit it's a fake, then."

A hush fell over the kitchen. No one was breathing. I didn't think any of them blinked while they waited for me to answer.

"Paige and I had very, very good reasons for getting married. I had mine, and she had some of her own."

"Yeah, for money," Isabel muttered.

"It's not my story to tell, but yes, she inherited money from her aunt, and in order to get it, she needed to be married. I helped her, and she helped all of us. That's the truth."

"Why not just tell us?" Molly asked quietly. Her eyes were shiny. "You didn't have to lie."

Four faces stared at me, and I felt the weight of that question like a tanker on my lungs. There was no good way to answer it. No defending that for the first time in my relationship with them, I'd chosen to lie. It didn't matter if I'd justified it in my head and thought I was protecting them.

In the end, I'd sacrificed the one thing that kept me afloat. The riskiness of the truth for my relationship with these four girls that I loved more than my own life.

"You're right," I said gruffly. "I didn't have to lie. And I shouldn't have."

I cleared my throat when I felt the bridge of my nose burn. Molly sniffed, her face turned down toward the floor.

"You four are the most important things in my life." I glanced around at all of them. Isabel swiped at her face again. The twins were uncharacteristically quiet, clearly understanding the weight of the conversation we were having. "Nothing will ever change that. Nothing. And I'd do anything to make sure you guys are loved and safe and taken care of the way you should be. If I thought that Nick and Cora were a better place for you, then I'd be man enough to admit that. But they're not. The best place for you is right here, in this family. And I'd lie to a thousand people a thousand times over to keep you right here." I swallowed, trying to get the damn brick out of my throat. "But I promise, I won't lie to you guys again when it comes to this. Okay?"

All four gave me varying degrees of a nod.

"Can you forgive me?" I asked.

"Yeah," said Lia. Claire smiled at me and nodded.

Molly walked over and wrapped her arms around my waist. I kissed the top of her head. "You're still in trouble," I whispered.

She was smiling when she pulled back. "I know."

Isabel regarded me steadily. "You promise? No more lies?"

I nodded. "No more lies."

"Are you in love with Paige? Because I'm not stupid, and our walls are hardly soundproof."

"Holy shit, Iz," I muttered, scratching the side of my face. Molly choked on a laugh.

"Are you?" she asked again.

I blew out a breath. "It doesn't matter if I am or not until I talk to her."

Lia lifted her eyebrows. "No shit, Sherlock."

I slid the swear jar toward her silently. She grinned.

"Is this the right time to tell him she left?" Claire whispered to Lia.

My head snapped in her direction. "What? Paige did?"

"When?" Molly asked.

"Molly was in the kitchen, freaking out on the phone to her friend, and she came in and woke us up, kissed us on the forehead and said goodbye. I figured she was going to run errands or something, but she was all crying, which was weird. But since I was still waking up, I wasn't even trying to make sense of it."

My hands curled up in fists, and my stomach made a similar motion. Anger and disappointment warred inside me because this was the easy way out. But I knew her. I saw the way she reacted to Isabel's outpouring of emotion of love.

The thought of damaging that fragile connection would probably be too much for Paige.

"Are you going to go after her?" Molly asked.

Isabel crossed her arms over her chest again but didn't say anything. Sometimes it freaked me out how similar she and I were, and the way she stared at me, it was like I could read her thoughts.

She's the one who left, why would I chase her?

We can't trust her.

She's too much.

There's no way she'd settle down anyway.

"Right now, we just need to get you guys to school, okay?" I said. I hated that those were the thoughts sticking in my throat. I wanted to wash them away with a strong gust of memories, the moments with Paige that made up the in-between. The steps she'd laid down for me, the ones that brought me to her.

But at that moment, as I tried to pick up the pieces in front of me, I couldn't remember them.

CHAPTER 24
PAIGE

"Never pegged you for a coward, McKinney."

I rolled my eyes and hitched my overnight bag higher on my shoulder. "Have you met Allie? I can't stay there. I'd never sleep with her cackling *I told you so* over my bed."

Ava sighed and let me into the Seattle penthouse apartment she shared with defensive star Matthew Hawkins.

I didn't know her well, but we'd hung out enough that I felt comfortable showing up on her doorstep and begging for sanctuary, even if it meant being subjected to entirely unnecessary name-calling.

Uh-huh.

The words almost crossed my brain without a hitch, except for that giant voice screaming, you are president of the country called Denial, population one.

While Ava showed me to a guest room, large and bright with a beautiful view of downtown Seattle, I couldn't scrub the image of Logan's face twisted in anger and accusation.

I'd slapped him.

I'd slapped him so freaking hard.

Not that he hadn't deserved it for what he said, but in my entire life, I'd never raised my hand against someone I loved before. For all the tough talk I did, all the fighting I trained for, the thought of striking someone had never been as lightning quick as when he called me Saint Paige.

Because the hurt. The hurt was so real and so unfiltered.

In a way I didn't know was possible and in a spot that I hadn't known existed. It was further down than my heart.

I wasn't even sure that spot had a name. To say that it cracked my soul even seemed inadequate.

"Are you okay?" Ava asked quietly.

I blinked because I forgot she was standing there. I forgot a lot when I was waxing poetic in my stupid heartbroken brain about my stupid heartbreaking husband.

Carefully, I sat on the edge of the bed. It wasn't as big as the one I'd left. "I don't know."

She sighed and smoothed her hands down the front of her red skirt as she sat next to me.

"I'm guessing this is about Logan," Ava said.

Since my last-minute marriage and the new routine I'd found myself in, I'd barely seen or talked to my friends. I blew a raspberry through pursed lips. "You could say that. We got in such a bad fight this morning. I slapped him." When she gasped softly in shock, I held up my hands. "In my defense, he super deserved it. But ugh, there was yelling and name-calling and crying and entirely too much sarcasm for how early in the morning it was happening."

Ava rubbed her temples. "Hang on. Logan was yelling? Like … *yelling*?"

I sighed. "Yeah."

She blew out a breath. "Having a hard time reconciling that one. He's so steady at work. Almost too steady, if you know what I mean."

I closed my eyes. "He's different outside of work. Not that you'd know that."

"Erm, well, I kinda do," she hedged.

"What do you mean?" I asked, giving her a sidelong look.

"Remember when my family came to town a couple of months ago? Before preseason started?"

"Vaguely. Why?"

Ava turned on the bed, and I had to blink at how serious she looked. She took a deep breath, and on the exhale, the words came out in a rush. "I sorta lied and told them Logan was my boyfriend, and he agreed to pretend that he was, but I didn't know he was doing it because he thought he liked me and wanted to ask me out."

I was off the bed before I knew what I was doing. "You dated my husband?" I hissed. "Did you sleep with him?"

Ava stood, hands raised. "Whoa, slow your roll, okay? It's not like I knew he was going to marry you. Or that you'd even spoken to him before."

Visions of Ava—tall and lithe, pretty dark hair and eyes—with Logan, had me seeing her through an icy white haze of jealousy. This was someone I liked, and I wanted to rip the hair off her head at the mere thought she'd touched his body or that he'd touched hers.

Allie clapped her hands from the doorway. "Excellent, I'm not too late for the cat fight."

I glared at Ava. "You called her?"

"Sorry not sorry, chica." She shoved Allie in front of her and then crossed her arms over her chest. "Besides, now that I've got a jealous supermodel imagining all sorts of violent things about me, I'm glad I have a witness."

A perfectly manicured finger, courtesy of my best friend, pointed in my direction. "Calm down, Paige Katherine McKinney. Right now."

"Sure, as soon as she explains what the eff happened between her and my husband."

Allie raised an eyebrow. "My, my, look at possessive Paige.

Methinks that someone has crossed that line, and it's not so fake anymore."

I slicked my tongue over my teeth. "We're not discussing me at the moment. Aren't you curious why we didn't know about this?"

"A little, but it's Ava's business, not ours. She's not required to tell us every little detail about her life if she doesn't want to." Allie looked over her shoulder at Ava, who looked remarkably brave now that there was another person standing between us. "However, in the spirit of friendship and female empowerment and blah, blah, I'd think once Paige did marry Logan, we should have heard about it."

Ava sighed. "It's embarrassing, okay? I had no clue Logan liked me when I asked him to pretend to be my boyfriend." I must have growled because she gave me a nervous look. "But I don't know that he really did. Or not much, anyway. He never seemed perturbed by much any of the times we interacted. And I was so in love with Matthew by that point, Logan didn't even really register, I swear."

"Paige," Allie said patiently, "wipe the inner assassin look off your face, and let's talk like normal, well-adjusted adults, okay? No one is taking Logan." She tilted her head. "Except maybe you."

My shoulders drooped.

"You didn't hear him, Allie." I shook my head. "And you didn't see the girls' faces. I broke their hearts. How can I walk back in there and pretend everything is okay?"

"You don't."

"Excellent advice. And you wonder why I didn't call you?"

She rolled her eyes. "That's your problem, you know?"

"Oh please, do explain to me what my emotional damage is, Sutton." I worked my jaw back and forth, but my bravado was failing quickly in the face of the human being who knew me best in the entire world and would not hesitate to call me on my shit.

Friends were the worst.

Ava glanced between us. "I'm going to give you two privacy. I think this is a conversation for besties only."

"You can stay," I told her. "I'm sorry I imagined punching you in the throat."

She laughed. "Umm, you're forgiven. I'm glad I didn't know that five minutes ago."

"It was just … imagining you two." I wiggled my fingers up by my head. "Made me go a little wonky."

Ava smiled a little. "I'm aware."

I deflated, plopping back down onto the bed with a bounce. "Fine. Tell me what my problem is because I don't see it."

Allie crossed the room and took a seat on the bed with me, but as I was sitting with my back straight, she made herself comfy against the mass of pillows up against the wooden headboard. "I think you see it, but I just think you don't want to dig too deeply into it."

I rubbed my temples. "Can you cut the cryptic, please? If you're going to psychoanalyze me, just get it over with."

"See? That right there." She shook her head. "A hint of bad or hard, and you flee like there's an atom bomb about to go off behind you."

"I do not," I said weakly. Except I did. I so did.

She gave me a look.

"Ugh, fine." I shifted uncomfortably on the bed. "It gives me the creepy-crawlies when I think about having fights with him or having to work through all the damage we both just caused those girls." My hand rubbed at the spot over my heart.

"You can't run from everything, Paige. Sometimes, you have to plant your feet and work through it and not just pretend everything will be fine. Yeah, that's worked okay for you up until now, but nothing you've walked away from has been as important as this."

"I didn't walk away, per se."

"Well, you didn't exactly stay either," Ava said. When I narrowed my eyes at her, she shrugged. "Hey, you said I could be in here."

Allie sat up and swung her legs over the edge of the bed,

planted herself so close to me that our thighs touched, and our shoulders were even. "I love you, Paige. Family, ride or die, I'll always bail your impulsive ass out of jail love."

I snorted. "But?"

"But packing a bag and disappearing without a word is running." She nudged me. "And you can't do stuff like that if you ever expect them to trust you. Especially with the girls," she said quietly.

My eyes welled up, so I pinched them shut as I sniffed. Isabel's face made my stomach shrivel when I imagined it behind closed eyes. My arms curled around my middle when I thought about hugging her on the floor of the gym, her tiny frame shaking with sobs, the outlet of crushing grief that she'd been carrying around for years.

"I know," I whispered. A tear slid down my cheek, and I did nothing to stop it. They'd earned my tears. They'd earned my heartache and were worth so much more than my cowardice. I pressed a fist to my heart. "Right here, there's something all twisted up because I left without thinking about what it would do to them. I just … I felt like I was causing harm by being there, and that they'd be better off without me."

Allie slid an arm around my shoulders and leaned her head on my shoulder.

"Paige," she said quietly.

I sniffed in response.

"That's … that's such bullshit."

"Hey," I protested in a watery voice.

She kept her grip tight on me, so I couldn't escape, even if I wanted to. But, really, I didn't. I wanted my best friend to hug me, even if she was being a giant meanie while she did.

"What's the worst that can happen?" she asked. "You love them, him and those girls. What's the worst that can happen by pushing through the hard?"

My eyes were closed so tight that I could see starbursts pop brightly in the black. My heart was hammering, and my hands were clammy.

When I finally felt brave enough to answer, my voice was hardly above a whisper, but it was thick with tears. "That I fall fully in love with him, and more in love with them, and it's still not enough. That *I'm* not enough for them. That for the first time, I've found a place that doesn't feel like a resting stop. Then we get to the end of this, and they'd be just fine without me, but I'd shrivel up into nothing without them. That I'd keep wandering forever, trying to find something like it again, but I stay … empty."

I heard a sniff from the corner, then another one next to me. Oh goody, contagious tears.

"Don't you feel better now?"

I gaped at her. "*No*. I feel awful."

She laughed; her eyes bright with tears. "That's good."

"I swear, you are a sadist behind all that blond hair and perfect makeup. You revel in other people's pain."

Allie hugged me tight. "Just yours."

"What are you going to do?" Ava asked.

I blew out a slow breath. "First, I'm going to go back to the house. The girls are probably at school, but maybe I can talk to Logan."

Allie hummed. "I saw his truck pulling into the training facility when I left to come here."

I nodded because it didn't surprise me. My brain whirred and whipped through what I wanted to do. How I wanted to do this. And how, impossible though it seemed, I could smooth over the damage that had been done today, by both of us.

The two women watched me, and an idea took root. "I'm going to need both of you to help me with something."

"Whatever you need," Allie said.

"Including use of the practice field?"

Ava lifted an eyebrow. "You mean, the practice field that's being used by the team today?"

"That very one."

"Coach won't be happy," she said.

Allie cleared her throat. "Then it's a good thing I own the team, isn't it?"

I grinned.

Ava laughed. "Indeed. What do you need from us, Paige?"

CHAPTER 25
PAIGE

WASHINGTON WOLVES

The house was quiet when I let myself back in. For a few minutes, I stood at the base of the stairs and glanced around, desperately hoping that my previous memories of being there wouldn't be the last ones I experienced. Isabel flying down the stairs, the vitriol in her dark, little eyes as she looked at me. The sight of Logan going after her, the casual barb that it wasn't my responsibility to go after her.

I took a deep breath and went upstairs to unpack my bag.

Briefly, I thought about texting Logan, but from experience, I knew that once he was at the facility for PT, he didn't look at his phone until he was done. Today, I was actually okay with that because it increased the odds of me being able to pull this off.

I stopped by the twin's bedroom and looked in with a smile. It looked like a bomb of purple and blue and green exploded in there. There was a lamp on the white dresser that matched the one downstairs. I rubbed at my chest again because those were the things I'd miss if I wasn't part of their lives anymore.

Mismatched lamps picked out by pre-teen girls.

My phone buzzed. Even though I was fairly sure I wouldn't be hearing from Logan, my heart still thudded until I saw my lawyer's name on the screen.

Maxine: Everything is set. Just need your signature. I'll add the rush to my billable hours.

"I'll bet you will," I said under my breath.

It didn't take me long to unpack my clothes since I'd only taken enough for a day or two. But when the last hanger was in place, I squared my shoulders and took a deep breath. That shirt was gonna stay there for a long ass time if I had any say.

With that thought in mind, I trailed my fingers across the line of my clothes and didn't stop until I found the outfit I wanted. My battle armor, if you will.

Because while Allie and Ava were pulling off their end of the bargain, I had a stop to make.

I used the printer/scanner in Logan's office to send the signed documents back to my lawyer before I searched the address for my first stop. While I waited for it to show up in the search results, I ran my finger along the edge of a framed picture he had next to the sleek computer monitor.

The girls were little, and he looked impossibly young but still just as handsome as he was now. I picked up and worked through the emotional log jam happening at the base of my throat.

There was a time in my life when falling in love felt impossible and unattainable, and now I was in love with five people in different ways. How did parents do this? The thought of one child was overwhelming, felt like they'd take up your entire heart, which you had to share with your spouse, and here I was, staring at a group of faces so dear to me that I couldn't imagine doing life without them.

Not so impossible, as it turned out. It just took its time clicking into the empty spot in my life, the place it fit perfectly.

I set the picture down with a sigh, then gathered my papers and tapped the address on the computer screen into the app on my phone.

When I arrived at the sleek building, all mirrored windows and chrome, I smoothed my hair and gave my best strong walk into the doors. Not too much hip, no smile, and just enough spark in my eyes that I didn't look like a complete bitch. Very Michael Kors Spring 2014 New York Fashion Week, except this time, I wasn't wearing a blue dress with a slit up to my crotch.

"Paige McKinney Ward to see Nick Ward," I told the expressionless receptionist with an earpiece. She hit a button on her keyboard and relayed the message, probably to another receptionist who also hated her job.

"I'm sorry, but Mr. Ward is in a meeting," she said after a second.

"Did she relay the message to him?" I asked with a cock of my head. "I'd really appreciate her doing so because he'll see me if he knows I'm here."

There was nary a wrinkle on her face as she did what I'd asked. She nodded to whatever she heard through the earpiece, then gave me a practiced smile. "His offices are on the fourth floor. The elevators are to the left."

"Excellent. Thank you."

Before I walked away, her eyes betrayed her stoic nature, and they flicked down the front of my nude, high-collared dress that slicked over my curves like it was made for me. Because it had been.

Made for me.

The Louboutins were purchased, as was the Nars lipstick in Dragon Girl, both in a bright blood red.

If Nick wanted to hit me where he mistakenly thought it would hurt, I'd give him the biggest damn target I could manage.

When the elevator doors slid open, he was waiting just outside the glass doors leading into the financial consulting firm where he worked.

He smirked, arms crossed tight over his chest. "This is a surprise."

"Isn't it fun when people show up where they're not invited?" I asked with a sweet smile.

His smirk melted off his face. "What do you want?"

I pulled out two manila folders and handed him the top one.

For a second, he didn't take it, just stared at it like it would bite him. I rolled my eyes. "You want dirt, right? Here you go. I'll make your life easier and hand you whatever ammunition you think you need to undermine my marriage to Logan."

For a moment, his mouth fell open, but he recovered quickly, snatching the folder out of my hand. Nick ripped the paper out, and his eyes scanned the words, mouth moving as he read. "What is this?"

"The inheritance I received upon my marriage," I told him.

He froze. "You're admitting you got paid to marry my brother? Why the hell would you do that?"

"No," I said slowly, very "bless your heart, I'll speak more slowly." "I wasn't paid to marry Logan, not specifically, at least. It was a strange condition of my aunt's will. I would've married him regardless. This just sped up the process."

"Yeah, right," he scoffed. "You expect me to believe that."

"No, I don't because you're an asshole."

It was true. When I thought back to the hospital, the way Logan looked when he talked about his sisters, I could easily believe that I would've done it, even if there hadn't been a single red penny riding on it. Because of the adventure, because it would help someone who I found intriguing, and because, for good or for bad, I did crazy shit without thinking it through.

And wasn't I glad about that? Look what it had gotten me.

I'd marry him a dozen times over for the days and weeks it had earned me with that family.

His mouth set in a grim line. "I'm not sure what you're playing at here, but I'll take this to my lawyer as soon as your skinny ass gets the hell out of my office. If this doesn't prove fraud, I don't know what does."

I held up my finger. "Uno momento, Nicholas." I handed him the second folder.

Nick slicked his tongue over his lips and made no move to take it.

"Oh, come on now, don't stop playing simply because the rules just changed. All the times you showed up at the house, I think you've more than earned this stop."

After he swallowed, Nick took the envelope and pulled that paper out much more slowly than the last one.

There was no triumphant smile. No moving mouth. No eyes zipping over the lines. It was all clear enough, and as the color leeched from his face, I felt the smile curl my lips.

"Clear enough?"

"This isn't real," he said.

I leaned over and tapped the top of my lawyer's letterhead. "Sure is, I'm afraid. The girls are going to get a copy later. My aunt's inheritance, set aside in a trust for all four girls in equal shares, to be distributed to them on their eighteenth birthday. Pending one exception, of course."

Nick might've been a dick, but he wasn't stupid. He read between the lines. Actually, he didn't even need to read between them because it was all laid out in black and white. The provision of the trust was that, in case of a legal guardianship battle that granted custody to Nick, they would all get early access to the funds, thereby affording them the opportunity to fend for themselves, if they chose to.

He shook his head and looked up at me. "Why would you do this? You barely know them."

"That's true," I said slowly. "But only an idiot would get to know those four and not be willing to do whatever it takes to do what's best for them." I took a step closer to Nick, and his jaw popped from holding it so tightly. "Believe me, I won't say this to you more than once. You are never to step foot on our property uninvited again. You don't want to cross me, Nick, because those girls, and your brother, mean everything to me. And while Logan has to walk some invisible legal line that you've drawn, I don't." I smiled. "You feel me?"

He tucked the manila folders under his arm and flicked a derisive glance down the front of my body.

"You can see yourself out," he said between gritted teeth.

"I'll take that as a yes." I wiggled my fingers over my shoulder. "Have an excellent day!"

As the elevator doors slid shut, I could stop the satisfied grin. There were better things in life than kneeing an asshole in the balls. Go figure.

I drove to my next stop with an irrepressible smile on my face. The sun was shining, and there wasn't a cloud in the sky. Doing that, signing the papers and knowing that Molly and Isabel, Lia and Claire would be taken care of, no matter what happened next, was the best thing I'd ever done.

And somehow, when I felt the warmth of the sun on my face, I knew Aunt Emma would heartily approve.

This time when I walked into the building, a smiling face greeted me. "Hi. How can I help you?"

"I know school isn't over yet, but I'm wondering if I could have five minutes with Molly Ward. I think she's in study hall right now."

The secretary smiled and tapped a few buttons on her computer. "Sure thing. Let me call down there. Can I tell her who's here?"

I inhaled. "Her sister-in-law."

It didn't take Molly long to rush down to the office, and she flung herself into my arms when she burst through the door. I laughed as she almost knocked me over.

"Where did you go this morning?" she asked with her face still buried into my neck.

I kissed the top of her silky black hair and then set her back. "I had a little freak-out, but it's okay now."

She nodded, eyes bright. "Why are you here?"

I bit my bottom lip. "Well, I'm hoping you might be willing to do two things for me."

"Anything," Molly said earnestly. So earnestly that I laughed.

"First, you have to promise not to climb into any more bedroom windows of neighbor boys," I said with a raised eyebrow.

"I'm still trying to figure out how you thought that would end well, young lady."

She hung her head. "I don't know. It just seemed like a good idea at the time."

"I get that more than you know, trust me."

"I promise. No more windows." She glanced at the secretary to make sure she wasn't listening. "What's number two?"

I gave her a crooked smile. "How do you feel about kidnapping your sisters and taking them out to the training facility after school? Not a word to your brother. He has no idea."

Molly face split open in a blinding smile. "I feel *really* good about it."

I hugged her again. "Perfect. This might just work, kid."

CHAPTER 26
LOGAN

WASHINGTON WOLVES

"Come on, Ava, what is this?" one of my defensive rookies asked. "Not that I don't mind getting out of practice early, but this ain't the shit we should be doing during game week."

I had the same question, but I simply rubbed at my forehead and shifted in my seat. Ava smiled at Carter, then flipped her attention back to her phone. "Just doing what my boss commands of me. Allie will be here in a second."

Rows of chairs were lined up in front of a makeshift stage with Wolves press banner stretched out behind it, and in the center stood a podium and a small black mic. For some reason, only the defense had been called to this little gathering, and if I wasn't so annoyed at the interruption to my PT, I would've laughed at the sight of them wedged into the seats, shoulders jammed up against each other.

"How's the knee?" Hawkins asked from his seat next to me.

I shifted. "Fine, until Maggie channels her inner dominatrix and makes me cry every single session."

He chuckled under his breath. "I remember those days."

I glanced over at him. "Your back?"

Hawkins nodded. "Worst recovery I'd ever had. Months of PT that made me wish I was passing kidney stones instead."

That drew a grimace to my lips. "Maybe that's because you're a pansy-ass."

He laughed outright. "Glad to see you're always in such a sunshiny mood, Ward."

Oh, little did he know. I'd been a bear all day. Maggie snapped at me more than once that if I wanted to infect the mood of the PT room, she'd have stayed home.

Getting the girls off to school after the debacle of the morning had been a good temporary distraction, but once I arrived at the practice facilities, it took everything in me not to go beat the shit out of my body just to be able to release some of the tension rippling through me.

All day, my body had been pushed to the limit, even as my head was stuck back at the house in the moments that Paige and I said such awful things to each other. Yeah, she needed to take ownership of what she said to Molly, but never, not once, had I imagined that she'd leave. That she'd bolt at the first sign of hard.

That was what had me on edge to get this day over with. My phone was still in my locker, where I'd tossed it as soon as I walked in. I didn't want to see it. And I did.

Had she tried to call? I wasn't sure if it was better if she had. I didn't know what to say to her yet, other than that if she was ready to walk away from us, she wasn't the woman I thought.

"Hey, guys," Allie said, crossing the small stage with a smile on her face. "Thanks for being here. I told Coach that I owe him extra vacation days."

"He gets vacation days?" Hawkins snickered. "I thought it was called a bye week."

A couple of guys around us laughed, and even I smiled.

"What's going on, boss lady?" someone asked from the row behind me.

"We have a couple of special guests today, actually." She

nodded to the side, and all eyes moved to the four people who cautiously walked in front of everyone.

As in, my four sisters.

I stood, and Ava's hand clamped down on my shoulder. "Don't you dare interrupt her," she warned.

Molly grinned at me, waving excitedly. The twins were looking around like they'd never seen the practice field, and Isabel tried desperately to look unimpressed when the entire defense started yelling and whistling for them.

"Allie, you bringing in new taskmasters?" Ramirez yelled.

Allie laughed, and Isabel tried to smother her smile.

There were five empty chairs in the front row, and Allie guided them to sit down. Then she lifted her chin at me. "You, too, Logan."

Oh, the guys loved that. They smacked me on the back, and a few shoved my shoulders. My face felt hot because surprises like this weren't exactly my favorite thing in the entire world.

I reached the row of chairs where my sisters sat and bumped knuckles with the twins before I sat down next to Molly. "What the hell is going on?"

"That's a buck," she whispered back.

"Oh, I'll shove a ten in there to cover me, depending on what's about to happen."

She laughed. "I don't know either. I was just told to bring the girls here."

My eyes narrowed. "By who?"

Molly mimed pulling a zipper across her lips.

But the second I heard guys start whistling and heard the click of her heels hit the stage, I knew who it was.

My wife ascended the steps and crossed the stage with confident, long strides. Her body was covered by a nude dress that, while it covered from her neck to her knees, was one of the sexiest damn things I'd ever seen. Her feet were capped in scarlet, and so were her lips. Her hair, that glorious red hair, spilled over her shoulders and tumbled down her back in effortless waves.

If I'd been standing, there's no way my knees would've held me.

Among the whistles, a few guys catcalled, and I couldn't help my growl. "That's enough, Davis. Don't think I don't know it's you," I snapped.

Paige paused and gave me a loaded look, one I couldn't quite decipher. All I knew was that her blue eyes held everything. Maybe she wasn't smiling, but I felt the look in her eyes like a kick to the chest.

"Gentlemen, I know you all know my best friend, Paige," Allie said into the mic. "She's a fixture at most Wolves' events, and in a couple of weeks, she'll be the keynote speaker at the first annual event for my foundation. Some of you will be there, which I appreciate, and I've got commitments from a number of your wives and girlfriends. We're fortunate at the Wolves to have a strong group of accomplished women who can help shape the next generation of girls to know they can achieve anything they put their mind to."

"Even me?" someone called from behind us.

"Even you," Allie said with a smile.

Laughter rippled through the guys.

I watched Paige because I had no idea she was doing that, but it made sense. She'd achieved success that was incredibly rare in her industry, and not just success, but a career with longevity. Her chin was up, a slight smile on her lips. Next to me, the girls shifted, probably wondering, just like me, what in the hell we were doing here.

Allie gestured for Paige to take the mic, and I found myself holding my breath. She smiled at everyone staring back at her, and there wasn't an ounce of nerves showing anywhere. Here she was, faced with an entire defense worth of massive guys, and the five people who she hadn't seen since a really ugly fight earlier that day, and she was perfectly in control.

I wasn't sure if that made it better or worse.

"Thanks for having me, guys." She smiled and set her hands on the black and red podium. "Like Allie said, originally, we'd talked about doing a dry run of my speech for the Team Sutton annual event that'll be held at the fifty-yard line of the arena, but I had something else that felt more important. And the only reason that the entire team isn't gathered here, as well as the entire front office staff, is that I think my husband would kill me."

Laughter rolled through the rows because they all knew me well enough, and apparently, Paige did too.

"Yeah, 'cause he's a grump," someone called.

"He is," Paige said with a soft smile. "He's the hardest person to get to know, isn't he? Harder than anyone I've ever met. I'm not sure if it's because he's so self-contained, or if he's too concerned with what will happen if he lets too many people in."

I crossed my arms over my chest and took a deep breath. I was torn between wanting to hide under the chair and soaking in every word like a new tattoo because her words had that same sweet sting of a needle hitting my skin.

Paige took a deep breath. "But regardless, what I know, from being around this team for the last year, is that even though he flies under the radar and might not be the guy with life-size posters gracing bedroom walls all across the country, he's respected by all of you to an incredible degree. Yet he's never had anyone shouting from the rooftops about all the things he does for the people he cares about, and make no mistake, every player on this team is part of Logan's inner circle, whether you realize it or not." She paused and swallowed hard. "I've been fortunate to meet that inner circle. Not just you guys, the coaches, and the assistants and trainers, but the four young women who are sitting up there next to him."

I had to clench my jaw against the swell raging inside me. Molly gave me a shy smile. The twins bounced in their seats, unabashed in how much they loved this attention. Isabel sank lower in her chair, but she was staring intently at Paige.

"Those of us who know him, who know what kind of man Logan is, and the way he sacrifices for the people in his life, we want to be able to shout it from the rooftops. We want everyone to know what he does, and we want to know that he's recognized for it in a way he'd never recognize himself."

Molly snuck her hand through mine and sighed happily.

"Logan Ward is one of the most steadfast and loyal men I've ever met," Paige continued. "He's tough when he needs to be, which all of you know, because I heard about the way he got in your face, Marcs, when you dropped that interception last week."

A chorus of "Ooooooh" echoed through all the guys, good-natured ribbing because I had gotten in his face.

"But he'll never seek the spotlight, sometimes to his detriment. He won't hold it against the people who are there underneath the bright light of attention, but considering what I've learned about him, I thought it was time to force his hand. Just a little. And I know his sisters feel the same. That no one realizes just how good he is. How kind and how loyal. How far he'd go for the people in his life. So today, we're celebrating you, Logan. We're shouting from the rooftops about how amazing you are."

I swiped a hand over my mouth and stared at her. Briefly, she met my gaze, and her apology was so clear in her eyes, I could've sworn she mouthed it.

"The reason I'm up here is that I've convinced Allie to start a new Washington Wolves tradition." She took a deep breath, and I saw her hands shake slightly until she gripped the edges of the podium. "Today, I'm proud to award the first annual Guardian Award to Logan Ward. This will be a family given, family-nominated award to celebrate the people in our lives who don't hesitate to step up when someone in their circle needs help, needs a hand, or needs a swift kick in the ass. It's to celebrate the people who will never, ever celebrate themselves."

Everyone seated burst into applause—yells, cheers, and obnoxious whistling. A few guys clapped me on the back while I smiled. Molly sniffed, and I wrapped an arm around her. Immediately, she laid her head on my shoulder.

"The Guardian Award presentation will have as many or as few people as the family thinks should be present, and because I'd really, really like Logan to speak to me after this," she said meaningfully, "I kept this one with the second branch of his family. The first branch, the most important, is sitting in the front row with him. If I'd taken longer to plan this, I would've flown his mom in too, but Allie was kind enough to FaceTime with her so that she could watch." She waved over at Allie, who was standing at the edge of the stage. "Hi, Nancy!"

"Hi, Nana!" Lia yelled.

I tipped my head back and laughed.

Paige sobered and found my eyes again. "Being part of Logan's family is the greatest gift I've ever been given, and I'll never take it for granted. Neither will his sisters because they've got the absolute best big brother in the entire world. And I've got all of them."

The breath left my lungs in a slow, controlled exhale. I stretched my hand beyond Molly and patted Isabel's shoulder. When she glanced over at me, her eyes were shiny with tears, and she nodded.

Paige paused, and I realized that she saw the exchange. She stared down at the podium for a long moment, clearly collecting herself. When she looked up, her smile was brilliant.

Brilliant. And mine.

"Now, for the part that he'll hate the most, I'd like the first ever winner of the Guardian Award to join me up here."

The noise level rose exponentially as I made my way slowly up the stage. In her hands, she held a small trophy, probably something she picked up at the dollar store.

I didn't give a shit what the trophy looked like.

Paige stepped away from the mic to meet me halfway, and I knew why.

"I'm so sorry about how I left this morning," she said. "I came back a couple of hours later, but it doesn't matter. I shouldn't have left."

My hands slid around hers where they cupped the trophy. I laid my forehead against hers and breathed her in.

"I'm sorry for what I said," I told her.

Her answering grin was wry. "We're pretty equally matched there."

I pulled her in my arms, amidst the whooping and hollering of my teammates. "I think we're pretty equally matched everywhere, Paige."

She sighed, her whole body melting into mine. "Can we go home?"

"And miss my celebration?" I asked, pulling back to grin at her. "No way."

I lifted the plastic trophy over my head, and the girls clapped and yelled.

My arm wrapped around her shoulder, and she buried her face into my neck. "This is insane. It's been less than a day, and I missed you like crazy. The girls too."

"Yeah?" I smiled down at her.

She pinched my side. "This is where you're supposed to say that you missed me too."

I laughed and dropped a kiss on the top of her head. "I missed you too, Paige."

"Such a good husband."

I paused, and since everyone in the chairs had started chatting, not really paying attention to us anymore, I gently turned her in my direction. "And how do you feel about me keeping that title? Indefinitely, I mean."

She sucked in a breath. "I will hunt you down if you tried to do it any other way, Logan Ward. You're mine, and I'm yours. And the girls … they're mine too."

I cupped her face and drew it up, breathing her in deeply before I touched my lips to hers. Then I paused.

"Am I going to get lipstick on my lips?" I whispered.

"That's not the right question to ask."

"No?" I asked, a smile spreading over my face.

"My lipstick is always the good, smudgeproof stuff." She tilted her head. "But that's not why it's the wrong question."

My thumbs rubbed over her cheekbones. "Tell me why then."

"The right question is, will my wife murder me if I don't kiss her right now?" she asked calmly. "Because the answer to that is yes."

I wrapped my arms around her and brought her in tight, my lips fitting against hers for a hot, hard kiss. Another cheer went up, but I didn't care. One quick slide of my tongue against hers, and I pulled back.

"Shit," she whispered.

"What?" I said. Her eyes were filled with tears, and I pulled back even further. "What is it? Are you okay?"

"No, you idiot," she cried. "I'm in love with you, and kissing you makes me want to cry. Are you happy?"

I laughed deeply, tightening my hold on her. "Yeah, Paige. I'm happy." I kissed the tip of her nose, the center of her lips, the crease of the frown between her eyebrows. "And I'm in love with you, too."

Her face smoothed out. "You are?"

"Am I going to have to repeat every major declaration in this relationship?"

She nodded earnestly. "Probably."

"I can handle that," I said around my widening smile. "Come on, let's go get our girls."

When I glanced down, they were waiting at the edge of the stage. Paige broke away and strode toward them. Molly and Isabel hit her with a hug first, then the twins followed suit.

"I love you guys," I heard Paige say in a cracking voice. "So much that it's stupid."

"Love isn't stupid, Paige," Lia said with a roll of her eyes. "It's awesome."

She looked over at me and smiled. "Yeah. It is."

"Ready to go home?" I asked them.

Isabel pulled her face away from where she had it buried in Paige's stomach, and she nodded shyly. "Yeah, let's go home."

With my hand in Paige's, and the girls running in front of us, that was exactly what we did.

EPILOGUE

WASHINGTON WOLVES

Logan

Not quite 5 months later

My knee felt like complete and total shit. My shoulder was wrecked from a hard block. And I was ninety percent sure I had a person size bruise blooming on my side. But there was no way I'd utter a word to my defensive coordinator, because he'd bench my ass.

And this was the Super Bowl.

If there was any game where I'd suck it up, where I'd grit my teeth, dig my heels in, and play through every screaming ache and pain in my beat-up body, it was this one. We were less than three minutes away from becoming champions. Less than three minutes and a mere six point lead from beating the Tampa Tarpons. Three minutes was an eternity in football. Six points was absolutely nothing to overcome in that amount of time.

Which meant I'd ignore what was happening in my body, even if I was playing on two broken feet.

From the sidelines, shoulder pads jostling against those of my defensive teammates, bodies tense with no place to put our restless energy, we watched Luke Pierson direct an offensive series. Hopefully one that would last every second of those three minutes, shave every precious second from the clock and end in another score.

A field goal would do it, but we wanted another touchdown. We wanted that end zone.

Luke lined up behind Gomez for third and five, hands frozen in position for the snap as he barked out the play to the offense. Receivers shuffled, the tight ends crouched in readiness, our rookie running back moved into position behind Luke, and the offensive line dug their hands into the grass, ready to protect whoever would get the ball.

Next to me, Coach crossed his arms over his chest and took an audible breath. It was a long five yards, and Luke called a run play, one that had worked perfectly in the previous series.

As a defensive player, there was always a part of us that wanted to end the game with some Top-ten worthy play. An interception. A pick-six. A strip-sack or flattening the opposing quarterback when the time ran out.

But more than that, I just wanted us to win. Nobody on the defense needed to play the hero, like Hawkins had in the game that brought us to this one. We wanted to win in the same way that we'd played all season, as a team, no single man more important than anyone else.

Gomez snapped the ball, Luke faked a throw, then pivoted and stuck the ball straight into the waiting hands of the receiver. Gomez plowed forward, opening a perfect lane through the defense.

The receiver's strong legs powered forward, chewing up grass as he ran. He cleared the first down line, drawing a triumphant roar from every player on the sideline, every Washington fan in the stands. Nimbly, he avoided a sack that would move him out of bounds, which would stop the clock, and he went down on the field.

The numbers ticked lower.

I glanced up at the screen and watched the replay, a grin spreading over my face.

This game was ours.

With unflappable precision, Luke ran another series, moving the offense down the field with unerring accuracy. The numbers on the clock got smaller and smaller. We stopped for Tampa's last time-out, and the team huddled up.

Coach waited for the offense to grab some Gatorade and then he set his hands on his hips. He glanced around the huddle.

"This win is ours," he said with steel in his voice.

"Hell yeah," someone said from behind me.

"Luke," Coach said, "you can kneel if you get that first down."

Luke nodded, his eyes lit with excitement and anticipation. The same anticipation that was making my skin buzz and my heart race.

"I can," Luke said.

"But if you want one more score, it's up to you."

The whole team held their breath, because it was crazy to even consider it. Kneeling was always the safest bet. Always.

Luke nodded, his eyes meeting mine for the briefest moment, and I grinned.

"Let's put the nail in the coffin, boys," he said. "They'll talk about this ending for years." The tension, strung tight and palpable through the entire team, had me bouncing on the balls of my feet. The entire stadium was electric with it.

Before we put our hands in, I caught a glimpse of the jumbotron. Allie had moved down to the sidelines, security surrounding her. Next to her was my wife, making the same jittery, excited movements that I was.

My heart could hardly be contained in my chest as I took a moment to study her. My jersey, the same white one we were currently wearing, was the first thing I'd given her after we renewed our vows. Real vows this time. In our backyard, surrounded by family and friends, just a few short weeks after she pulled her award stunt. That same night, she wore the jersey and nothing else when I took her to bed.

On the screen, pixelated and massive, she and Allie clung to each other. Ava was right next to them, and behind them, I saw my sisters holding hands with Faith Pierson, screaming at the top of their lungs.

A family. That's what we were on this team.

Luke thrust his hand into the middle of the circle.

"We gonna do this, boys?" he yelled.

"Hell yes," was our reply.

"Wolves on three!"

One, two, three.

The rest, as they say, went down in history.

Paige

Nine years later

The door to Logan's office was cracked open, and I approached it quietly when I heard the low hum of his voice.

Even after nine years of marriage, that voice made me want to rip his clothes off, much to the chagrin of the other members of our family. Isabel said she'd finally moved out simply because she couldn't handle hearing us have sex anymore.

Whatever. She'd understand eventually.

"See what he did there?" my husband said. "No one saw it coming. That was the beauty of it."

I breathed out a soft laugh. Before I pushed the door open, I knew exactly what I'd see. I'd caught him watching the clip of the game-ending play from that Super Bowl win more times than I could count over the last nine years.

"Everyone thought he was going to kneel, so when he starts down, the defense automatically relaxes. Look, right there, see how their shoulders go down?"

"Yup," a small voice answered diligently, like they hadn't heard this explanation a dozen times. "I see it."

"Always expect the unexpected, okay? Because boom, right there, Luke snaps back up before his knee ever touches the ground, throws a shovel pass to the receiver out to the left, and he's gone before the defense even realizes what's happening."

"Touchdown!" came the gleeful reply. "Washington wins the Super Bowl!"

I dried my hands with the kitchen towel and then slung it over my shoulder as I carefully pushed the office door open.

Logan was in the large leather chair facing the computer monitor on his desk, our eight year old son in his lap, and they stared at the screen with matching expressions that did funny things to my heart.

When Emmett was born, he had a shock of black hair, which Logan proudly commented on to anyone who would listen. But I remember sitting in the hospital, nursing him quietly, and I saw dark, dark red roots on that tiny head.

He had his dad's eyes, bright emerald green, and hair that was a deep, burnished mahogany. My red, and Logan's black perfectly mixed together.

His love of football was straight from his dad, and his unbelievable stubbornness came straight from me.

"Whatcha doing?" I asked.

Logan grinned in my direction. "Caught me."

"Mmmhmm. How many times have you watched that this season, Coach?"

"Only five, Mom," Emmett piped up. "It's the best Super Bowl ever."

I rolled my eyes. "Go wash your hands. Lia and Claire just

pulled in. The other two said they're running late, but they'd be here in time for dinner."

Emmett tore past me. "Woohoo!"

Logan turned his chair to face me. "Everyone's coming?"

I walked up to him and sank to my knees on either side of his lap. "Mmmhmm." Up the line of his neck, I planted soft, wet kisses. I nipped at the edge of his jaw.

Logan's hands smoothed up my back and tangled in my hair. "You trying to get us caught?"

I lowered my lips to his and gave him a lingering kiss. "Maybe. They do hate it, don't they?"

His mouth spread into a smile and I bit his bottom lip.

Logan's tongue slipped across mine and I wrapped my arms around his neck. When he pulled away, I hummed happily.

Honestly, my husband was so freaking delicious, I could hardly stand it.

"Just think," I said quietly. "In ten years, Emmett will be in college, and we'll have the house to ourselves. We can screw on every surface if we want to."

He tipped his head back and laughed.

When he dropped his chin, his eyes were warm and happy on my face. "I love you."

My finger traced his full lips. "I love you too."

"Want to watch that play again?" he asked.

"Nope."

"You remember when we won?"

"Yup," I said around a widening smile. "I had no idea you were such a narcissist when I married you."

He kissed me again, slow and sexy and sweet, and I melted into his lap. "You would've married me anyway," he whispered against my lips.

I pulled back and cupped his face. "You're right."

Logan groaned. "Sexiest thing you ever say to me."

As I laughed, I wrapped my arms around his neck again, and marveled, for the millionth time, that this was my life.

The last one I was looking for, and the only place I was meant to be.

The End

ACKNOWLEDGMENTS

These will be short and sweet, you guys. I SWEAR, next time, I'll plan ahead and give myself more than fifteen minutes to do this right at the last minute (LOL, and other lies I tell myself, like I'll fold the laundry as soon as it's done). If I forgot to mention you, PLEASE FORGIVE ME because I'm the worst.

To my husband Zak, and my boys, who are spectacular human beings that I love more than life itself.

To my family and friends for being so incredibly supportive, no matter what that support looks like.

To Fiona Cole (#dreamteam) and Kathryn Andrews, for giving me unwavering friendship, solid insight, critical feedback, and pushing me to write the best version of Logan and Paige's story that I possibly could. I couldn't do this without you two.

To Caitlin Terpstra and Michelle Clay for setting valuable reader eyeballs on this puppy and showing me where I could make it better.

To Tiffany for the lamp throwing scene idea because she knows Paige on such a soul deep level.

To Staci Hart, Kandi Steiner, and Amy Daws, for pushing me, listening to me, encouraging me, even if you didn't set eyes on the book. What you do for me every single day is just as valuable.

To Jenny Sims and Amanda Yeakel for cleaning up my MULTITUDE of errors.

To Najla Qamber and the rest of the design team at Qamber Designs, for my covers, and all the pretties that go with it. You're SO talented, I can hardly stand it.

To Ena and Amanda at Enticing Journey for all the promo help.

To my reader group, and the bloggers and bookstagrammers who make this journey so much more incredible than it already is.

A big, huge, sweaty shoutout to my newfound family at CKO Kickboxing. You've given me strength, sore muscles, support, encouragement, laughs, and a place that allows me to leave all my stress in one safe place. Maybe no one has cried at the bags like Isabel, but damn if it might not happen someday.

And to my Lord and Savior, Jesus Christ, for all things, all the time.

OTHER BOOKS BY KARLA SORENSEN

(AVAILABLE TO READ WITH YOUR KU SUBSCRIPTION)

Wilder Family Series

One and Only

The Wolves: a Football Dynasty (second gen)

The Lie

The Plan

The Crush

The Ward Sisters

Focused

Faked

Floored

Forbidden

The Washington Wolves

The Bombshell Effect

The Ex Effect

The Marriage Effect

The Bachelors of the Ridge

Dylan

Garrett

Cole

Michael

Tristan

Three Little Words

By Your Side

Light Me Up

Tell Them Lies

Love at First Sight

Baking Me Crazy

Batter of Wits

Steal my Magnolia

Worth the Wait

ABOUT THE AUTHOR

Karla Sorensen has been an avid reader her entire life, preferring stories with a happily-ever-after over just about any other kind. And considering she has an entire line item in her budget for books, she realized it might just be cheaper to write her own stories. She still keeps her toes in the world of health care marketing, where she made her living pre-babies. Now she stays home, writing and mommy-ing full time (this translates to almost every day being a 'pajama day' at the Sorensen household…don't judge). She lives in West Michigan with her husband, two exceptionally adorable sons, and big, shaggy rescue dog.

Find Karla online:
karlasorensen.com
karla@karlasorensen.com
Facebook
Facebook Reader Group